D1284350
Christmas

ALSO BY TILLY TENNANT

From Italy With Love series:

Rome is Where the Heart Is

A Wedding in Italy

Honeybourne series:

The Little Village Bakery

Christmas at the Little Village Bakery

Mishaps in Millrise series:

Little Acts of Love

Just Like Rebecca

The Parent Trap

And Baby Makes Four

Once Upon a Winter series:

The Accidental Guest

I'm Not in Love

Ways to Say Goodbye

One Starry Night

Hopelessly Devoted to Holden Finn

The Man Who Can't Be Moved

Mishaps and Mistletoe

A Very Vintage Christmas

TILLY TENNANT

bookouture

Published by Bookouture
An imprint of StoryFire Ltd.
23 Sussex Road, Ickenham, UB10 8PN
United Kingdom
www.bookouture.com

ISBN: 978-1-78681-083-0
eBook ISBN: 978-1-78681-082-3

For Olivia. I'm bursting with pride every day
for the extraordinary young woman you've become.

One

Harvey. An old film and a ridiculous story some might say, but boy was it good. Something about it spoke to Dodie in a way few modern films ever had. She couldn't count how many times she'd seen it – twenty, maybe twenty-five. But she still cried as Elwood P. Dowd said goodbye to Harvey in the expectation of leaving forever to care for Dr Chumley, not a flicker of bitterness in the pure, selfless acceptance of his loss. She cried every time she watched it, and she expected that she would cry even on the hundredth viewing. Some things were just like that.

Isla, stalwart friend who'd sat through the old movie with Dodie more times than she cared to recall, or so she kept telling her, rolled her eyes and shoved a box of tissues towards her. 'I just don't get it.'

She followed her statement with a solemn slurp of the banana and mango smoothie she'd picked up on the way over.

'He's saying goodbye to Harvey,' Dodie said.

'I know that. I don't get why you cry every time. You know it will all work out in the end.'

'Because at this moment, Elwood doesn't know it will work out so he's sad, but he doesn't make a fuss. It reminds us that life is loss and Elwood accepts this with a quiet dignity. It reminds us that nothing lasts forever.'

'This bloody film does.'

'It's nearly finished.'

'It's trite nonsense. An invisible rabbit? Six feet tall? The bloke's a nutter. This script would never make it past production execs if they tried to get it financed today.'

'He's not really a rabbit – that's just what he looks like to Elwood. He's a pooka. Pookas appear to people in different forms. And he's real because the doctor can see him too – that's why Harvey has agreed to help the doctor find his inner peace.' Dodie wiped the sleeve of an oversized sweatshirt across her eyes and reached for her cooling tea from the TV table. 'That's what Harvey does – he helps outsiders come to terms with their outsideriness.' She smiled at Isla, as if her statement was the most obvious thing in the world. But then it would be to her, who had spent her twenty-eight years on the earth feeling like an outsider in one way or another.

'I already know all this – you've told me before. I'll tell you what – I wouldn't have come over if I'd known you were going to put this on again. As soon as it's finished we're having that new *Star Trek* film on, right? Because if we're not then I'm going back to my flat to watch it. I feel like you're dating James Stewart sometimes. I have nightmares that *I'm* dating James Stewart I see him so often! And that's just weird… considering he's dead and everything.'

'I wish I was dating James Stewart,' Dodie said wistfully.

'You're about sixty years too late.'

'Fifty maybe.'

'And maybe you don't want to say that in front of Ryan, who might not appreciate coming second to a corpse. Quite honestly, I don't know how you two are still together. It must drive him mad having to compete with dead people all the time.'

'Ugh.' Dodie shivered. 'I don't like hearing it quite like that. I prefer to think of Jimmy in a non-corpse-like state.'

Isla pulled open a share-size pack of crisps and offered it to Dodie. 'Chris Pine... Now he's a man I could happily give my worldly possessions up for.'

'Who?'

'Oh yeah, I forgot that you don't know the names of any actors from after the sixties. He's in the new *Star Trek* films.'

'Is he?' Dodie asked vaguely, her attention back on the screen of a TV that almost certainly belonged in a museum. It worked just fine, even if it didn't have the sleek lines of a modern flat screen, and, as Dodie had said to Isla many times when her friend had nagged her to get a new one, or come over bearing news of some special offer in an electronics shop, she liked the cute chunkiness of its old shape. She'd stick with it until it died – and might even be tempted to try to get it fixed after that. The film was at the point where Elwood P. Dowd was discussing the whys and wherefores of Harvey leaving him with Harvey himself. Although to everyone else – characters and viewers alike – he was talking to what was effectively thin air.

Isla let out a sigh of exasperation, and Dodie shot her a crafty grin, prompting Isla to hurl an embroidered cushion at her. 'Cow! Stop winding me up!'

'Of course I know who Chris Pine is,' Dodie said, laughing. 'I do have some knowledge of the modern world. I just happen to prefer the not-so-modern one.'

'Figures. CGI must have cost a fortune on this film too,' Isla said wryly. 'If you're going to make all this fuss about a six-foot rabbit at least let us see it.'

'They didn't have CGI back then. Their special effects were so bad it was far more effective to rely on the power of your imagination.'

'What if you don't have any?'

'Probably best watching something else then. Like the new *Star Trek* film.'

'And that's why I like my entertainment to be made in the twenty-first century. It's all there in front of me and I don't have to imagine what it looks like. If I wanted to imagine it I'd read a book.'

'Hmm. I prefer the pace of old films. I just like the pace of old times; it feels less stressful and scary than today somehow.'

'It probably wasn't if you lived there. They had some pretty scary laws for a start. You couldn't even be gay in the old days. And everyone had rickets or consumption or something horrible.'

'Yeah, I know that. But it just seemed gentler, you know?'

'Tell that to Oscar Wilde.'

'I never said it was perfect,' Dodie replied, turning her attention back to the screen. Isla always won theoretical arguments. She soaked up facts about the world like trifle sponges soaked up sherry, and while Dodie spent all her time lost in another age, Isla spent hers reading books on sociology and psychology and just about any other -ology you could name.

'Speaking of old times, have you seen any improvements in sales since you refurbished the shop?' Isla asked, reaching to retrieve the crisps.

'Business is up a bit,' Dodie said, tucking her legs beneath her and smoothing her bobbed hair behind a pierced ear. 'I don't know whether it's because Christmas is coming but I'm hoping it's a bit more long term than that. When I take the books to my accountant he'll be able to do a projection for me; might give me a clue what to expect next year. I hope it's good news because I've sunk every last bit of money into redecorating so it has to work or it's curtains, if you'll excuse the pun.' She paused, her attention on an imaginary spot in the distance. 'And I'm not even exaggerating when I say that,' she added quietly.

'Most of the students from the university go home at Christmas too,' Isla reminded her, appearing not to have noticed Dodie's sudden melancholy. 'I would imagine they're your main customer demographic so I wouldn't worry too much, even if you're slow over Christmas, because it will pick up afterwards.'

'I was kind of hoping Christmas would save me, actually. I'm not sure after Christmas won't be a bit too late.'

'You have to have faith,' Isla said. 'I have faith that you can make this work, so you just need to have a little more yourself. This is Bournemouth – packed full of hipsters and bohemian types and the perfect place for vintage and quirky. Once people know about your shop you won't be able to move for customers.'

She stretched, scratching a fingernail through her tightly braided hair. Dodie had always considered herself to be reasonably decent looking, if perhaps a little ordinary, but Isla was something else. With her half-Nigerian, half-Scottish heritage, she was both exotic like a rare orchid and as hardy and streetwise as a dandelion. It was a potent combination, though Isla had never cared much for her many admirers, preferring to be single and independent. It would take a very special kind of man to steal her heart, and Dodie had often wondered if he even existed.

'So if you look at it that way,' Isla continued, 'it means things should get even better when the new term starts in January. Students love vintage clothes.'

'You don't.'

'Even though I'm technically a student, I'm far too old to be that hip now.'

'You're not old; you're only a couple of months older than me.'

'Not old, but not young enough to be a hipster either.'

'Well,' Dodie added, 'I'm not a student either but I love vintage.'

'I think we've established you're weird.' Isla swept a hand towards the bulky old television. 'I give you exhibit A.'

Dodie grinned. 'OK, guilty as charged.'

'But the town will be swarming with potential customers come the summer, so I reckon you'll be OK. You've only been open six months, and people still have to find you. If I could level one criticism it's the property you chose to open up in.'

'The shop is in a bit of a crap spot,' Dodie agreed. 'But the rents are ridiculous in the main town, and the seafront would bankrupt me.'

'I did try to tell you at the time. You'd have been better off inland; Ringwood or Dorchester, or somewhere – at least while you built the business.'

'But I love it here. And my gran is here too – she loves that she has someone living close by.'

'Hardly a reason to set up a business in the most expensive seaside town in the world – because your gran's here.'

'Bournemouth isn't the *most* expensive.'

'I'll bet it's in the top ten,' Isla said, folding a large crisp into her mouth with a grace that nobody else could possibly achieve doing the same thing. 'I can barely afford to park outside your place when I come over to visit.'

'Sorry.'

Isla threw her a sideways look. 'It's a good thing I like you, that's all I can say.'

'With that in mind…' Dodie began, turning the volume down on the television, 'I don't suppose you fancy swinging by to help me for an hour in the shop tomorrow? I wouldn't ask, but I'm expecting a crate of stuff I won at auction last week and I need to go through it.'

'Lucky for you I'm not doing anything tomorrow – lectures have been cancelled because the tutor has flu.'

'You can stay over at the flat, actually, save you driving back to Dorchester if you like.'

'I haven't got any stuff with me.'

'Borrow my pyjamas – that's no problem. And I have an unopened toothbrush you can have.'

'What about clean knickers? I'm not pulling on a pair of sixties nylon Y-fronts from your shop, so you can forget that!'

'Don't be daft!' Dodie giggled. 'I don't put the Y-fronts in the shop… I keep them to model to Ryan. Sixties nylon Y-fronts make him *so* horny.'

'Oh dear Lord! He's so normal and you're so weird – again, how is it you two are together?'

'I suppose opposites attract. Or maybe he was desperate.'

'I wouldn't say that. If anyone was desperate it was you – you're far too complex for him.'

'Are you saying he's basic?'

'As a single-celled organism.'

'But—' Dodie began. Isla held up a hand to stop her.

'I know – he's steady and normal and he makes you feel settled and it's good that you're so different because two people just like you would end up in a total mess. I didn't mean to start anything again and you already know my thoughts on him so let's avoid a disagreement about it now.' She repositioned herself on the sofa and gave Dodie a sideways smile. 'I'll go home and get my own knickers, if it's all the same to you. It's no bother to come back in the morning and you don't need to worry about it – Dorchester is hardly at the ends of the earth.'

'You're a star!' Dodie beamed. 'Thanks so much!'

Isla gave a vague shrug. 'It might be fun.'

'And if you see anything you like, you can have it, free of charge as a reward for helping me.'

'No offence, but I very much doubt I'll see something I like. My clothes are strictly first-hand, and that's how I'm going to keep it.'

'I bet you'll be surprised when we go through the delivery.' Dodie smiled. 'I bet we find something amazing!'

'If I end up with something from your delivery of dead people's clothes I'll be more than surprised. You've been trying to convert me for years and you haven't succeeded yet so you might as well give up. Much as I love you and want to support your business, I'm not wearing old-lady clothes.'

Dodie laughed. 'They're not all that old! I do have some stock from the eighties and nineties and it's really popular right now.'

'Oh Lord!' Isla clapped a melodramatic hand to her brow. 'Only thirty years old… what is this modern, newfangled witchcraft?' She looked back at Dodie and grinned. 'Still old enough to qualify as museum exhibits.'

Dodie folded her arms. 'I still say you'll be surprised. You need to give it a chance, have an open mind when you look through, use a bit of imagination. I guarantee you'll see something you fall in love with in my shop sooner or later, and then I'll be the first one to say I told you so.'

'If I find something in your shop, you have my permission to do the world's longest and most elaborate victory dance.'

'I might just hold you to that.'

Isla stretched and yawned. 'Is this film finished yet? I might go and make a sandwich while you watch the rest; I'm losing the will to live here.'

Dodie grinned. 'You know where the bread is. I'll get back to daydreaming about Jimmy Stewart and you go and stuff your face.'

Isla unfurled herself from the corner of the throw-covered sofa, limbs lithe and elegant as she poked her feet into a pair of flip-flops that she always kept at Dodie's flat. 'Got any decent ham?'

'In the fridge,' Dodie said. 'You're in luck – it's Waitrose. On special offer, of course.'

'Ooooh,' Isla squeaked. 'Lovely!'

Dodie turned back to the television as Isla left for the kitchen. Harvey had come back and Elwood was overjoyed to see him. Or at least, that was what the filmmakers would have us believe because nobody else could see him. Dodie smiled fondly at the screen; she'd always imagined, watching the film as she grew up, that Jimmy Stewart himself *could* see Harvey. But now she thought that he was simply such a good actor he'd convinced himself he could see Harvey. She was certainly convinced he saw something in front of him as he delivered his lines. A growl from her stomach interrupted her thoughts and she called after Isla:

'All this talk of ham has made me hungry now! While you're at it you can make me a sandwich too!'

Two

It was Monday morning and Dodie was in a red kind of mood. Perhaps it was the Christmas spirit working its way into her soul – the German markets had hit town and everywhere was a blaze of fairy lights and tinsel, frantic shoppers racing from store to store, those with more time on their hands settling in for the day at the temporary bar in the main square to indulge in Glühwein and mulled cider. As she made her way back from the local café, laden with breakfast muffins and cinnamon-flavoured coffee for her and Isla, the sight of the stallholders setting up for the day made her smile. If only she had a little more time to enjoy the markets herself, rather than working every day from the crack of dawn and into the evening. But the Christmas vibe taking over the seaside town of Bournemouth had ignited something in her and she'd spent an hour the previous Friday evening, once she'd closed the shop, dyeing her hair a vibrant scarlet to match her mood. It meant her whole wardrobe had to be rearranged to work with it, but she was used to working with a new hair colour every so often so it didn't necessarily bother her. Besides, her shop was filled with sartorial treasures to root through, and if you couldn't own a vintage clothes shop and treat yourself to the odd indulgence from the stock every now and again, there was really no point in owning one at all. Her chosen fashion era changed almost as often as her hair colour;

there was really no particular favourite, only a deep and abiding love for all things past. If she'd thought she could get away with walking along the seafront in a crinoline and bustle she probably would, but today she'd gone with a rockabilly-inspired look that suited her new red bob perfectly. She drew a lot of attention on the high street – some admiring looks, some puzzled – although that wasn't what she was after. By nature she was something of a wallflower, and Isla had often commented that the dressing up was almost like acting; Dodie pretending to be someone other than who she really was. This made a lot of sense to Dodie, who had always felt that the real Dodie Bright was a boring story that nobody would want to read. But Isla was clever like that, and when she got her psychology degree Dodie was certain the whole world would know it, too.

'Oi, Dodie! Red today, is it? Nice!'

Dodie looked around to see who'd called her. Sitting on the floor at the entrance to Debenhams was a man with a sleeping bag covering his legs, bundled up in a duffle coat and hat. Most would call him middle-aged, but perhaps it was the grey-flecked beard making him look older. Next to him sat a hefty kitbag that he was using as a makeshift cushion.

'Alright, Nick?' Dodie smiled, changing direction to go and talk to him. 'Watch out – they'll move you on from there. Remember what happened last time.'

'Probably,' Nick agreed. 'But it's early yet and the fat git who does security won't even be out of bed. Besides, I can run faster than that lump of lard.' He grinned. 'It's nice and warm under this heater so I'll take my chances either way.'

'You've been there all night?'

'More or less.'

'You must have been freezing!'

He sniffed. 'I like it under the stars. Police and social workers and all them religious types keep offering me a bed but I get all claustrophobic indoors. It's not so bad out here once you get used to it.'

Dodie gave him a patient smile. He always said the same thing, every time she asked him. Always some line about sleeping under the same sky as our ancestors, but our ancestors weren't usually huddled in shop doorways beneath a grubby blanket being peed on by drunks when they were sleeping outside. Dodie had got to know Nick a little since she'd opened her shop, had even invited him in for a cup of tea in the warm, but he always declined. She suspected that there was more to it than wanting to be outside, some internal conflict he needed to work through, some social anxiety that meant even though he chatted cheerfully enough to anyone on the street who offered a helping hand, he didn't want to get too close. It was only a theory, of course, and Dodie was no expert.

'Had your breakfast yet?' she asked.

'Expect I'll get something in a bit.'

Rooting in the paper bag in her arms, she pulled out an egg and bacon muffin and a hash brown. 'Here.'

'Aww, I don't want to take your breakfast, love,' Nick said, waving away the offer. But Dodie placed it on his lap.

'There's plenty in here,' she said. 'I'm not saying you need it more than I do but I know my waistline probably would, if it could talk.'

'I think your waistline is cracking,' Nick said, taking the muffin and unwrapping it. 'Not that I look, mind.'

'Don't worry, I'll take it as a compliment,' Dodie laughed. 'I haven't got a spare coffee here but if I leave you a couple of quid you can get one when the Christmas stalls open up, can't you?'

He stuck a thumb in the air. 'That'd be handsome. You're a good girl, one of the best.'

'Nah. I just wish I could do more.'

'Don't start that rubbish,' he chided through a mouthful of muffin. 'I appreciate everything. What I appreciate most is that we have a nice little chat from time to time. Most people don't even look at me.'

'That's alright; I like our chats.'

She stood for a moment, a quiet smile of understanding passing between them. Then Nick waved his hand to shoo her away. 'If you don't get that lot back it'll be cold.' He angled his head at the bag in her arms.

'Oh, yeah…' Dodie shook herself. 'My friend is helping me in the shop today; she won't be happy if I give her cold bacon sandwiches in payment.'

'She won't be back, that's for sure. Take it easy, sweetheart.'

'You too, Nick. Don't get too cold out here.'

He gave her a brisk nod and turned his attention back to his muffin as Dodie walked away. Despite having a bag full of rapidly cooling food, she found herself easily distracted by the shop windows, bright and lively with sparkling Christmas displays of toys, jewellery, clothes and cosmetics. She still had her own Christmas gift shopping to finish and she made a mental note of one or two items that might be suitable for people.

As she stared at the pastel window display of a shop selling organic cosmetics, her mobile rang.

'My stomach thinks my throat's been cut,' Isla said.

'I'm coming now. I thought you said you'd had some toast this morning before you left home?'

'I did but it's wearing off. I need bacon and I need it stat.'

'Right…' Dodie smiled. 'I'm ten minutes away, tops. I know you're hungry but please try not to faint into the seventies rack while I'm missing, won't you?'

'I can't promise it, but I'll do my best to hang on. Anyway, if I was going to faint into a rack of clothes I'd go for something a bit more stylish than the seventies. Some of it might stick to me and that would just be embarrassing.'

'I don't know,' Dodie said. 'I could see you rocking a pair of bell-bottoms.'

'*Nobody* has ever rocked bell-bottoms,' Isla replied stuffily and Dodie had to laugh at the note of utter horror in her voice.

'You wouldn't have had a choice if it was the seventies; you'd have *had* to wear them.'

'It's not the seventies, and quite frankly, the seventies can stay exactly where they are if that's the best they've got to offer.'

'Alright, alright… now I really know you're hungry; you've never managed to insult an entire decade before and, as insults go, you're pretty good at them.'

'I am not!' Isla squeaked, and Dodie laughed again. 'Who do I insult?'

'See…' Dodie grinned as she repositioned the phone against her ear, 'it comes so naturally you don't even know you're doing it.'

'Cheeky cow,' Isla huffed.

'No,' Dodie fired back, 'that one wasn't very good at all – you've done much better insults than that.'

'Oi!' Isla said. 'If you don't get back here with my bacon before it's cold I'll show you what an insult really looks like!'

Dodie's laughter only grew louder as she ended the call and stashed her phone in her coat pocket.

Forget-Me-Not Vintage was so far from the main shopping streets of Bournemouth town centre you could almost argue it wasn't in the town at all. Flanked by a decent sprinkling of bars and restaurants, however, along with a flower shop, newsagent-cum-convenience store, a Jewish bakery and an English-language school (of which Bournemouth seemed to have dozens), it promised just enough passing trade to make the location work. Dodie was relying heavily on the truth of Isla's promise that she just needed to get established, and once word got out people would seek out her shop so that she wouldn't have to worry about its location. So far the footfall had been stubbornly and disappointingly low, and it had led to a frugal summer.

The store had previously been owned by an elderly lady who had sold lingerie to even older ladies, and it had been in desperate need of repair by the time Dodie took possession of the premises when the old dear finally retired. Dodie had done much of the refurbishment herself – plaster knocked from walls to expose brick, polished wooden floorboards, old film posters dotted around the place, the shopfront painted a pretty forget-me-not blue – but there had been things she hadn't been able to do on a budget, like the wiring for the eclectic array of chandeliers that lit up the shop, drawing the eyes of passers-by to the windows like moths to the stars. By day it looked pretty, but when dusk fell over the streets it was magical. Despite rolling her sleeves up and doing a lot of the work herself, the final touches had still all but cleared out the coffers, and if she didn't turn a decent profit soon, Dodie knew she was going to have to make some tough decisions about the business she had poured her heart, soul and all her cash into.

As she stepped inside with their breakfast, she found Isla sitting in the middle of the shop floor surrounded by neat piles of fabric – georgette, denim, faux fur, wool and lace – all classified by colour.

'Lovely,' Dodie said, nodding at the arrangement. 'Looks very organised. It's a shame I'll have to undo all your good work.'

'I couldn't find the hangers…' Isla said in a vague tone, her gaze travelling the piles. But then she looked up sharply. 'Wait, why do you have to undo my work?'

'I can't just put it out for sale. I have to inspect everything first, repair it if it needs it, wash and iron. Some of it I won't even be able to use and that will either go to the charity shop or recycling. Then I'll need to catalogue every item so I know exactly what's going in and out and I can keep track of the profit – or losses, as the case may be.'

Isla scratched her head as she looked again at the hundred or so items she'd sorted. She let out a long, irritated sigh. 'No wonder it takes you such a long time. I thought it was odd you needed help on one little delivery.'

'Not little. This is quite big by my standards. I got it for a brilliant price though, so I'm hoping there will be some treasure in here.' Dodie shook the paper bag she was holding. 'First: breakfast. We'll have to take it in turns to eat upstairs in the flat, though. Don't want the shop stinking of bacon – gets in the clothes and then it's hell to get the smell out of the fabric. You can have yours first, if you like.'

'I was hoping you'd say that,' Isla said, leaping up and snatching the bag and her coffee with a grin. 'I won't be long,' she added, heading through the doorway that separated the shop from the tiny staff-room/office and stairs to the living quarters above.

Dodie smiled, turning her attention to the clothes Isla had sorted into piles. Judging by the sizes and colours, a great deal of the pieces could have come from the same original collection – there was a lot of rich forest and autumn shades in what looked to be a modern size ten, though some of it was clearly handmade and not traditionally sized. Unsized clothes were often a problem but Dodie had learned to gauge pretty accurately by looking at the item, and most people who shopped for vintage knew that they'd always have to try a garment on because of inconsistent sizing.

She unfolded a few items and held them up for inspection. There was a bit of a mixture, bundles that might have come from different places, but a good deal of it was forties and perhaps fifties fashion, probably from the loft of an old lady who had once put it away and forgotten about it. That often happened, and when the old dear died or went into a home and the family cleared the house, the treasure would be discovered. This particular batch was good quality and well cared for; some pieces even had mothballs in the pockets and tissue paper within the sleeves. These were the best sorts of hauls; it was likely Dodie wouldn't have too much repair work to do on any of it.

There was a tawny tweed jacket, which she couldn't resist slipping on for a look in the mirror – though it was a little tight around the arms so she quickly decided it wasn't a personal keeper. There were three brown hats complete with feathers, netting or a simple band tied in a bow. She tried these on too but decided against them. She unfolded various skirts and dresses with oversized collars and contrast stitching, some with plain blocks of colour and others in delicate florals. And then she came across the most fabulous forest-green coat; calf-length wool, cinched waist and flared skirt with a fur collar.

'Please let it fit,' she squeaked as she shook it out and pulled it on. It slid over her shoulders like a dream and fastened easily. It could have been made for her. As she stood at just over five feet it was a little longer than intended by the tailor, but Dodie was used to being swamped by the length of her clothes, and as long as she wasn't tripping on the hems she didn't let it worry her. She pulled the collar up and twirled to admire the back in the mirror, then turned around to take another look at the front. The colour looked amazing with her new hair. It was cosy too – nice thick wool that would be perfect for the winter. She plunged her hands in the pockets to see how deep they were and test just how cosy the coat was. Modern clothes had rubbish pockets – hardly anything at all – but old clothes were brilliant for hand storage space, and Dodie tended to pick up a lot of debris as she went about her day-to-day business: bus tickets, shop receipts, cough sweets, hair grips – you name it, she found it all in her pockets on a regular basis.

And that was when she found the letter. She frowned as her hand brushed against the paper and she pulled it out to inspect. The envelope was yellowed with age, browned and worn at the edges, and it looked as though it had been written with a fountain pen and ink. There was a heavy postmark she didn't recognise, but it almost looked like one or even two on top of another, as if the letter had been through many hands to get to its final recipient. She turned it over to see that it had already been opened. Perhaps it was an empty envelope, hastily stuffed into a pocket and forgotten once the contents had been read and remembered? Either way, it was clearly old and that fact alone was enough to pique Dodie's interest.

Lifting the flap, she peered inside and her heart almost skipped to see there was a sheet in there, a letter. The paper looked expensive, even if it was grubby with age. The colour was a slightly lighter cream than the envelope but they unmistakably matched. With nervous anticipation, as if her subconscious knew that something monumental was about to happen, Dodie drew the sheet from the envelope and opened it out. Her eyes skimmed over the first three words, words so personal, so perfect and full of love that it almost felt like a violation to be reading them: *Dearest Darling Maggie.*

Those three words stopped her heart. She felt cold, the hairs stood up on her neck and she knew she was about to read something so extraordinary and special that it would become a part of her too. Suddenly and inexplicably, it felt like her whole existence had been building to this moment, as if she'd simply been eating and sleeping as she waited for it to arrive. But surely that was crazy? So why, as she read further, was her heart beating in her ears? Like the words that followed *were* going to change her life?

Dearest Darling Maggie,

How I wish I could whisper those words in your ear, my love. I'll bet you're sitting by the wireless now looking pretty as a picture as you laugh at Band Waggon, just like the night before I left, and I wish I could see it. The way you laugh makes me love you all the more, and I love you more than life already. This damned war drags on and on, and I wish desperately for it to end. If only to come home and see you. I dream of you every night and think of you every day. I'm trying my very best to stay alive for you, my love, but when the bombs miss me by inches sometimes I fear I may not make it.

When I get home, at last we will be married and it is the thought of that day that keeps me marching on. I hope you believe me as I make that promise. I know you are scared about our little secret and I must confess to being shocked at your news, but I am happy – as happy as a man ever was. It only makes me more desperate to come home to you. I know people may talk if it gets out, but be sure of my love and my honest intentions. I would not abandon you to scandal, and all the scandal in the world would not diminish the love I have for you in my heart.

I ask every day about coming home on leave, and we will get married when I do. My darling, please write and tell me you love me, tell me you're not angry or upset about our little mistake. My heart is heavy with the thought that you might be, and I cannot be there to make it better. But I will be soon, and the thought makes my feet quick and my reflexes sharp as I dance between the bullets.

I cannot tell you where I am, but I can tell you there are lots of good-looking French girls here, though there is none here as beautiful as you. You are my precious and adorable sweetheart and I count the days until we are together again.

Always yours,
George

The love, the emotion, the promise pouring from every line was almost too much for Dodie. It felt like a crime, somehow, that she'd read such an outpouring, as if she'd directly spied on some intimate moment between two people who were strangers to her but who she already felt she knew. But what she'd read she couldn't now unread and the words on the page filled her head, inserted themselves into her memory, settled into the cracks as if they had now become hers. Except they weren't, because no man had ever made such a fervent declaration of his love to her; no man had ever bared his soul and offered his life in that way and she didn't expect any man ever would.

What she had in her own life with Ryan was safe and comfortable and she could rely on him to steady her sails as she navigated life's choppy seas, but he was hardly what you'd call romantic. And as for love, she supposed he must love her in his own way, as she did him in hers, but they were hardly Romeo and Juliet. But this letter, this declaration from George, was a precious glimpse into a kind of love she didn't even know she wanted until this exact moment.

Dodie wiped away a tear as she turned her thoughts to more practical matters. She shook her head and smiled vaguely at the silliest of notions. Really, Isla had a point when she told her – on many occasions – that she was odd. She almost certainly was if she thought an old letter could change her life that drastically. Still, she couldn't shake the strange feeling that it already had.

She checked the address on the envelope. It had fared worse than the letter inside; time had faded the print and worn the paper, but she managed to make out the name Margaret and a surname beginning with V, and then a Bournemouth address that looked like Wessex Road. She squinted at the number. It could have been a seventeen, or maybe an eleven. The date on the letter was 8 June 1944, so the war mentioned must have been the Second World War. In which case, it seemed safe to assume that George had been in the allied forces, fighting abroad, and that Maggie was his sweetheart back home. And if this haul of clothes had ended up in her shop, then it was probably also safe to assume that it had once belonged to Maggie and that maybe Maggie was now dead. Did that mean George was dead too? Quickly Dodie worked out what their ages were likely to be now and had to conclude that he probably was.

She found herself reading the letter again, letting each word burrow a little further into her soul. What had this couple been like? Had they known each other since childhood, perhaps? Or had they met at some genteel dance where Maggie had allowed George to walk her home and talk to her about poetry and the weather? Perhaps there'd been more irreverent flirting from out of a top-floor window, or a random conversation on a shared bus journey that had led to them seeking each other out on that same bus every day, eventually blossoming into something more. Dodie longed to be able to see beyond the letter, into the past, to see the rest of their lives play out. Had he ever come back from the war? Had they married? If they had, were there children… grandchildren? In the letter George talked about some news he'd had from Maggie, a shock, and how he was trying to get home so they could marry. Could that mean there *was* a child?

It was silly and pointless to try to figure it all out and it was even sillier to pine for love like that – it was a different age and love was different back then. The spectre of separation through war, the ever-present threat of death and loss, made love different. If you thought that every stolen moment might be your last together, you made each one count. Everyone was so comfortable now, everyone safe. Ryan was only ever a text message away if she needed him. There was no urgency in their love because there didn't need to be.

Dodie looked at the letter again. The emotion was so raw, so tangible, it was like she could grasp it from across the years and hold it to her own heart. It was exceptional and special and, even if it was silly and pointless trying to piece together George and Maggie's history, something about it wouldn't let Dodie be. A record of love this precious deserved to be back with Maggie's family, not in the drawer of a shop owner who knew nothing of the people who'd shared such devotion.

'I might have known you'd be trying everything on the minute my back was turned.' Isla's voice came from the doorway. Dodie looked around with a sheepish smile, the letter clutched guiltily in her hand as if she'd been caught reading a stolen diary. Which she knew was ridiculous, even if it was the way she felt.

'You know me too well. Isn't it gorgeous, though?' Dodie replied, trying to sound normal, though she felt far from it.

'It looks lovely on you,' Isla said, folding her arms and leaning against the doorframe. She raised her eyebrows. 'I take it you're keeping it?'

'I might,' Dodie said, turning to the mirror again. 'I'm not sure I can justify another coat but… well, it's weird but I feel very attached to it already, even though it's supposed to be stock; I don't think I can bear to sell it.'

'You're going to make a lot of money that way,' Isla said dryly. 'The shop isn't struggling because there's no business, it's because you're keeping all the stock for yourself.'

Dodie smiled. 'Not quite all of it. I have to admit to keeping a bit back, but I can't help it when everything is so lovely. You think this suits me then?'

'It does, though telling you so is just encouraging you.' Isla made her way around the counter to get a closer look.

'I won't hold it against you,' Dodie said. 'I found this too, in the pocket…' Grudgingly, but knowing that Isla would notice and ask about it sooner or later, she handed the letter to her friend, who took it with a vague frown.

'What's this?'

'If you read it you'll find out.'

'Sounds cryptic,' Isla said, opening the page. She was silent for a minute or two as she read it, and then folded it up and handed it back to Dodie.

'And that's why I don't get involved in old stuff; it's all too depressing.'

'I think it's romantic.'

'Romantically depressing. All angst and heartbreak and unfulfilled destinies. Poor sods.'

'They might have ended up getting married.'

'If that letter has come to you then it ended up as tragedy.'

'How do you know?'

'Because you're a weird tragedy magnet.'

'I'm a what?' Dodie laughed.

'A tragedy magnet. I don't know… something about you just invites drama. Not you – you're never dramatic – but you're always befriending people haunted by terrible secrets and angst. You're like an actual living, breathing women's fiction character.'

'So you don't think they ended up together,' Dodie asked, ignoring the jibes. She knew Isla didn't really mean any of it – that was just how they worked; Isla teased and insulted and Dodie loved the irreverent, dark humour in it.

'Absolutely not. I bet he didn't come home and she waited for a whole week before she married some slick American GI.'

'Not if the clothes have ended up with me, she didn't. Anyway, I prefer to think that they had true, everlasting love that could overcome anything. I bet it kept him alive and he came home at the end of the war to get married.'

'He died. You know it and I know it.'

'Well,' Dodie said, 'even if he did, it's still kind of romantic in its tragedy. You know that saying about it being better to have loved and lost…?'

'Yeah… I think that might be bull. I'll let you know my verdict if I'm ever stupid enough to fall in love.'

Dodie peeled off the coat with a grin and folded it carefully. 'I'm going to get my breakfast. Think you can hold the fort here for ten minutes?'

'I'm sure I'll manage.' Isla shot her friend a sideways glance.

'I know,' Dodie said, laughing. 'Just keep an eye on things but don't worry about any more sorting. Once I've eaten we'll go through it together and I'll tell you what needs doing.'

'Best if we do go through it together so I can stop you from trying it all on.'

'I'd like to see you do that. Many have tried and failed. Besides, I'm going to get you trying some stuff on later. I'll convert you to the joys of vintage clothing if it kills me.'

'God forbid, it will probably kill one of us,' Isla said.

Three

Dodie couldn't stop thinking about the letter, now stashed safely away in a locked drawer. The coat had gone to the dry cleaners, along with half a dozen other delicate items, after a careful check had revealed no more hidden secrets in the pockets. Inspecting and cataloguing the things that hadn't been discarded for the charity shop kept Isla and Dodie busy for the rest of the day, in-between serving customers. There were blouses, dresses, a couple of pairs of chic slacks and – to Dodie's utter delight – a cache of hidden brooches and costume jewellery stowed in a red leather clutch bag. Outside, the bright morning had darkened and, though it was barely 4 p.m., dusk was already throwing the corners of the street into shadow. The Christmas markets in town would be alive with festive music and the smells of bratwurst, roasted nuts and mulled wine while shoppers clung to cups of hot chocolate and sugared doughnuts as they strolled through the stalls. Maybe they'd wander down through the Lower Gardens where the trees would be strung with lights and hardy squirrels darted from branch to branch, then out to the promenade and the beachfront where bars and fairground rides came alive after dark. Dodie half wished she could close the shop early and join them, but if she didn't sort out this stock nobody else would – not to mention that she was supposed to be trying to sell some of it.

'But if it was you,' she said as Isla sniffed at a cashmere sweater and wrinkled her nose, 'if it was your grandma or mother, you'd want it, wouldn't you? I mean, it's sort of like an heirloom.'

'I suppose,' Isla said. 'Can't say I've given it much thought to be honest. I don't really *do* sentimental because I've never had much in the way of family heirlooms to treasure. That's kind of how it goes when your mother's family leave their homeland in a hurry with nothing more than the clothes on their backs and your dad cuts himself out of your life entirely. You're probably asking the wrong person about it.'

'But you would,' Dodie insisted.

'Maybe. But as you don't know where to find them it's a bit of a moot point.'

'I *do* know where to find them – the address is on the envelope.'

'*An* address is on the envelope. You know where this Margaret *used* to be. I don't suppose she'll have lived there for years, and she's certainly not living there now if you've got all her clothes.'

'What makes you think she hasn't lived there for a long time?'

Isla rested her hands on her hips. 'It was 1944. Who stays in the same house that long?'

'Lots of people,' Dodie said stubbornly.

'It might even have been her parents' house. Probably was if she wasn't married to George.'

'But a relative might live there now – a descendant or something.'

Isla gave a vague shrug. 'Maybe, but I doubt it. Do you know where the street is?'

'No, but I could Google it. Shouldn't think it's that far away.'

'Wouldn't hurt to try, I suppose. Or you could put it in the post to that address. Job done, as far as you're concerned. And if Margaret isn't there it's someone else's problem to find her.'

Dodie shook her head. 'I couldn't do that – what if the current owners aren't members of the family and don't know where any of the family has gone to? They might just throw it away.'

'Well if the people who live at that actual house don't know, you can hardly be expected to know, can you? I suppose they'd just send it on to the post office as "Not known at this address" and the post office could track the person down.'

'How would they track down someone who lived on Wessex Road in 1944?'

'How are *you* going to track down someone who lived on Wessex Road in 1944?'

'I don't know,' Dodie said lamely. 'I just feel as if I should have a go.'

'It's sweet, and just the sort of thing you'd do, but personally I think it's a waste of time and you've got enough to do here in the shop.'

Dodie was silent. 'You're probably right,' she said finally. 'When I think about it properly it does seem a bit daft, doesn't it?'

'A bit. But it's cute that you wanted to try.' Isla offered Dodie a black chiffon blouse. 'This is a bit saucy – you should try it on; would totally go with your new red hair.'

Dodie wrinkled her nose. 'I don't think I can pull off saucy. You should try it on if you like it.'

Isla was thoughtful for a moment as she studied the blouse. 'You're bloody determined to get me into second-hand crap, aren't you? Oh what the hell…' She sighed as she snatched it back. 'I'll be back in five minutes.'

Dodie grinned as she watched her head for the changing rooms. 'I knew I'd convert you!'

Isla had left at around seven and Dodie sat alone in front of the television in the tiny flat above the shop watching *Mr Smith Goes to Washington*. But she was seized by a strange restlessness that even Jimmy Stewart couldn't distract her from. She'd tried making a camomile tea, and she'd tried listening to Billie Holiday on her iPod, but she couldn't settle. A walk might do it, and the night was still young enough for there to be lots going on in town.

Peering into the fridge, she pulled out the pack containing the last of her posh ham and made a sandwich from it. The ham wouldn't be any good if she didn't use it today and you never knew who you might run into when you were out and about. She wrapped up the sandwich in cling film and dropped it into a bag with some crisps and a can of cola before locking the flat and heading out.

If anything, the main town and Lower Gardens were busier than they would have been during the day. The outdoor skating rink and disco set up for the Christmas period probably had a lot to do with that, not to mention the carousel and street-food stalls. Dodie stood for a while at the edge of the rink watching families and couples go round to the music, breath curling into the air and gales of laughter erupting as people ended up on their bottoms or slammed into their companions when they couldn't stop.

'Are you having a go, love?' a man asked her as he wobbled past on his skates to get onto the ice.

Dodie smiled. 'Not today. Looks a bit full for me. I need to be able to cling onto the rails at all times.'

'Me too,' he laughed. 'I'll be on my arse in a minute, but you can't let the kids have all the fun, can you?'

She watched as he launched himself into the fray and was every bit as unstable as he'd promised. He was enjoying himself, though, and that was the main thing. Catching up with a woman already on the ice, he grabbed her from behind and swung her around to face him, planting a kiss on her lips that left her giggling. Then they continued to skate together, holding hands to steady each other. They were probably in their late forties, maybe early fifties, but both looked as if they lived active, healthy lives and were very much in love.

Moments later they were joined by two teenage children who laughed at the man's ineptness, though he didn't seem to mind. They dared the woman to let go of his hand, and eventually she did, laughing as his arms went in windmills until he lost his balance and his bottom connected with the ice.

This time last year Dodie would probably have been on the ice with Ryan, but he lived out in Dorchester and she didn't see him as often as she used to. He cited the distance, the fact that she was often working into the evening and that he often worked weekends – just about anything, it seemed – to avoid driving over, and she found it difficult to make the journey to his house for the same reasons. It was a relationship, of sorts, but though neither of them had ever mentioned breaking it off, sometimes it seemed to Dodie that, rather than go out with a bang, it would just tail off quietly until one day they quite forgot they were supposed to be together at all. Not that she wanted it to, of course, and not that she actively sought a break-up, but she was strangely philosophical about the prospect, and she didn't think Ryan felt that differently. During her endless defences of him to Isla she wasn't lying when she said he was good and steadying for her, but maybe he was just a little too steady… But then, who said love always had to be fireworks? Couldn't love sometimes be more like a comforting hot-water bottle?

It was getting colder, and Dodie shivered slightly. With her beautiful new coat off to the cleaners, she'd hastily pulled on a short woollen pea jacket to come out, but it wasn't as luxuriously heavy and snug as her new one. It would probably help to get moving again, so she decided to make her way down to the beachfront promenade and get a caramel latte to warm her up.

A two-minute walk along winding paths, flanked by perfectly manicured shrubbery and lawns, took her past the glowing terraces of a hotel playing live music, down beneath a flyover taking traffic out of the town, and out to the entrance of the Victorian pier. At either side the promenade hugged a beach to take you towards Studland in one direction and Christchurch in the other. You could ride the cute land train in the summer along seven miles of golden sand and, if you fancied a bit of an adventure, lifts that looked like clockwork toys waited to take you up the sheer cliffs for a leisurely view of the impressive panorama of the bay. On a sunny day it was breathtaking.

The promenade was also home to seaside rides and stalls, including a beautiful Victorian carousel that Dodie often wished she could shrink down to fit in her flat so she could look at it all the time. Brightly painted horses, each with their own name, gilt poles and furnishings, baroque mirrors and piped music evoked a beautiful sense of the past, when life's pleasures were as simple as whizzing up and down on a steam-powered fairground ride. Dodie could squint her eyes in the lights and imagine it full of women in empire-line dresses and huge feathered hats and men in stiff-collared suits. But it was always packed, even in the twenty-first century when people wore jeans and had smartphones and access to hundreds of theme parks and TV on demand. People clung onto simple things more than even they realised, and the carousel was proof of that.

She wandered for a while. Down to the beach where she loved to see the twinkling lamps stretched along the sweeping shadow of the coastline, and where strollers on the pier gazed out to where the bobbing lights of distant boats flickered on the black sea and the moon sent silver ripples over its surface. On a night like this, there was nowhere on earth she'd rather be. No wonder she'd felt an odd pull to this place; ever since she was a girl visiting her grandmother at weekends, she'd known she'd end up living here herself one day. Some days it was tough forging the new life she'd promised herself – master of her own ship, maker of her own future – but on nights like this it was worth it.

If only she could get the business established so she felt financially secure, life would be just about perfect. God only knew she'd been through hell trying to get it on track – a battle with a bout of depression and anxiety had sealed her fate on her time studying dress history and fashion at university, ensuring she flunked the course before she'd even got halfway through. Despite this, she counted herself luckier than most that a supportive and loving network of family and friends had helped her through the dark days and nudged her to get back on her feet. Without them her life would have been very different to the one she had bright hopes for now. Never turn back, her mum had said, and Dodie hadn't. Terrified that re-entering education would send her down the same path again, she had done the next best thing – fulfilled another dream she'd harboured as a girl; to own a shop, full of the things she loved with a passion. She tried not to let the image of a dozen red-topped bills on the shelf at home invade her thoughts. There would be a time to worry about them properly, but she wasn't going to let them ruin her mood tonight.

At 9.30 p.m., too cold to stand much more despite the sense of contentment being out had brought, she decided to make her way home. It was as she was returning through the gardens that she noticed a shuffling figure dragging a huge shopping bag, kitbag and blanket over his shoulders. He looked as if he was casting around for a place to sleep.

'Nick!' she called, hurrying over.

He turned to her and his weary frown cleared into a smile. 'Twice in one day – must be my birthday.'

'I was hoping I'd see you – I had some ham left at home so I made you some sandwiches. You like pickle, don't you?'

'You remembered.' He smiled as she handed him the bag she'd made up earlier. 'Other goodies too – you're a sweetheart, you know that?'

'Not really – it would have gone to waste and I hate that. Where are you sleeping tonight? It's freezing – I know what you're going to say but do you think you ought to go to the shelter for once?'

'My mate Barry has something lined up, I think… if I can find him, that is. You haven't seen him anywhere tonight?'

'I'm not sure what he looks like,' she said doubtfully. 'And I don't recall the name.'

'To be fair he's pissed most of the time so if you have come across him on your travels, he'd have been too drunk to tell you his name. In fact, you wouldn't get much sense from him at all, but he does have a talent for sniffing out a good place to bunk.'

'What does he look like? If I see him I can tell him you're looking for him.'

'I wouldn't worry about it, love. He won't remember what you've said anyway. I'll find him sooner or later. Been for a walk, have you?' He nodded at the sand on her boots.

'Oh.' She laughed. 'I might have let my inner child out for an hour on the beach. It's when I see all that lovely sand, I just can't help it.'

'Was a time you could sleep on the beach.' He wiped the back of his hand under his nose. 'Not now – at night these days the beach is busier than it is during the day. Students everywhere having parties. Madness in the summer.'

'It's not too bad tonight,' Dodie said. 'Maybe you could try under the pier? The tide doesn't come right up, does it?'

He sniffed. 'Might do that if I don't find Barry. Probably just find somewhere in the park, though.'

Dodie gave a brisk nod. 'Right… well… I'll probably make my way back then. Early start tomorrow.'

'You take care. And thanks for the sandwich – made my night.'

'No problem; I hope you like it.' She held up a hand in farewell and turned to leave. But then she stopped a few paces on and spun around to call back. 'Nick…' she said slowly as the idea occurred to her. 'Do you happen to know where Wessex Road is?'

Four

It was easier to walk to Wessex Road than drive, mainly because Dodie got flustered when she was driving to new places, and walking allowed the luxury of checking street signs carefully and making mistakes without the stress of an angry motorist banging on his horn behind her. Nick had told her it would be about ten minutes from her shop; the reality was more like twenty, but the evening was milder than the previous one, and it wasn't so bad once she'd wrapped up. Besides, the stroll gave her time to unwind from a day in the shop that, while not particularly busy, had brought stresses in the form of a call from her accountant that had tied her brain up in knots and a difficult customer who had brought a ripped dress back for a refund. She'd insisted it had nothing to do with her, but Dodie distinctly remembered checking the item thoroughly as it came into the shop and finding no faults. It was tempting, given also that the woman was clearly bigger than the dress, to mention that a size sixteen body fitting into a size twelve garment was quite contrary to the laws of physics and would undoubtedly lead to something giving way, but in the end they'd negotiated a credit note rather than a refund and Dodie had taken the dress to a pile she'd put aside for repairs.

As she left the town proper for the suburbs, larger, gated properties hidden behind curtains of fir trees where the millionaires lived gave way to smaller, Victorian-built detached houses with magnolia trees, the winter skeletons of rose bushes in the gardens and mock Tudor-painted eaves. Then came smaller turn-of-the-century semis with neat frontages and too many cars spilling from too-small driveways. It was the end of November, and though Christmas was a little over three weeks away, most already had their decorations up.

Number 11 Wessex Road was not one of these. As she stood outside the gates, looking up, she saw no Christmas decorations cheering the windows, no magnolia trees in the garden and not even the tiniest stump of a rose bush. There weren't any cars in the driveway either.

The hefty period door was sheltered by a porch, and a quick inspection of the doorbell revealed that at some point the house had been converted into two flats. Dodie's heart sank at the sight – she was unlikely to find Margaret's family there, if it was no longer a single home. She peered at the names inside plastic squares beneath each of the bells: a Mr Albert Chan and an Edward Willoughby. Chan didn't sound a likely surname for someone related to her Margaret V, though she couldn't rule it out, of course. But her finger hovered over the bell for Mr Willoughby until she finally took a deep breath and pressed it.

The silence as she waited was lightly punctuated by the hissing of a car on a distant road and a dog barking somewhere in a neighbouring garden, and then a deep voice came through the intercom.

'Who is it?'

She'd already decided that she was going to sound quite mad to anyone who heard her story, so there didn't seem much point in dressing up the request for information. She took a deep breath and came straight out with it. 'You don't actually know me but my name is Dodie. I was wondering if you could help… This sounds crazy but I'm trying to track down a woman who may have once lived here. A long time ago, actually…'

'I don't know anything about anyone who lived here before me. And I rent it, so I'm not likely to anyway.'

'Oh.' Dodie hesitated. Not that she'd expected much more but still she felt oddly disappointed. 'But you might be able to give me some details for your landlord, though?' she added hopefully. 'They might be able to help.'

There was no reply, and after a moment Dodie hesitantly pressed the buzzer again. She didn't want to be a nuisance but not to respond to her question was a bit rude. She hadn't come all this way to give up at the first hurdle.

'I've told you I can't help!' the man snapped.

'I know, I just wondered...' She frowned. 'Never mind,' she sighed. It was clear Mr Willoughby was a grumpy, misanthropic loner who was best left to the solitude of his tarmac-gardened flat. She might have felt sorry for him if he'd even tried to be a bit polite.

Bracing herself, she went for the other doorbell, hoping to speak to Mr Chan instead. He might have no more information than Edward Willoughby but at least he might be civil about it. But there was no reply.

She could try down the road at number seventeen, of course, and see how she got on there, but as she turned her phone light on to study the address on the envelope once more she was more convinced than ever that it was number eleven she needed. She had to be sure, and she hadn't come all this way to do half a job – it was either a thorough investigation or none at all. *No you don't, Mr Scrooge McWilloughby – you're not putting me off that easily*. She buzzed for Edward Willoughby's flat again and waited for the onslaught.

'Are you still here?' His voice came through the intercom, full of barely contained irritation. Clearly he wanted to tell her to piss off and she half wished he would – at least she'd have a good excuse to do the same to him.

'I'm sorry…' she said, trying her best not to let him hear her own vexation. 'I'll try not to take up much of your time and after tonight I'll leave you alone, but this is quite important and I would rather get as much information as I can before I try another line of enquiry—'

She was interrupted by the front door being flung open.

'Oh… s-sorry…' Dodie stammered, looking up at him. 'You're Mr Willoughby?'

The man's glowering expression softened instantly as he looked down at her. He had to be five eleven, maybe even six feet tall, and to a squeak of a girl like Dodie, that was pretty intimidating. Perhaps he realised this quickly, because he gave her an unexpected and reassuring smile that showed slight dimples in his cheeks.

'Ed,' he said.

'Sorry?'

'My name is Ed.' He paused, seeming to appraise Dodie for a moment. She took the opportunity to do the same. She'd guess he was in his early thirties but it was hard to tell with the light spilling from behind him out onto the step. His hair was reddish brown, short at the neck but longer and tousled at the top so that it curled over his forehead. His eyes were hazel, maybe even green in daylight, but they had kindness and intelligence in them, despite his brusque attitude over the intercom. His nails were short, bitten down to the quick on fingers that looked lithe and delicate enough to play piano or perhaps guitar, and the T-shirt he shivered in now that the door was open hung from a well-toned frame.

'Look… I'm sorry I snapped earlier but I really don't know that I can help you,' he said. 'What exactly is it you need again?'

'I'm trying to track down a lady, or the family of a lady… I think she once lived here. It would have been in 1944, so I know it's a while ago but …'

He scratched his head. '1944? More than a while ago. I bet this house has changed hands a dozen or more times since then.' Then he narrowed his eyes slightly. 'Are you related to her? Doing a family tree or something?'

'No. I just know her name was Margaret and I think she lived here.'

'Margaret? Don't you have more than that? I'm not sure what you're going to find armed only with the name of Margaret. Aren't there websites for this sort of thing?'

'I don't know… I just thought I'd try the address first before I did anything else. It kinda made sense to me.'

He folded his arms. 'I don't have a clue about anyone who was here before me, and I only moved to the area two months ago. Sorry.'

'Perhaps your landlord would? He or she must have had some information when they bought the house – deeds or Land Registry papers or something that might give a clue? They might even be related to Margaret, inherited her house or something?'

'I deal directly with a lettings agent – not a clue who owns the house.'

'Do you think your neighbour would? Mr Chan?'

'Albert?' Ed swept his hand over a light dusting of stubble, deep in thought. 'I doubt it. I suppose I could ask him. He's away for a couple of days though, and I don't have a phone number for him.'

'I'd appreciate it – I could leave you my phone number in case he does know anything?'

'This must mean a lot to you.' Ed pulled a mobile from his pocket and swiped the screen to access his contacts list. 'It's a lot of trouble to go to. Can I ask what it's about, or is that private?'

'Oh, no, it's not private at all. I found this letter…' Dodie rummaged in her bag and produced the envelope. She held it up for him to see. 'There's the address, but as you can see some of it's worn off and so has the surname. But it's a very important letter as far as I can tell, the sort of thing that would have a great deal of sentimental value.' She shrugged as he took it from her and turned the envelope over to look at the other side. 'I wanted to return it to… whoever it belonged to really, though I'm not entirely sure who that would be.'

'No sender's address on the back,' he said, studying it. 'Where's it from? Can I look inside?'

Dodie hesitated. They were old words, shared between people neither of them knew, but they felt somehow deeply private. She wasn't sure she wanted just anyone reading them. She'd barely felt comfortable reading them herself. To let him read them felt like an insult to Margaret and George, as if making light of the intense love on the page for the sake of entertainment or idle curiosity. And yet, who knew, this man might be able to help if he did look.

'OK,' she decided. 'Go ahead.'

'If you want to step inside for a moment while I read, be my guest,' he said. Dodie hesitated. 'I am freezing, to be honest,' he added, 'and it might be nice to shut the cold out for a minute before I get hypothermia. I won't jump you, I promise.'

'I didn't think you would,' Dodie said, feeling stupid for her doubts as she stepped in and set the door ajar behind her. 'Anyway,' she added with a defiant jut of her chin that looked braver than she felt, 'I carry hairspray in my bag for that sort of thing, so I don't worry.'

'Hairspray?' He raised his eyebrows as his thumb slid under the flap of the envelope. 'What are you going to do with that – style your attacker into submission?'

'Spray it in their face,' Dodie replied indignantly. 'It's not as stupid as it sounds; would you like a ton of hairspray in your eyes?'

'I suppose not,' he replied with a faint smile before turning his attention to the letter. Dodie couldn't decide whether it would be an overreaction to give him a swift kick in the ankle for being so patronising. In the end, she decided maybe an arrest for grievous bodily harm wouldn't help her cause all that much, whether she was being patronised or not.

While he was occupied, she took the opportunity to give the house a quick once-over. It was like most rented houses she'd been in: lockable doors separating the entrance to each flat, one at the top of the stairs and one at the end of the hallway, which served as a shared entrance to the property. The hallway was painted in a sort of dirty beige colour that was probably called 'wheat field' or 'truffle' or something equally romantic that in no way resembled the drab, uninspiring colour it really was. This sort of décor was Dodie's worst nightmare; the sort of colour she imagined her own personal hell would be if there was such a thing and she was unfortunate enough to end up in it. The only saving graces were the rather nice terracotta tiling on the floor, which looked like an original feature, and the distinct smell of pine air freshener that showed someone had, at least, made a bit of an effort to make it welcoming. But then she wondered if, rather more disturbingly, they were trying to mask a nasty smell?

She didn't doubt that it once would have been a lovely family home. It made her sad to see it reduced to lets, where people came and went year in year out without so much as two words to their neighbours or a single thought for the way it looked. Houses were bricks and mortar but they could be so much more – they stored memories and they became entwined in lives. How could somewhere so temporary ever become entwined in anyone's life? It was somewhere to sleep and eat and nothing more.

'I was in the army,' Ed said quietly, his voice bringing Dodie back from her musings. He was still staring at the letter. She frowned at his tone, suddenly so melancholy and introspective. Then something in him jolted and he handed back the letter. 'It's tough being separated from your loved ones and not knowing whether you'll ever see them again, or whether a bullet will get you.'

'You were at war?'

'I was out in the Middle East… Iraq, Afghanistan… I saw a bit of action, yeah.'

'What about the letter?'

'What about it?'

'I thought you said you might get some clues from it – where I can try next.'

He shrugged. 'There's not much in it. Even George says he can't divulge his position. I suppose we might be able to find records to say where any particular battalions were stationed during June 1944 in France. But we don't even know whether he's army, air force or navy. I would say army, but I couldn't be certain. Even if we could find out who was stationed where and sift through it to get the right one, we have very little information about George apart from his Christian name and the fact that he's dating Margaret someone or other. I would imagine both names were quite common at that time. So we don't have a lot to go on when you look at it all like that.'

Dodie let out a sigh. 'Well, maybe I can go and see your letting agent. Could you give me their number?'

'I can, but I doubt they're going to be interested in helping you. They probably have some sort of data protection obligation or something to their client… y'know?'

'I suppose so.' Folding the letter back into the envelope, she stowed it carefully back in her bag. She turned and pulled the front door open again, letting a blast of cold air roll through the hallway.

'Are you going to give me your number or not?' he asked.

Dodie turned back, her hand resting on the doorknob. 'My number?'

'You did say you would.'

Dodie held back a frown. He'd just told her he couldn't help.

'I would,' she began awkwardly, 'but I have a boyfriend you see…'

He grinned. 'I don't doubt it. But you wanted me to talk to Albert when he got back and let you know what he said. I can hardly do that without your number, can I?'

'Oh… of course!' Dodie felt the heat rise to her face as she fished in her bag for her mobile. She held it out with her number displayed on the screen so he could copy it into his own.

'What did you say your name was again?' he asked.

'Dodie. Dodie Bright.'

'Dodie Bright,' he repeated. 'Cute. Well, Dodie Bright, if I find anything more I'll let you know.'

She stepped out onto the street and pulled her jacket tighter. The porch went dark and as she turned to speak again she realised he'd already closed the front door. So she didn't find a Margaret V but she did find an Ed Willoughby. She couldn't quite decide what she thought of that.

Dodie had visited number seventeen as well in the end. As she was on the street anyway it made sense to investigate every lead, even if she wasn't quite convinced of it. But the young woman with a screaming baby clamped to her hip who'd answered the door had even less information, or inclination, to help than hot-and-cold Ed at number eleven. In some ways Dodie was annoyed at herself for thinking her wild goose chase had been a good idea. People were busy, wrapped up in their own lives. What did they care for a nutty girl who turned up on their step bleating about lost love and ancient letters? What difference did it make to anyone if Dodie's letter never made it back to Margaret, or her family? It mattered to Dodie, but then she cared about a lot of things that never troubled most people and, if she'd been pushed on the reasons, even she would have found them hard to put into words. All she knew was that she'd gone to sleep thinking about it and woke the next day still thinking about it. In between she'd probably dreamed about it too, if only she could remember.

As the sun rose in a pearl-grey sky and the town awoke, it was business as usual. Dodie threw herself into wet-dusting the shop in between customers, the radio blasting Christmas songs in the corner. As it wasn't yet December she'd probably be sick of hearing them long before the main event arrived, but for now they took her mind off the miserable failure of the night before. By lunch she'd managed to shift two blouses, a leather satchel and most of the previous week's dirt from the store shelves. Working on her own for most of the time meant she rarely got time to stop for lunch – not wanting to close the shop or make it smell of any food she might be eating – but today she was ravenous, so she surreptitiously broke off bits of cream cracker from a pack beneath the counter, munching on them as she read through a listing for an online auction site. It was mostly furniture and bric-a-brac rather than clothes, but for some time now she'd had the notion that she might quite like to branch out into retro household furnishings, and there was certainly a market for it from what others had told her. It was all a question of outlay, of course, and she couldn't afford to have too much money tied up in stock on the shelves at any one time. Then again, it might be a risk worth taking if it turned things around. Perhaps she'd talk to her accountant about it next time she saw him.

Absently, her gaze flicked to her phone, sitting on the counter beside her laptop. It had been silent all morning. She hadn't really expected anything exciting to come through and it was probably far too soon, but part of her had been hoping she'd hear from Ed Willoughby. She'd thought about him a lot over the course of the morning, when she hadn't been thinking about George and Margaret, and each time he seemed more of a mystery than before. He'd been like two different men: the one who'd barked at her over the intercom, and the one who'd almost flirted with her on the doorstep. Not for the first time she decided that if men thought women were an enigma, women had twenty times more reasons to think the same of them. And at least a woman would talk to you and tell you what she was thinking, whereas men simply expected you to mind read, and even then the signals weren't very good.

Her thoughts were interrupted by the bell of the shop door jingling and she looked up to see her gran stagger in under a pile of plastic-wrapped garments. Dodie's gran was even tinier than Dodie; a dynamo of a woman with steel-grey hair that still had good slices of black and cheeks that were smoother than most women half her age.

'I called in at the dry cleaners on the way here,' she said. 'I knew they'd have some of your stuff and they know me.'

'I know they know you,' Dodie said as she raced around the counter to take them from her. 'But I've told you before there's no need to go and fetch it for me – you'll do yourself a mischief carrying all that up the road.' Her gran followed her as she went into the back with the newly cleaned stock. And then followed her back into the shop.

'Your hair is red,' she said as she threw a critical gaze at her only granddaughter.

'It is,' Dodie replied. She could have done it with a lot more sarcasm but she loved her gran, despite the constant criticism of her hair. *And here it comes…*

'I don't know what's wrong with your own hair – it's very pretty. Everyone used to say so when I took you to school.'

'You took me to school twice when I was ten and Mum had the flu,' Dodie reminded her. 'I don't think you could possibly have managed to talk to *everyone* about my hair.'

Gran shook her head sombrely, as if she was witnessing the destruction of the Great Wall of China or someone ripping up the Magna Carta rather than the result of her granddaughter's hair-colouring whims. 'I like it natural.'

'I know you do but I happen to like changing it.'

'I think it's a crying shame. It'll fall out if you're not careful.'

'I'll be careful then.'

Gran wandered over to a rail of tweed suits and jackets and began to rifle through it. 'Have you sold anything this week?'

'It hasn't been too bad actually. Although it is only Tuesday, you know.'

'Is it? I lose track of the days. Comes from being at home all the time.'

'You've been at home all the time since you retired ten years ago.' Dodie couldn't help a wry smile. 'And you're still not used to it? Besides, you're barely in.'

'It's the dark evenings,' she replied absently, and Dodie decided it wasn't worth trying to figure out what that even meant. 'Ooooh, this is nice,' she added, pulling a long plum-coloured coat from the rail and holding it against herself.

'It buries you, Gran,' Dodie said. 'Far too long.'

'You think?' Gran said, disappointment edging her tone.

'It'd be too long for me, and you're a good inch shorter.'

'But you could take it up for me…'

'I'd ruin the cut with an alteration that big. Best to leave it, Gran.'

'Shame… I fancied a nice coat. What else have you got?'

Dodie took a deep breath. She loved her dearly, but Gran was definitely her worst ever customer. Once a week she'd turn up at the shop and spend the afternoon trying on clothes she had no intention of ever buying. Dodie had even offered to give her something she liked free of charge, but whatever she pulled from the rails, it was never quite right once she had it on. There must have been dozens of discarded items over the months; Dodie had once gently suggested that her gran continue to get all her clothes from the Victorian department store that was a stalwart of the town and her gran's usual garment provider of choice, a suggestion which had wounded her gran so deeply that Dodie had never broached the subject again.

'I had a big pile of forties and fifties stuff in yesterday. Quite a lot of it's in the dry cleaning you've just brought in. Feel free to rummage if you want to… although the green coat is mine so don't take that.'

Dodie turned the radio down and closed her laptop as her gran went through to the back room where they'd just left the dry cleaning. She gave her phone a quick check for new messages or calls, but there was nothing. At the sound of her gran coming back into the shop her head flicked up, and she had to hold in a groan as she saw that Gran was wearing the very coat she'd just told her not to pick up.

'This is nice,' Gran said, plunging her hands into the pockets and snuggling into the fur collar. 'How much are you going to put this out for?'

'I said I was going to… oh, never mind. I'd let you have it for free if you wanted it.'

Gran tripped over and kissed Dodie on the cheek. 'You're so kind to your old gran. It's very warm. I'll bet it cost a pretty penny when it was new.'

'I think it must have done. It was a worthwhile investment too – just look how it's lasted. It still looks new.'

Gran went to the full-length mirror and studied her reflection for a moment. 'I don't know whether I like green,' she said thoughtfully. 'Perhaps I'll try something else on. Have you got any beige? Beige goes with everything.'

Dodie gave her a patient smile. 'I've got something that's sort of brownish dogtooth, and something a bit tweedy. Any good?'

'Camel…' Gran said firmly. 'Camel is what I'm after. I saw a lovely camel coat in town.'

'At the department store, by any chance?'

Her gran stared out of the window for a moment. 'Yes!' she said, swinging round with surprising speed, as if she'd suddenly been struck by the meaning of life. 'Yes, it was! Do you have one like that?'

'I don't know because I haven't seen it,' Dodie replied patiently. 'It might be easier for you to look through the rails yourself and see if there's anything similar.'

'Good idea,' Gran said, shrugging off the green coat and handing it back to Dodie. 'First I'll put the kettle on for a nice cup of tea, eh?'

Twenty minutes later Gran had forgotten about looking for a coat, much to Dodie's relief, and they were sitting together in the shop with mugs of tea watching the traffic on the road as it rumbled past the window. Gran had left the teabags in too long, distracted by a pigeon fight on the roof of the newsagent opposite, but Dodie never liked to waste anything and now held back a grimace as she swallowed a mouthful of liquid that could very likely strip the paint from her shop front.

'I remember when this place was an underwear shop,' Gran said. 'My mother used to come here for her girdles.'

'No girdles now, so don't even think about asking me to find one,' Dodie said, raising her eyebrows over the rim of her mug as she took another sip. She was going to drink this tea if it killed her. And it probably would.

'Oh no, I couldn't bear to wear one. But my mum was never without hers, even in bed. Never liked my dad to see her wobbly bits. It's no wonder she was dead at sixty, all that squeezing of everything in…'

Dodie had learned to smile patiently at this story. She'd heard it many times before and at first wasn't quite sure how she was meant to respond. She soon learned that it was the telling of the story Gran was interested in, not necessarily the reaction to it.

'I suppose it's changed a lot around here,' Dodie said.

'Oh yes, from what it looked like when I was a girl it's barely recognisable now. All that new building and shops and students everywhere you look. Foreigners too with all the English-language schools that have popped up. Not that I mind foreigners, of course; I'm not one of those National Front types.'

Dodie laughed. 'I didn't think you were.'

'And my grandmother was half Spanish you know.'

'I know.'

Gran's tea sloshed dangerously close to the lip of her cup as she reached to pat Dodie's hand. 'I'm ever so happy you came back to live here. I was lost the day your mother said she was moving to Dorchester.'

'I know you were, and I know you missed her at first, but Dorchester's not exactly Greenland, is it?'

'It's ever so hard for me to get there now I'm not so good on my legs.'

Dodie had seen Olympic athletes slower on their feet than her gran, but it wasn't worth arguing the point. Some people smoked and others drank, but her gran's vice was gaining the sympathy of whomever she was with, even if that took a little exaggeration of problems that weren't there in the first place.

'You don't have to get there – Mum comes to you.'

'She's too busy most of the time.'

'She comes every fortnight… it's a lot more than some people get from their relatives.'

'I know…' Gran slurped at her tea as she gazed out of the window. 'Your grandad – God rest his soul – has a cousin in Poole who never sees her son from one week to the next but when he wants money…' there was a pause for added drama, though it was hardly dramatic when you'd heard the story ten times before, 'when he wants money he's there, making a fuss and bringing her chocolate biscuits. When she's got a packet of Hobnobs in her cupboard then she's usually got a hole in her bank balance.' She patted Dodie's hand again. 'But you'd never do that to me, would you? And I'm ever so glad that you live here now so I can see a lot more of you.'

'Me too,' Dodie smiled. 'I love it here. And I can't afford luxuries like Hobnobs so you're quite safe.'

'You need money...?' Gran plonked her tea on the counter and reached for her bag, but Dodie placed a hand on her arm.

'No, Gran... I was just joking. I'm fine; I don't need any money.'

'Well you'd better tell me if you do. Don't want you lining up at the soup kitchens when I could help.'

'Don't worry, I will,' Dodie said, giving her a fond smile. 'The minute I'm down to my last Pot Noodle you'll be the first to know.'

'Good girl.' Gran reclaimed her tea and turned to the window again. 'Don't let me forget that green coat before I go.'

'I thought you didn't want the green coat.'

'Oh no, it's beautiful. It'd look lovely with my black shoes.'

Dodie's gran owned only black shoes – about ten pairs that were virtually all cloned from the same court shoe that had been cobbled some time around 1965, but like many things where her gran was concerned, it was easier not to open up a debate about it.

'But I thought you wanted a camel coat.'

'Oh, I saw a camel coat in the big store... the one I like...'

'Yes, I know which store. I could take you over there later if you want to try it on.'

'I might do. What time will that be?'

'I can't go until the shop's shut, but I think the rest of the town's doing late-night opening tonight so it would be no bother to go.'

'Oh, I expect *Countdown* will be on then. Best leave it.'

'OK.' Dodie tried to swallow some more tea, if only so she wouldn't have to keep looking at it. 'So... do you want the green coat or not?'

Gran was silent for a moment. 'I don't think I completely like green,' she said finally. 'Makes me look peaky. And your grandad hated green.

I had a green skirt once and he sulked every time I wore it. So I wore it all the more. One Sunday he spilled gravy all over it on purpose because I wouldn't take it back to the shop.'

Dodie smiled. Another story she'd heard before, though she often wondered how much of it was true and how often it had been embellished over time. But talk of the green coat brought to mind again the letter she'd found in the pocket.

'Gran… do you know the area around Wessex Road at all?'

'I had a friend who lived in Casterbridge Road and it's quite nearby. Why do you ask?'

'Was there a woman named Margaret living there at the time? Or a man named George?'

'How should I know? I hardly know everyone who lives there. This is a very strange question!'

'I suppose it is. It's just that I found a letter to someone named Margaret who lived there in 1944 and I wanted to find out where she'd gone.'

'Blimey, I know you think I'm old but I'm not that old! I don't know what happened to someone in 1944!'

'I thought you were born during the war?'

'Well, I was but I was only a babe in 1944. I'm hardly going to know anyone if I'm still sucking on my dummy, am I?'

'I suppose not. It was just a thought.'

Gran ran her eyes over the interior of the shop. 'About time you got your Christmas decorations up? It'll soon be upon us.'

'It's not even December yet.'

'Still, all the other shops have theirs up.'

Dodie paused. She supposed Gran had a point, and perhaps it was a much more productive use of her time than fretting about an old letter written by a man she'd never met.

'I'll do it this week,' she decided. 'Want to come and help?'

'Depends when you decide to do it. You'll have to give me some warning so I can cancel arrangements.'

'Don't cancel anything on my account; I just thought you might want to. I'll ask Ryan if he's free and we'll do it together.'

Gran nodded, then drained her cup and plonked it down with a smack of her lips, seemingly blissfully unaware of the awfulness of her tea. She reached for her handbag. 'Best be off,' she said. 'I'm calling bingo for the old folks at the home later.'

Dodie smiled broadly as she gave her a peck on the cheek. Gran was probably older than most of the people in the home she was visiting but the irony seemed genuinely lost on her. 'Thanks for coming. Be careful going home, won't you?'

'Oh yes,' Gran said cheerfully. 'I expect Alastair will be passing with his mobility scooter in a minute – I'll hop on and catch a lift home.'

'You're not still flirting with him, are you?' Dodie wagged a finger at her. 'If you've no intention of dating him it's not kind to lead him on.'

'He doesn't mind one bit and I do like those custard tarts he brings over every Thursday.'

'Hmmm, I'm sure...' Dodie said, arching her eyebrow disapprovingly as she saw her out of the shop. Though it was hard to be disapproving with any level of serious commitment where her gran was concerned. 'Phone me when you get home!' she called after her, but Gran was already marching down the street.

Five

It had started to rain. Not the sort of rain you could walk about in either, but rain that bounces from the pavements, holds up traffic and soaks you to the skin in minutes. The shop had been closed for an hour and Dodie had hardly tasted the quick meal of beans on toast she'd eaten while she watched the teatime news. She didn't know why she watched the news at all, because it only made her miserable, but it was a duty, somehow, like checking on the elderly neighbour in the next street she'd got talking to one morning the month before or making sure that Nick got a sandwich from time to time... Somehow she felt an inexplicable obligation to know what was going on in the world, like by knowing it was in some way helping.

There had been a report from Syria, and the sight of bombs going off and the sounds of bullets cracking through a smoke-filled skyline had reminded her of something Edward Willoughby from Wessex Road had told her the night before. He'd seen action in the Middle East, he'd said. She'd never met anyone who'd served in a conflict zone before, and it had always seemed like a distant thing when she'd seen it on the news, a thing that happened to other people and affected other lives. She wondered how it might have scarred him, made him into a different person, because as she watched the TV images she realised that nobody could walk away from that without being affected by it.

She wondered what George, her letter writer, had been through, and whether the war in France in 1944, though the technology was very different, had been every bit as traumatic and brutal as what she saw on the reports now. She supposed it must have been, but when she'd learned about it at school in history lessons, it had never seemed so real and so tangible as it did now she was in possession of a letter written by the hand of one of the men who'd actually fought there. George sounded so ordinary, so unremarkable, that he could have been any of the men she knew now, and it pained her to think of the love on that page never being seen again by the people it mattered to. It was the least poor old George deserved from her, and she owed it to him as the custodian of such a precious thing to somehow get it to the family who would cherish it and all it represented.

Checking her phone again, she noted that there was still nothing from Ed Willoughby. Either he hadn't been able to talk to his neighbour or letting agent yet, or he'd just decided she was a nutter worth nothing but instant dismissal from his mind. It looked as if she'd have to tackle the problem in a different way. Curling into a corner of her sofa under a duvet by the fire, she opened up her laptop and logged in. Every search made in the world these days started with Google, so it seemed sensible for Dodie to start there too. What to use for search terms – that wasn't quite so obvious. Using George's name and Margaret V, the street and the year turned up hundreds of results that barely seemed relevant at all, and trying to find out which British units were serving in France during 1944 turned up various archived documents, history lessons and contemporary eyewitness accounts, but only a handful of individual names pertaining to the men who served in them. As far as she could tell, her George wasn't one of them. It seemed like an impossible task, but after an hour she went off to make herself a milky coffee and started again, trying to locate the local marriage records in case George and Margaret had got married in the end and she'd be able to trace them that way. That didn't yield any clues either. It had gone ten by the time she gave up, and she was no further forward than she had been when she'd started three hours earlier. In fact, as she looked at her watch, she couldn't believe three hours had passed so quickly. Shutting the laptop down, she made one last check on her phone, but apart from a daft photo of a rude-shaped carrot Isla had found in Tesco's and a text from Ryan saying he was feeling kinda anxious (his favourite *Beetlejuice* quote, which meant he was in the mood for sex) and that he was going to pop over to see her at the end of the week, there were no messages. Time for bed. Perhaps sleep would bring her some inspiration, because she sure as hell wasn't getting any awake.

As it turned out Ryan was very anxious indeed. He arrived the next evening after closing time with a bottle of rosé wine and a cheeky grin.

'I wasn't expecting to see you tonight,' Dodie said as she let him in, trying to bite back the tone of vexation at being surprised. She supposed he'd thought it would be sweet and she'd love it, but she'd made plans to do some more internet research into her mysterious wartime sweethearts and with Ryan there she certainly wouldn't be doing that. Perhaps her reaction was unreasonable but she couldn't help it. His dark hair was still wet from the shower he'd clearly had before rushing over, and she didn't always get a freshly washed Ryan, so at least that was something.

He didn't seem to notice the sharpness of her tone, though.

'I know,' he replied cheerfully, 'but that's the point – you're always going on about how I'm not romantic enough. Isn't this the sort of thing that's supposed to be romantic?'

'But it's Wednesday…'

'Yes, I had noticed.'

'I have to go to bed early.'

'And I was hoping you'd say that…' Ryan handed her the bottle with a slow smile, and Dodie couldn't help but throw one back. How could she be annoyed when he was trying so hard?

'Red hair?' he added, nodding at the now scarlet bob she'd clipped behind an ear with a delicate diamanté grip.

'Oh…' Dodie smoothed a hand over her tresses. 'I forgot to tell you I'd dyed it again.'

'I like it better than the turquoise.'

'That's not hard as you had no issue with telling me how much you hated the turquoise.'

'It was weird; people stared. But red… at least it's almost normal.'

'Thank you – I think.'

'It looks great,' he said, wiggling his eyebrows suggestively. '*You* look great whatever colour your hair is.'

Dodie folded her arms. 'I'm not staying up late no matter how much you try to persuade me. And if you're thinking of staying over just remember that I'll be up at the crack of dawn and I'm not going to tiptoe around the flat just so you can sleep in.'

'That's OK, I've got an early start anyway…' He stepped forward to kiss her. 'I just wanted to see you.'

'Hmmm…' Dodie didn't want to give in, but she could feel her resolve to be annoyed at his impromptu appearance starting to melt.

Whatever he'd used in the shower had left him smelling *very* good. 'OK. But don't forget… no keeping me up past ten.'

'Wouldn't dream of it.'

His expression was all innocence, but Dodie knew that, despite her warning and his promise, she would most definitely be up past ten.

They shared a pizza that Ryan had fetched from the takeaway along the road and the wine flowed. There had been flirty double entendres all through the meal, and almost as soon as the last slice had left the box, Ryan made his move and they went to bed at just gone nine thirty. When he was done, he rolled away from her and kicked the bedsheets off.

'Wow. It feels like forever since we did that.'

'It's not,' Dodie laughed. 'You were over last Saturday, remember?'

'It's because you're so good, babe – it feels like forever because I can't get enough.'

Dodie propped herself on an elbow and turned to face him with a frown.

'I know, I know…' He laughed. 'You hate it when I call you babe. I forgot… sorry. I don't know why it's such a big deal, though.'

'It's not a big deal. I don't know why I don't like it, I just don't. Not *babes* or *baby* either. I'm a grown woman, not an actual child, and to call a sexy woman *baby* just sounds a bit weird to me. Dodie will do just fine because that's my name.'

'You don't complain when people call you love or sweetheart in the street.'

'That's different.'

'How?'

She shrugged. 'Just is.'

He shook his head and shot her a sideways grin. 'You're weird.'

'Isn't that why you like me?'

'I suppose it must be.' He pulled her into his arms and she nestled there, listening to his heartbeat. When she looked up again his eyes were closing.

'Oi!' She prodded him. 'At least give me ten minutes of conversation before you fall asleep.'

He opened his eyes with a lazy grin. 'OK; talk to me.'

'How about you talk to me?'

'What do you want me to say?'

'I don't know… whatever comes into your head.'

'How about *I'm knackered and I want to go to sleep*?'

'You must have something to say.'

'I could tell you about my week at work but you'd soon be falling asleep yourself. If you want to chat, you'll have to think of something to talk about and I'll just nod in the appropriate places.'

'That's a cop-out if ever I heard one but I suppose it's better than listening to you snore.'

'I don't snore.'

'You wouldn't know.' There was a pause. What she wanted to talk about – the thing that seemed to be most on her mind lately despite not fully understanding why – was George's letter to Margaret. But she knew Ryan well, and he wouldn't understand either. Not only that, but he'd probably make her feel silly about it. Ryan was practical, head firmly in the real world, and although he tolerated her whimsies, she could tell he didn't have time for them. Not many did, and Dodie had learned to keep a lot of it to herself for the sake of an easy life. But she wanted to talk about this, to share it with him – after all, he was her boyfriend, and if she couldn't share her thoughts with him, who could she share them with?

Opening her mouth to speak, she looked up to see that his eyes had closed again, and already his breathing was slowing. She could wake him up but what would be the point? Reaching for the lamp, she turned it off and let the darkness lull her to sleep.

Six

Ryan had left at six that morning, and although Dodie should have been tired getting up with him, she was surprisingly perky. Perhaps it was the flurries of snow set against an impossible blue sky that made her smile. For the first time that winter, the cold weather brought beauty with it. As long as it didn't turn into a blizzard, the snow would make people feel festive and perhaps bring them into town to splurge on gifts for their loved ones, maybe even a cheeky one or two for themselves. Dodie was certainly counting on the latter as most of her customers purchased things they intended to keep – as Isla had often commented, surprising your friend with a beige seventies Crimplene trouser suit was always going to entail an element of risk that they might want to throw it on the fire once you'd gone.

While she was feeling festive, she thought it might also be a good day to do the decorating Gran had mentioned. So she lugged two boxes of tinsel and other Christmas odds and ends snaffled from her parents' loft down from her living room and began to arrange them around the shop in between customers. She had to admit that she wasn't entirely sure whether she was making the shop look more festive or just an almighty mess, but as the radio played swing arrangements of Christmas classics, she certainly felt more festive, even if her shop didn't look it. Then she began on the white plastic tree she'd found at a car boot sale. Tacky was what Isla had called it, but Dodie felt it fitted the aesthetic of the shop perfectly. Nothing said Christmas vintage quite like a white sparkly plastic tree hung with glittery baubles and topped with a fairy that looked like Barbie's well-endowed alcoholic older sister.

By twelve she'd had four customers – one looking for a print of the lady with the green face that had seemed to grace every living room wall between 1971 and 1979, another one after a period costume for a school production of *A Christmas Carol* (Dodie had directed them to the costume shop), one who bought some eighties dungarees and one who'd spent almost an hour trying on the same two dresses with her friend, mumbling how both looked equally good every time she emerged from the changing room again, only to announce that she'd think about it and come back. There were days when Dodie wished she'd had a bit more patience with her university course and maybe she'd be working in the fashion industry now rather than painting on smiles for the customers from hell. Cranky moods aside, however, she loved her little shop, and when she really thought about it, that wasn't how she felt at all. She simply needed her shop to perform well enough to stay open and sometimes the stress and frustration attached to that could be overwhelming, especially when there were days when nothing seemed to go her way. Lunchtime wasn't for another hour and she probably wouldn't be stopping anyway, so she pulled her box of cream crackers from the drawer and munched grouchily as she stared out of the window, the snow now spitting to a halt, and her Mary Poppins mood turning into Miss Trunchbull.

As she contemplated closing up for an hour at one and taking a walk down to the seafront – something she rarely did but today seemed to call for drastic action – her phone rang. Retrieving it from the drawer to answer, she smiled, her maudlin thoughts forgotten as she heard the voice of Ed Willoughby. She'd just about given up on him, and a bit of good news was what she needed to lighten her mood. At least she hoped it would be good news.

'Hello, Ed. How are you?'

'I'm good, actually,' he said. 'I thought I'd better catch up with you. Any further on with the search for your mysterious letter writer?'

'No. To be honest I haven't really had as much time as I'd like, though.'

'That's a shame. I can't offer much help either, I'm afraid. Albert came back from his travels and I had a quick word with him, but he didn't know any more about any of our house's previous residents than me. And I phoned the letting agent but, as I thought, they wouldn't give me any details about the landlord. They did say they'd get in touch with him and ask, which I thought was good of them.'

Dodie munched on a cracker thoughtfully, staring out of the window. 'Oh,' she said, swallowing. 'And I suppose you haven't heard back yet?'

'It was only at the start of the week and I expect they're busy. I just wanted to let you know where I was at… it seemed important to you.'

'Thanks; I appreciate that.'

There was a brief silence. Was that it?

'Oh, and I did have a word with the people at number seventeen,' he said, breaking into the pause, 'but they told me you'd already been to ask them about it.'

'Yes.'

'They weren't very helpful – looked a bit pissed off, to be honest.'

'They were like that with me too,' Dodie said. 'But they'd got their hands full with a baby so I suppose they haven't got time for people knocking to ask them silly questions.'

'No need to be rude, though.'

'At least you know which of your neighbours to avoid when you need a cup of sugar,' Dodie said with a faint smile. 'So you didn't speak to anyone else on the road?'

'No.'

'Right…'

'Maybe it would help? I mean, some of the residents are older… they might know about the family who lived there.'

'That's not a bad idea,' Dodie mused. 'I might even go later today when I've shut the shop.'

'Shop?'

'Oh, I work in a shop. I mean, it's my shop…'

'What sort of shop is it?'

'I don't think you'd be interested. Just clothes.'

'Just clothes? What, like women's clothes? Men's? Both? Is it in Bournemouth?'

'Yes, but I don't think you'd want to shop here.'

'Are you trying to put me off coming to buy something?' he asked. Dodie couldn't be sure, but something in his voice sounded like he was teasing her and she wasn't certain what to make of it. He was there again, this intriguing, unfathomable man. He'd seem like he didn't care one minute, and then was fascinated the next.

'No… of course I'm not. You just didn't strike me as the sort of man who'd wear vintage clothes.'

'It's a vintage shop? I've never been in one.'

'It's definitely an acquired taste, as my best friend keeps reminding me. But we're doing OK so far,' she lied. 'There's definitely a market for it.'

'Maybe I'll check it out one day.'

'That'd be nice...' She looked up at the sound of the bell over the door chiming and smiled briefly at the customer who'd just walked in. 'Listen, thanks so much for trying the landlord for me.'

'I'll let you know if I hear anything else.'

'Brilliant. Well... got to go. Bye for now.'

'Bye. Dodie, I—'

She ended the call and stashed her phone back in the drawer behind the counter. Ed's idea about talking to other people on Wessex Road wasn't half bad. Or at least, it wouldn't be if it didn't involve making her look like a complete nut-job with the added risk of her getting chased from properties by pensioners hurling slices of Dundee cake at her. Would any of them know enough to make it worth her while? She mulled the idea over as the customer flicked through a rack of coats and then gave her head a little shake. Door-to-door enquiries like an overzealous salesman? Worst idea ever.

Dodie huddled in a pool of lamplight, phone pressed to her ear. The temperature had dropped sharply as the sun sank below the horizon and now, at ten past six, with clear star-strewn skies above her, even her beautiful old–new coat wasn't quite cutting it. She had some deeply unglamorous thermal underwear sitting in a drawer in the flat that she'd purchased for a trip to Lapland a few years before, and right now she wished more than anything she was wearing it.

'I was counting on you being here,' Dodie hissed into her phone. 'I wouldn't have come if you hadn't agreed to come with me!'

'I know. I said I'm sorry but something has come up. I did try to phone you to let you know I wouldn't be there.'

'About ten minutes ago, yeah. I was already on my way up here then.'

'I can't help it.'

'So this something is more important than your best friend?'

'No, but…' Isla's sentence trailed off.

'Thanks a bunch. Let's hope I don't get mugged because you'll feel bad then and I won't care.'

'Don't be ridiculous,' Isla snapped. 'I can't hold your hand every time you go out and it was your stupid idea to go knocking on doors and asking about a stupid old letter that nobody but you cares about.'

Dodie stared into the distance. While Isla could be forthright at times, she'd never been quite so vitriolic in a response before. She didn't know how to respond to it.

'I'm sorry,' she said finally. 'You're right and I'm out of order. It's just that I feel like a prize plum already doing this without doing it on my own. I probably ought to just forget about it.'

'*I'm* sorry,' Isla said, her tone softening now. 'I know it matters to you and if I could be there you know I would.'

Dodie smiled thinly. 'I know that and I shouldn't have doubted you. Do you want to tell me what's going on?'

'I can't yet.' Isla sighed. 'It's sort of complicated and I don't even know myself what I think about it right now.'

'That sounds bad. I can leave this here and come over to yours if you need to talk.'

'I'm better off alone this evening. Mum and I need to talk and she's probably not going to like what I have to say. Which is all the more reason to get it over with as soon as I can. Thanks, but not tonight. Sorry.'

'Don't be sorry, although I'm worried now about you more than anything else.'

'Don't be. I have Mum here and we'll work it out between us. When I can say more I'll let you know. And I promise I'll try to get over soon. Maybe you want to put your little door-to-door exercise off until I can get to you?'

Dodie was silent for a moment as she mulled it over. 'OK,' she said finally. 'That's probably a good idea. I don't suppose it will make any difference what day I come.'

'Right then. I'll call you tomorrow if I can and let you know more.'

'OK… I'm sorry for sounding annoyed at you.'

'I'm sorry for not turning up. If there was any way I could have avoided standing you up I would have done. Hey, maybe you want to call Ryan to go with you? It's about time he shifted his slovenly arse and did something useful.'

'No… Can you imagine him walking the streets with me asking about a letter from a couple who are both probably dead by now? I'm sure he'd think that was a cracking night out.'

'You could try explaining to him why it's important.'

'I could, but I honestly don't think he'd understand.'

Isla was silent for a moment. 'Probably not,' she agreed finally. 'So I'll call you tomorrow and hopefully I'll be able to tell you more.'

'OK. But don't stress about it.'

'I won't,' Isla replied, and Dodie could hear the fond smile in her voice. 'Take care out there, won't you?'

'Always,' Dodie said. 'You too.'

She ended the call and slipped her phone into the pocket of her coat as she stared along the rows of houses flanking Wessex Road. Shadowed shrubs hung over garden walls and windows glowed yellow or flickered with lights from television screens. She was here now and she could still do this, but somehow she didn't have the heart. Isla was clearly in a state about something and she couldn't even discuss it. What kind of friend was Dodie to have been so quick to judge? Isla had never let her down before and Dodie had been completely unfair. What had felt important just ten minutes ago now seemed not to matter. George and Margaret – their time had been and gone, but Isla needed Dodie now. Her friend was right – this obsession over the letter was stupid and nobody else cared. They were right not to, because who had time to care? Her first instinct earlier that day to ignore Ed's well-intentioned suggestion was probably the right one. The best thing Dodie could do was to hand it to a museum or a local historian to see if they wanted it. They'd decide if it was valuable and, after that, what happened to it was none of her concern.

Pulling her collar up against the cold, she sank her hands into her pockets and turned to leave. But she hadn't gone more than ten steps when she heard her name being called. She turned to find Ed Willoughby jogging towards her, wrapped in a thick double-breasted coat, a beanie hat pulled tight over his head.

'Where are you going? Wessex Road is that way!' With a wry smile he flung an arm out in the direction she'd just come from.

'I know,' she said, stopping to wait for him. 'I'm going home. At least, I was about to.'

'You've done the street already?' he asked, coming to a halt in front of her. 'What did you find out?'

'Nothing. I'm not going to knock on anyone's door – I doubt anyone knows anything and it'll only annoy people.'

'You don't know until you try. I thought you were desperate to find out about this couple? You want to give the letter back, don't you?'

'I know but who cares really? It's nearly Christmas, people are having their tea and nobody wants to know.'

'You've changed your tune.'

'Yeah, I suppose so.'

He scratched his head, glancing up the street and then turning his gaze back on Dodie again. 'So… I was going to come with you,' he said awkwardly.

'You were?'

'I thought… I wasn't up to much and I knew you were coming tonight, so I thought I'd keep a look out for you.'

'You waited for me to arrive?'

'Sort of… Does that sound creepy?'

Dodie smiled. 'I think the fact that you recognise it might sound creepy means it's not. It's sweet.'

'I've been called a lot of things but sweet has never been one of them. So… I guess I'll just go home then.'

Dodie hesitated. It was strange, but he looked disappointed. 'I suppose I'm here now. It wouldn't take more than an hour I expect…'

'Less when most will take two seconds to slam the door in our faces.'

'Probably,' Dodie said. 'So even you admit that everyone will hate us?'

'Maybe. But why let a little thing like unpopularity get in the way?

'OK then,' Dodie laughed, suddenly feeling brighter and strangely fired up again. 'Let's do this!'

It felt a lot safer knocking on doors with someone, especially when that someone was a six-foot-tall man who already knew the street. Although Ed clearly didn't know his neighbours well, some of them recognised him and it meant they were more willing to engage in a conversation about Dodie's query. There wasn't a lot of help, though. Most had no idea who'd been in their house before them, let alone seventy-odd years ago, and even the older ones struggled to give much useful information. People simply hadn't lived in the street long enough to know anything about a girl who'd walked the pavements in 1944 or a boy who might have called at her house with flowers every Sunday afternoon before war had taken him away. It was beginning to feel like Dodie's quest was every bit as stupid as Isla had told her, even though it had been uttered in a fit of pique.

Eventually they ran out of houses to visit and they both had to concede it had been a futile exercise.

'I'm sorry I dragged you out here,' Dodie said as they walked the length of the road to his house, breath curling into the night air, footsteps echoing strangely on the frosty pavement.

He gave a slight shrug. 'Hey, it was my idea – no need to apologise. Anyway, I quite enjoyed the excuse to be out.'

Dodie shot him a sideways glance. 'I'm not sure what to make of that. You must have more exciting reasons to go out.'

'I don't bother much to be honest. For a start I don't really know anyone here and my mates are all up north.'

'Sad.'

He grinned. 'I know. No need to feel sorry for me though – I'm happy enough with my own company.'

'Where are you from?'

'Blackpool.'

'Blackpool? And you came to live in Bournemouth? Wasn't there enough sea for you in Blackpool?'

'Mad, eh?' He laughed. 'One seaside resort to another. There are more palm trees in Bournemouth.'

'So what made you move?'

'I haven't actually lived in Blackpool for a few years now. Not properly anyway. I've been posted abroad with my unit for most of the last five years so I've been backwards and forwards but never stayed at home for long. I suppose that's why…'

Dodie waited for the next bit. He paused, looking towards the sky as if to find the words hanging there. But then he shook his head. 'It doesn't matter now.'

'So you like it here?' Dodie asked, aware of a sudden tension and desperate to diffuse it. 'You don't regret leaving your home?'

'It's nice.'

'As nice as Blackpool?'

'Yeah. Posher, that's for sure.'

'It's not actually that posh… I live here for a start.'

'You sound posh compared to me.'

'That's down to the circumstances of my birth and nothing else. Believe me, I'm not.'

At Ed's gate, they halted. Dodie looked up at the house. A light burned behind the blinds of the downstairs flat, but the upper floor was in darkness.

'Looks as if Albert's in,' he said, angling his head at the lit window, though Dodie suspected that he was simply filling the awkwardness of their parting with words – any words would do.

'Hmm. Thanks for helping me tonight. It made things a lot less scary to have company.'

'It's just a shame it didn't work out in the end. We could try some of the surrounding streets if you wanted to have another go—'

She shook her head forcefully. 'I don't think so. It doesn't seem very productive, does it? In fact, none of this is very productive; I should probably just forget about it.'

'Maybe. So what are you going to do now?'

She gave a vague shrug. 'Home, I suppose. I came straight from work and didn't manage to eat so I might get something on the way back… Know any good takeaways nearby?'

'Depends what you want. There's a decent chippy around the corner. Although they don't do gravy and what's with that?'

Dodie blinked. '*Gravy?* Why would they need to serve gravy?'

'That's what they said when I asked. You've never had chips and gravy?'

'God, no!'

He grinned. 'It's like I've moved to another planet.'

'So what street am I looking for if I want this decent chippy?'

'You're going there now? I'll walk with you.'

'There's no need, I—'

'Don't be daft. To be honest I could eat some chips too so we might as well walk together.'

'OK,' Dodie replied uncertainly. 'I suppose it couldn't hurt.'

'I'd feel better knowing you weren't wandering around alone anyway. I mean, I know you have your hairspray and everything but…'

She smiled. 'Yeah, I have my deadly hairspray. You'd be surprised how much it stings if you get it in your eyes and you'd be laughing on the other side of your face if I had to use it on you.'

'I imagine my face would be stuck solid if you had to use it on me.'

'Nah, it's only light hold,' she laughed. 'I think you'd survive.'

'I don't think I want to put it to the test. Shall we?' He motioned for her to start walking and fell into step alongside. She was used to independence since she'd moved to Bournemouth and it didn't bother her one bit walking around alone after dark, but oddly she did feel so much safer in his company. It wasn't just that he was a man, but there was something solid and dependable about him, and not in a boring way – like with your dad or favourite uncle, who were obliged to look out for you – but in a way that you knew if you ever needed help he'd have your back and it would be totally because he wanted to. Maybe it was the fact he'd been a soldier that put the notion into Dodie's head. They'd got off to a less than auspicious start, and at first he'd seemed rude and arrogant, but the more time she spent in his company, the more she liked Ed Willoughby.

'So if you can't have gravy,' she began as they turned the corner and emerged onto a busier road lined with shops and cafés, 'what are you going to have with your chips?'

'I expect I'll just have them au naturel.'

'In my opinion the best way.'

'Lots of vinegar, though.'

'Oceans of the stuff.'

'So much you're almost choking on it.'

'Eyes watering like crazy.'

'Best chips ever.'

She turned to see him grinning. But then it faded just as quickly and he stared resolutely ahead. The mood had changed in an instant. Had she said something wrong? What the hell was it now? She could have asked if he was OK, because it felt very much as if he wasn't, but how to approach that without making the change more obvious and awkward? Was it best to just ignore it and hope the cloud passed?

She was spared the agony by him breaking the silence. 'Just ahead there on the corner. You'll be OK from here?'

Dodie blinked up at him. 'I thought you were getting some.'

'I don't think I'll bother after all… I've got some soup in the cupboard…' He pulled his hat down around his ears and hunched into his coat pockets.

'You're not hungry?'

'That's it… weird, not so hungry now…' Without another word, he turned to walk back the way they'd come, lifting a hand in farewell.

'Right…' Dodie replied, more confused than ever. 'Thanks for everything.'

He didn't look back, merely bowed his head in acknowledgement, and Dodie watched for a moment as his figure grew smaller before going to get her chips.

Seven

She'd walked slowly back with her chip paper open, the sharp tang of vinegar trailing into the air, munching solemnly as she went. They were good chips – worth going back for in the future – and they warmed her hands as well as providing just the stodge she needed to feel human again. It didn't bother her to walk home alone but Ed's strange behaviour did. Try as she might to identify the cause, she couldn't think of any reason why he would have taken off so suddenly when they'd been getting on so well. She certainly couldn't think of any insult she might have given or any upset she might have caused and, if anything, she'd felt as if they could end up becoming good friends. If it was going to be like this every time they met up then it really wasn't worth bothering again. But then, if the manner of their parting was anything to go by, perhaps that was the last she'd see of him anyway.

Later, back at the flat as she cleaned down the kitchen surfaces ready for bed, her phone had bleeped the arrival of a message from Isla, apologising again for her no-show. Dodie had sent an immediate reply telling her not to think of apologising and that she hoped everything was OK. Isla hadn't replied, and so it looked as though Dodie was going to be kept guessing for a little while longer. When her friend was ready to talk, Dodie knew she would be the first to hear about it.

Then it had been Ryan's turn to text, the message coming through just as she was about to set her alarm and turn in for the night. He asked if he could come over to see her again the following evening. It wasn't like she had anything else to do, although Friday nights were never full of partying for her as she had to open up the shop on Saturday morning just like she did every other morning. In fact, she was even thinking about opening up on Sundays during the Christmas build-up. Though she wasn't sure how much more custom that would bring in, the spectre of those reminder bills kept floating around in front of her face and perhaps even an extra fifty quid was better than nothing. Maybe it was something she needed to work out properly with a notepad and sums and all the weighing up that grown-up business people did, and her evenings were just about the only time she had free to do that. But in the end she'd sent him a reply saying that she'd see him around eight and decided that, out of weighing up her odds against bankruptcy and listening to Ryan harp on about the latest Premier League signings, the latter was probably the lesser of the two evils.

The following evening she was turning the key in the shop door to close after an uneventful Friday, during which she'd managed to sell two handbags, a belt and a jacket, when her phone rang.

'Hey,' she said brightly, determined that whatever cross words she'd had with Isla the night before would be put firmly behind them. 'Everything OK?'

'I can't honestly answer that, but I could do with a chat. You got time?'

'Always for you. Fire away.'

'It's a long story that I think would be better face to face. Can I come over?'

'Sure, when?'

'Are you free tonight?'

Dodie was about to explain that Ryan was due when she checked herself. She could hear something in Isla's voice she'd never heard before, and it almost sounded like desperation. Whatever it was, she clearly needed to sound off. How could Dodie say no? She'd have to call Ryan and explain, but she was sure he'd understand, and it wasn't as if he hadn't seen her that week anyway. He could come on Saturday night instead, or even Sunday, and it wouldn't make any difference.

'Tonight's OK,' she replied. 'Can you give me an hour to cash up and sort the shop?'

'I'm about that far away anyhow,' Isla said. 'I'll pick up some Chinese on the way if you like.'

'Sounds good.'

'Your usual?'

'Perfect. See you soon.' Dodie ended the call and dialled Ryan's number. There was no reply, so she left him a voicemail to explain and then sent a text to do the same. It wasn't really good enough, and she'd try again after she'd cashed up to speak to him in person, but hopefully the messages meant he wouldn't start driving out before she'd had a chance to speak to him.

Once the till had been emptied and the money stowed in her tiny safe, she switched the lights out, save for the security lamps, and retreated to her upstairs flat. Halfway up the stairs, Ryan's smiling photo lit up the screen of her phone. But his voice as she answered suggested that the real-life version wasn't doing much smiling.

'What's happened?' His question was brusque. 'I thought we had plans.'

'I'm sorry, something's come up.'

'What?'

'I don't know yet… Something's going on with Isla – she phoned and she needs me. We can do something tomorrow instead, can't we? It wasn't like we had something set in stone.'

'We still had plans.'

'Not proper plans; it was just you coming over. You can do that any time.'

'So can Isla.'

'I know, but I think it's something really important.'

There was a heartbeat's pause. 'So your mate is more important than me?'

'Of course not!'

'But that's what you're saying.'

'It's not what I'm saying at all.'

'Then what exactly are you saying?'

'Ryan, why are you being so unreasonable? You know I wouldn't let you down without a good reason.'

'I'm not hearing any reason except that Isla matters more than I do.'

'That's not true and you know it. These are exceptional circumstances.'

'What's up with her then?'

'I don't know – she's going to tell me when she gets here. But she sounds stressed.'

'That's alright then,' he replied, his voice dripping with sarcasm. 'You can totally drop everything for a reason you don't know and because someone *sounds* stressed. Don't worry about your boyfriend because he doesn't sound stressed, even though you had arrangements to meet him.'

'But I saw you a couple of nights ago!'

'Rationed to once a week now, am I?'

'Of course not! I just meant it's more than we usually manage.'

'If that's the way you feel it's no wonder we're not going anywhere.'

'What does that mean?'

There was a long sigh at the other end of the line. 'I don't even know. Forget it. See you whenever you can next fit me in…'

Dodie was framing a reply when the phone went dead. She stabbed at the screen to redial his number so they could slug it out, but then she paused, staring at it for a moment before finally locking it. Idiot. Let him stew. Ryan might have thought he was the centre of the universe but he was the only person who did.

As promised, an hour later Isla arrived with a bag of foil cartons and a mound of free prawn crackers. There was far too much – there always was – but Isla had a huge appetite for such a tiny girl, and what they didn't eat now she'd happily hoover up after an hour's grace. Dodie was constantly in awe of how her friend processed such vast amounts of food – her metabolism must have been something to rival the speed of the Hadron Collider. Dodie was still smarting from her spat with Ryan and she didn't feel much like eating, but Isla always had the opposite problem and stuffed her way back to happiness whenever she was fed up. Judging by the bulging bag, she was very fed up indeed.

'Lemon chicken for you,' she said as she placed the items on the kitchen table. 'Retro food to go with your retro shop.'

'Lemon chicken is the only thing I like from that restaurant.'

'But it *is* naff.'

'What have you got?'

'Pancakes, spring rolls, Szechuan chicken, special fried rice…'

'Bloody hell! You could feed the street with that lot!'

'The street's not getting it. I'm going to eat until I'm sick. And then I'm going to eat some more.'

'Like the Romans used to?'

'Exactly.'

'Go on then…' Dodie took the plates she'd been warming from the oven, 'tell me what's happened.'

'You know how I haven't seen my dad since I was five? And I didn't know where he was because Mum forbade me to talk about it for all these years? Well, I mean, I had a rough idea that he was in France but that was about all.'

'Yes…' Dodie said slowly. She had a feeling she knew what was coming.

'He's been in touch.'

Dodie's eyes widened. It looked as though her own problems were going to have to go on the back-burner for this evening, at least while she gave Isla the support she clearly needed to cope with such momentous news. But the way she was feeling right now that wasn't necessarily a bad thing.

Ryan had phoned later that night, but Dodie wasn't in the mood to pick up. Isla had raised her eyebrows as she noted Dodie look at her phone and then place it back on the table again, Ryan's name flashing on the screen.

'I don't want to talk to him and I don't want to talk about it,' Dodie had told her, mostly because if she'd told Isla the whole story then it might have made Isla feel responsible for the spat and she didn't want that. The rest of the evening was devoted to Isla's dilemma, about how and why her father might have ended up living in the French Alps, about ski suits and drinks overlooking the pistes and what her dad might have done to get so rich. They discussed, at great length, whether it was a good idea for Isla to go and see him to find out about an inheritance from a gran she could barely remember, and Dodie was far happier to think of all that than her own problems.

But the next morning when she woke there was a text message.

Sorry about last night. New restaurant opened in Poole harbour, could drive out and have dinner tonight if you want. My treat. X

Dodie couldn't help a small smile. It was nice to know he hadn't stewed too long and for once she hadn't needed to back down. A new restaurant did sound tempting and it would be nice to have a change of scenery. She loved Poole harbour; on a summer's day you could almost imagine you were in Nice or St Tropez, only with fish and chips and without the need to speak French. But even though it was only half an hour down the coast she didn't get time to visit nearly as often as she would have liked. Most importantly, she couldn't remember the last time Ryan had taken her out and treated her, so it meant he was making a real effort.

Sounds good. X
I'll pick you up at 7. That OK for you? X
Perfect. X

Early December, with a harsh wind whipping up the waters of the harbour, it couldn't have felt further from St Tropez, but the quayside was lined with restaurants and pubs all decked in pretty Christmas finery, and the warm smells coming from each doorway were enough to make Dodie forget the cold. Ryan, having made an effort to scrub up for her in a powder-blue shirt and smart trousers, led her to a whitewashed building where bay trees standing sentry at the entrance were decked in fairy lights and Christmas baubles. A sign painted in scrolled writing above the door read *The Sandbank*. The interior was a chic mix of rustic wood and wrought iron, ambient spotlights dotted around the ceiling and modern art on the walls.

'Looks lovely,' Dodie said as he guided her towards it.

'Nice food – or so the paper said.'

Dodie turned to him with a raised eyebrow. '*You* read a restaurant review in the newspaper? Have I stepped into a parallel universe or was it stuck to the sports pages and cunningly disguised as a football score?'

'Come on, I'm not that bad!' he laughed as they stopped at a sign requesting new customers to wait for seating.

'Did you book?' Dodie asked as she glanced around the packed room.

'Yes.'

'Oh Lord, now I know I've fallen into a parallel universe! You actually booked a table at a restaurant!'

'I knew it would be busy. Proud of me?'

'Staggered is what I am. There's hope for you yet.'

A waiter arrived and swiftly showed them to a table for two by a window that looked out onto the quay where boats of all shapes and sizes, from tiny dinghies to sleek yachts, danced on the darkness of the choppy waters. Dodie ran her gaze over the menu as he left them again.

'Everything looks so good I don't know where to start. Better than crackers and ham sandwiches, which is all I've eaten today. I might go for fish, seeing as we're by the sea.'

'You're always by the sea.'

'I'm too busy in the shop to see much of it these days, so it hardly feels like it.'

'All the more reason for a night away from it,' he said. 'Order what you like, my treat.'

'In that case I'm having one of everything.'

Ryan grinned over his menu before turning back to it again. 'So,' he asked, in a voice that sounded far too nonchalant, 'do you know what Isla is going to do?'

On the drive over, they'd briefly touched on the reasons for Isla's impromptu visit. They'd needed to if they were going to clear the air, and as Isla hadn't exactly told Dodie to keep it a secret she felt it would be OK for Ryan to know. He was her boyfriend, after all, and it wasn't as if he knew anyone who knew Isla, even if he did want to gossip about it. Ryan wasn't a gossiper anyway, he was more of a down-the-pub, at-football, silently-glued-to-the-telly kind of guy. He'd been surprisingly sweet about it, especially since he'd never really been a big fan of Isla, and said he hoped that things worked out whatever she decided to do.

Dodie wanted to believe him, she really did, but there was just something suspicious about the way he was acting this evening. She could feel a bombshell coming; a reason that he might want Isla, with whom Dodie spent almost as much time as she did him, out of the picture.

'I don't think she knows yet. When she left me last night she was going to sleep on it.'

'That's good. Do you think she'll go?'

'No idea.'

'Gut instinct?'

'I think she'll go. She's got too many unanswered questions and she's got the sort of mind that needs answers. She doesn't do mysteries or blind acceptance.'

'You'll miss her.'

'Like crazy.'

'So… you might get a bit lonelier than before…'

'I doubt it.'

'But you might. You're with her a lot when you're not with me.'

Dodie lowered her menu to look at him. 'Where's this going?'

'Does it have to be going somewhere?' He held up his hands in a gesture of surrender. 'Why does it have to be going somewhere? I'm just asking.'

'Sorry, it's just… I doubt she'll be gone long.'

'But what if she loves her dad and ends up staying? What if there's a house in France for her? I don't know… a huge family she wants to get to know?'

'She loves her mum way more than she could possibly love her dad. She doesn't know her dad and she's not going to get that close to him that quickly after all that's gone on. She's going to come home.'

'But what if she didn't?' he insisted. 'You'd miss her, right? You'd be lonely.'

Dodie narrowed her eyes slightly. This was definitely going somewhere but where was anyone's guess. 'I suppose I will be a bit lonely. I mean, it's proving difficult for us to get together as much as we used to and most of my old friends are too busy to drive out to Bournemouth. But I'd get used to it. Besides, the shop keeps me too busy to worry about being alone.'

The waiter returned with drinks, and they were occupied for a couple of minutes with placing their food orders. When he left them again, Ryan leaned across the table.

'Cos I was just thinking… we don't see that much of each other any more – not since you moved – and it's a shame because we have a laugh when we do.'

'There's nothing to stop us driving over to each other a bit more when the weather improves. And I know I've been a bit busy with the shop and everything, but that will get better when things pick up, hopefully.'

'But it might be better if we were closer – right?'

'Well, yes but—'

'So I was thinking maybe we could move in together.'

Dodie blinked. This was not what she'd been expecting. Ryan, by nature, was a nomad not a settler, and she'd accepted that very early on. In fact, she was happy with the arrangement because she quite liked her freedom. The only thing that could have shocked her more was a marriage proposal. If she got one of those now she might just pass out.

'I can't afford a mortgage for a house,' she said slowly, trying to work out what sort of reaction she was meant to give.

'We don't need to buy a house,' he replied in a triumphant voice, as if he'd just made an incredible scientific discovery. 'You've got the flat above the shop! I'll move into the flat!'

She stared at him. 'You want to move into the flat? That's crazy!'

'Why?' he asked, his expression darkening. 'Why is it so crazy? Why can't I move into the flat? Because I suggested it, and I'm too stupid to have good ideas?'

'Of course not – that's not what I mean at all. But it's far too small for a start. And then there's the inconvenience to the business—'

'*Inconvenience?* Is that what you think I am?'

'You're not listening. I said inconvenience to the business, not to me.'

'Aren't they one and the same?'

'No, they're not. I need the space up there for stock. And there's the extra costs for heating and electric and whatever else.'

'I'd pay my way.'

'I know you would but…' Dodie paused. That was a white lie because she couldn't be certain of just how much Ryan intended to pay his way. He didn't pay his parents anything to live in their house – he just assumed they'd soak up the costs. But without laying it on the line and possibly insulting him into the bargain, she couldn't ask whether he thought the same was going to happen if he moved into her place. After all, the rent itself wouldn't change whether he was there or not and she could probably manage at least that. But the principle of the matter, that was a different thing altogether. And she certainly couldn't afford any of the other extras his presence at her flat might bring.

'It's just difficult,' she sighed. 'I only live up there myself because I can't afford the rent on the shop and another place to live but it's just not practical as a home – it's hardly practical for me, let alone a couple. It's a lovely idea but…'

'But what? I don't need a lot of space.'

'You're not listening to me. It's not a place designed for anything but to run a business from. It's crap there, it's like living in a warehouse with a bit of old furniture and you'd soon hate it.'

'You don't hate it.'

'I make sacrifices because I want the shop to succeed.'

'You always seem happy living there. And you've got it cushy. You don't have your mum nagging you about socks on the floor and dirty dishes and where you keep your work tools. I mean, I'm nearly thirty and I shouldn't be living with my parents, should I? None of my mates live with their parents. It's not right.'

Dodie eyeballed him in silence for a moment. She could have replied that the only reason he was still living with his parents when his friends weren't was that they'd all had enough get-up-and-go to actually get up and actually go, and that he liked his money too much to spend it on a mortgage. But perhaps that was an argument that was guaranteed to inflame things and best left alone. Instead she shook her head. 'Where's this suddenly come from? You've never shown an interest in any sort of commitment before, so why now?'

'You're the one who keeps saying we're stuck in a rut. You're the one who thinks we're not going anywhere so I thought—'

'I've never said we're not going anywhere! If I remember correctly you said that last night, not me!'

'So you don't want to live together?'

'I want to be consulted first. You can't just assume it's OK to move into my flat.'

'I wasn't assuming, I was just asking.'

'It didn't sound like asking to me; it sounded very much like you'd decided it was OK and that I would agree.'

He folded his arms tight across his chest and looked across the restaurant. 'Forget it,' he muttered.

'We've got my flat for visits any time you like but it's not big enough for the both of us to live in… It's just not practical.'

'I said forget it.'

Dodie held in a sigh. 'I would forget it, but it's clear that you can't.'

He turned to her. 'Then why am I the one saying forget it?'

'You can say it but you don't really mean it! For God's sake, Ryan, grow up! You're so passive aggressive it's painful!'

'I'm passive aggressive? Is this another one of your fancy terms you've learned from Isla?'

'Don't be ridiculous.'

'*You're* ridiculous.'

Dodie turned to the window. If he said another word she was quite sure she'd throw her drink right over his stupid head. Which would be a shame because it was a very nice Zinfandel. She grappled for something to change the conversation, something they could talk about that might diffuse the tension, but she couldn't leave it because something about the situation still didn't stack up.

'Is this something to do with living with your parents?'

'No.'

'Because I know you've been complaining about it for a while now...'

'It's got nothing to do with my parents. I thought the girlfriend who's supposed to love me might want to spend more time with me.'

Dodie ignored the jibe, feeling that she was perhaps getting to the real heart of the issue despite his denials. 'So you're happy at home?'

'I haven't been happy there for a couple of years and you know it. Like I said, it's not right, a thirty-year-old bloke still shacked up with his parents.'

'Your mum would be inconsolable if you left.'

'She'd have a spare room.'

'Is that what she said?'

He turned back to face her. 'What does it matter what she said? You've told me no, so that's the end of the discussion, isn't it?'

'I was just asking; that's all.'

'Let's change the subject, eh? You've made it clear you don't want me.'

'I want you – the flat just isn't a practical solution.' This time the sigh escaped. 'Look... Ryan... I wasn't trying to put you off because I don't want you, I just thought... the flat's very small and I wasn't sure how we'd manage. But if it means that much to you we could give it a go.'

His frown lifted. 'Honestly. You're not saying that because you feel sorry for me? You really want me to move in?'

'Yes, of course I do. But I do need some time to sort things out. Can we hold that thought until after Christmas?'

'After Christmas.' He nodded, a smile spreading across his face. 'I can do that.'

Eight

Monday mornings arrived with alarming regularity and this one was no different. With her promise to Ryan still hanging over her head, Dodie stood in the kitchen of the flat above Forget-Me-Not Vintage and reflected, as she had many times that weekend, on just how tiny it was. She was tidy and Ryan was a slob. She was eclectic and he was minimalist. She liked quiet, introspection, history documentaries and monochrome films and he liked shouting at football on the TV. How in the hell was this going to work? Maybe if they had a huge house where they could lose each other every once in a while, but here…?

Her life as she knew it was about to change beyond recognition. Most people would see this kind of commitment as a good thing, but Dodie wasn't most people and she rather liked her life just the way it was. Perhaps she was being unreasonable and perhaps she was being stubborn, clinging to a life she'd grown to love. Perhaps Ryan moving in was just what she needed to spark some changes around the place, and perhaps it would be good for her. She tried to focus on the positives, as difficult as it was to spot them on the choppy seas of her looming new future. She tried to convince herself that she was being a selfish cow and that Ryan moving in was exactly what she needed. She'd reacted badly at the restaurant, the very least she owed him now was to give it a chance to work.

She opened at nine on the dot to find a young girl on the doorstep who'd passed by the previous day and had seen a lime-green kaftan through the window. She explained it would be perfect for a bad taste party she was going to so had come back as soon as the shop had opened in case it was sold. Dodie had to agree with the bad taste bit – she'd only put it in the window as she thought the bright colour would catch people's eyes – but she couldn't imagine how it would have been sold before the girl returned. She'd learned since she'd started this business that there was no telling what would sell, and as she rang up the sale she gave silent thanks for bad taste parties and prayed for many more over the festive season.

The second customer of the morning was her gran. Dodie suppressed a groan as she heard the bell go on the door and turned to find her smiling in the doorway.

'You're early,' she said as Gran tottered over to the counter.

'The gas engineer is coming tomorrow and I've been invited to go bowling the next day so I thought I'd pop in while I got the chance.'

'Bowling?' Dodie frowned. 'You mean bowls? On grass? It's a bit cold for that, isn't it?'

'Oh no,' Gran said amiably. 'That sort of bowling when you throw it down an aisle at some sticks and knock them over.'

'*Tenpin?* You're going tenpin bowling?' Dodie raised her eyebrows but her gran was fast running out of ways to surprise her these days. 'Who are you going there with?'

'Alan Lawrence.'

'Who the hell is Alan Lawrence? I can't keep up with your boyfriends!'

'They're not my boyfriends,' Gran said as she started to peel off her coat. 'They'd like to be, but I'd rather keep them guessing.' She handed her own coat to Dodie, who took it with a questioning look. 'I thought I might try that lovely green coat on again,' she clarified. 'The one you had in the other day. You haven't sold it, have you?'

Dodie chewed her lip for a moment. It wasn't that she minded giving Gran her coat – she'd happily give her anything she had – but she wasn't sure she could cope with the going around in circles that trying on would have them doing.

'I did sell it,' she said, making a mental note never to wear it when her gran was around. 'Sorry.'

'Oh.'

'But I thought you wanted a camel coat anyway? I've been looking out for one for you.'

Her gran's expression brightened. 'Have you? That's sweet of you.'

'So if I see one I'll get it in stock and then you can come and look at it. There'll be no obligation because I'm sure I could sell it anyway.'

'Lovely.' Gran rubbed her hands together. 'Cup of tea?' she asked, going through to the back of the shop without waiting for a response.

Dodie shook her head. There was no point in replying because her gran would make her a cup of tea no matter what she said. Besides, she quite liked her gran's visits to the shop, even if they did sometimes leave her reeling. But then her mind went back to Ryan's imminent moving in and she realised that even the nature of her gran's visits would change with him living there. It wouldn't be just her place, and she wouldn't be able to let her gran loose in it just as she liked. And what if Gran visited when Ryan was there? Upstairs in his pants watching telly and scratching unnameable parts while Gran pottered around making tea and checking her cupboards for digestives?

She shook herself. Morose wasn't her thing, but how she was feeling today came pretty close. But the fact was she'd agreed and she couldn't very well back out now. Besides, she ought to be happy about the prospect of spending more time with her boyfriend; anyone else would be. It would be good for them, and hadn't she always said it sometimes felt like a part-time relationship? This would cement things, make them into a real couple. She couldn't complain about that. She just wished that sinking feeling wouldn't keep plaguing her every time she thought about it.

Ten minutes later Gran reappeared with two mugs of tea and handed one to Dodie.

'Isn't it funny?' Gran said as she took the spare seat behind the counter.

'What?'

'I've just seen a green coat upstairs exactly like the one I tried on in here. In your wardrobe. I didn't know you had another one.'

Dodie clung onto the internal groan so it wouldn't escape, cursing the fact that she hadn't bolted upstairs to make sure the coat was firmly stashed in a carrier bag under her bed.

'Still,' Gran continued, 'I expect it looks nicer on you than it did on me.'

'Hmm.'

They lapsed into silence as Dodie took a sip of her tea and Gran bit into a chocolate digestive. Then she spoke again, spraying crumbs over the counter. Dodie stared at them, fighting the urge to run and get a dustpan to clean up the mess.

'I wanted to tell you something.' Gran screwed up her brow in concentration. 'What was it? Oh!' she cried, causing Dodie to almost throw the tea she was holding over her shoulder. 'Your letter!'

Dodie sat forward. Finally a subject she could think about and not feel down. An outcome she might have the power to influence when everything else seemed to be slipping from her grasp. With all the drama around Ryan's announcement the letter had been pushed to the back of Dodie's mind. Hiding there, not forgotten, but waiting patiently until she had time to pay attention again. Now looked like that time, and it was just what Dodie needed to cheer her mood. 'You found something?'

'I think… now let me get this straight. I was at salsa dance class and I was talking to Winnie, and I was telling her about your letter. And then she shouted to Arthur who came to listen. And then Arthur called Gloria over and she said that her dad's uncle had a friend who fought in France during the war and he was supposed to marry a Margaret somebody or other, but he never came home and she spent the rest of her life mourning him. Such a terrible story.'

'Gloria told you this?'

'Oh yes.' Gran nodded cheerfully.

Dodie blinked. She'd been expecting that George or Margaret or both would be dead, and she had even been ready to hear that he hadn't made it back from the war, but to hear it confirmed still left a sense of numb shock. 'Does Gloria know the family?'

'Not really.'

Dodie frowned slightly as she processed the new information. Now it seemed more important than ever that Margaret or her family got the letter back – it might be the only thing they had left of George.

'Well, could she find out Margaret's surname? Could you ask her?'

'I can ask her. Of course her dad and his uncle are both dead now so it wouldn't be much use asking them.'

'Probably not,' Dodie agreed wryly. 'But will you let me know if you find out?'

'Yes.' Gran reached for another biscuit from the plate.

Dodie turned her gaze to the window and tried to temper the feeling of excitement building inside her at the thought that she might just have a clue. She wanted to leap up now, lock the shop and rush to Gloria's house to grill her. It was a silly notion, of course, and real life had to come first – shutting the shop and rushing to Gloria's house wasn't going to pay the bills. Still, the idea that she was just that little bit closer to the truth had Dodie's insides fluttering. So much for letting the mystery go.

Gran stayed for an hour, during which time she'd managed to try on four pairs of shoes, two jackets and a tweed skirt and not take any of them away with her. But she'd had fun trying on so Dodie couldn't see the point in complaining, and all the while they'd talked over the possibility of learning more about George and Margaret. Gran's information was patchy and not much better on more in-depth scrutiny, but Dodie was hopeful that more would come soon once Gran's friend had done some digging.

At five Dodie turned the shop sign to closed and locked the world out with a thankful sigh. Something from the freezer would do for supper and then a soak in the bath, she thought, if only because she knew that her days of soaking peacefully in a bath for hours on end were numbered. Afterwards, hair coated in scrummy-smelling banana conditioner and wrapped in a fluffy towel, she curled into the corner of the sofa with her laptop to do some more digging into George and Maggie.

Research wasn't as easy as it looked on the TV where they pushed a few buttons and – hey presto! – the result you wanted was right there in front of you. The reality was rather more laborious and less glamorous. Dodie had read some mind-numbingly boring stuff as she trawled through endless obscure pages ranging from census records to lists of schoolchildren. Nothing.

Isla's name suddenly flashed up on her phone.

'Oh, hey! I was just thinking about you; how's everything? You're feeling happier?'

'Better, thanks. I think it really helped having our evening together – just talking to someone who doesn't have their own agenda, y'know?'

'And has it helped you come to a decision?'

'Maybe. I'm closer, even if I haven't quite made up my mind. Honestly, it's more about what other people will say than what I want now.'

'It's really not,' Dodie began, but Isla jumped in to change the subject.

'So… are you OK? Sorted things out with Ryan?'

'Oh, he's fine,' Dodie said, deciding not to tell her about his request to move in and her mixed feelings on the subject. Isla had enough to worry about, and the more she thought about it, the more Dodie could see that she might have overreacted to the news.

'Did he stay over?'

'No, went home. Early start. I probably won't see him until the weekend now; we're both a bit busy.'

'So what are you up to?'

'Oh… this and that.'

'Your letter?' Isla asked, and Dodie could hear the wry smile in her voice.

'OK, yes. I've been searching again.'

'I thought you weren't going to bother.'

'I wasn't, but then my gran came over with some news and made me think about it again. One last go, and if I don't get anywhere by the end of this week I'll give up. I'll be too busy to worry about it over the next few weeks with Christmas coming up. So if you do go to the Alps…' Dodie continued, hoping to turn the focus of the conversation back onto Isla, 'when were you thinking?'

'I've got to go soon, to be honest. Like in the next week or so.'

'A bit short notice, isn't it?'

'I think it's to do with the timing of the will reading. That, and it took a while to track me and Mum down, apparently, so they're up against it now.'

Dodie's glance went back to the laptop, the screen open to show a page of black-and-white photos from a VE Day street party. If Isla's father's solicitor had had trouble finding two people living in twenty-first-century Britain with more technology than ever before, what hope did she have of tracking down George or Margaret?

'So you might be gone for Christmas? Your mum *will not* be happy about that.'

'She would go nuclear! No, I'll have to get back somehow, even if that means leaving France and going back to finish off afterwards.'

'Expensive business, four flights instead of two.'

'Hey, but my dad is paying, right?'

'In that case can you go via the Seychelles?'

'I can try,' Isla laughed. 'Screw the old goat for as much as I can get.'

'And you'll need a chaperone; can't just go flying around the world all by yourself.'

'Absolutely. Know anyone?'

'Let me think about it and get back to you.' Dodie grinned down the phone.

'I wish you could come,' Isla said, serious now. 'I'd appreciate the company.'

'Even if I had the money for the flights I couldn't leave the shop at this time of year. Otherwise I'd have bloody loved to. Just one thing… under no circumstances must you hook up with a hot ski instructor named Jean-Luc and decide to stay there because I will not be impressed.'

'I seriously doubt you need to worry about that. I'll be keeping a low profile, getting my head around meeting my dad and possibly a whole new family for the first time. I have so many questions; I don't even know where to start.'

'Sounds to me you've already decided you're going.'

'Maybe. But then I'm more like you than you realise so there shouldn't be any surprise there…'

'How do you mean?'

'Well, we both find it hard to settle when there's a mystery to be solved.'

'I never thought about it that way.' Dodie glanced back at the laptop. 'I suppose it's true. I suspect your methodical way of dealing with things is better than mine though.'

'I don't feel very methodical right now. In fact, I'm an emotional wreck and I don't much care for the feeling.'

'Even more than when we watched *Titanic*?'

'I wasn't crying, it was your bloody air freshener getting in my eyes.'

'Of course it was. How silly of me to forget that. Listen,' she added, serious now, 'if you need to come over and talk, any time at all, then just come. I'll always make time for you.'

'I know you will,' Isla said. 'I'm so lucky to have you. But right now I need to get things straight in my own head.'

'A bit more talking might help?'

'A bit more talking might tie me up in bigger knots. I feel as if all I do is talk about it and I must be driving everyone nuts. Thanks, but this is for me to figure out now. But as soon as I know what I'm doing, you'll know too.'

'I'd better!' Dodie said with a smile. 'The title of best friend has to come with some privileges you know.'

'Always. So, you want to tell me what's going on with your letter? Anything more from your gran? Turned up anything new?'

Dodie glanced back at the screen again. If Isla thought her predicament was boring then Dodie's current painstaking line of investigation was likely to put a room of insomniacs to sleep.

'Trust me, you really don't want to hear about what I've been reading.'

When she was a little girl, Dodie's gran and grandad used to take her to the Lower Gardens at the heart of the town to see the brass band play. They'd sit on the grass in the sun eating ice cream, and while other children fidgeted next to their parents or ran about playing tag, Dodie would sit, mesmerised by the musicians with their starched uniforms and gleaming instruments, nodding to tunes that had been penned long before she was born. She'd sit still for hours, snug in her gran's arms watching the show, and would always feel sad when the applause died and everyone started to drift away. Looking back, she often wondered whether her love of old things had started that very first time her grandparents had sat her down on the yellowing grass one roasting July day to watch that brass band play.

The night after Isla had poured her heart out there was a concert – a medley of Christmas hits by a local orchestra ensemble – and Dodie was determined not to miss it. She'd even phoned her gran to see if she wanted to go, but she had made arrangements to try out a pottery class with someone named Kay she'd met in Waitrose. Dodie didn't even ask what the hell that was about, because she was used to her gran muscling in on every social occasion going. Besides, it was good for her; when Dodie's grandad had died everyone thought Gran would wither to a shadow within a year, but she'd faced her grief head-on and fought it. Her way of coping with the loneliness was to make sure she never spent a minute alone.

It didn't matter that her gran was busy, though, because Dodie was happy enough to stand in the park and watch the band by herself. It might be the last opportunity to do anything much by herself before Ryan moved in – not that he'd be seen dead at an open-air brass band concert.

So at seven that evening she was huddled in her new green coat, unglamorous thermals finally put into use and hot chocolate in her grip as she stood on the grass and waited with the crowds for the show to begin. The smells of the nearby bratwurst stall lingered in the air, and further down the gardens the disco music from the ice rink could be heard along with shrieks of laughter from its customers. Maybe she'd have a look later; maybe she'd even be persuaded to have a go this time.

It was then that her phone rang, and she juggled with her hot chocolate as she tried to retrieve it from the depths of her bag.

Edward? She'd almost put him out of her head, expecting not to hear from him again after their strange parting at the chip shop. She swiped to take the call and clamped the phone to her ear, trying to hear above the hum of the crowds.

'Ed? I didn't expect to hear from you…'

'Didn't you?' he asked, sounding vaguely surprised. 'I did say I'd keep in touch.'

'I know but…' She gave a mental shrug and left it at that.

'I was just wondering…' he continued. 'Have you got any further with your letter?'

'I've got one or two bits of hearsay but not a lot else.' She sipped at her hot chocolate. 'Did you get a reply from the letting agent?'

'They called me today, so I thought I'd better let you know… bad news, I'm afraid.'

'They can't tell you anything?'

'Not a dickie. The owner of the house bought it at auction about seven years ago and has zero knowledge of the previous owners.'

'Oh. I don't suppose we could have expected anything different really. But thanks for trying.'

'No worries.'

There was a silence. Dodie was just about to say goodbye when he spoke again.

'What will you do now? You said last time I saw you that you might give up.'

'I don't know. George and Margaret are proving very elusive so far. I still don't have so much as a surname for either of them. I've searched online and… well, it's like looking for a needle in a haystack. Worse than that, like looking for an invisible atom in a haystack.'

'Isn't the haystack completely made of atoms and therefore all of them completely visible in the form of the hay?'

'Huh?'

'Never mind – nerdy joke and not even funny. Ignore me.'

The fact that he was joking at all had Dodie flummoxed. Here he was again, unpredictable Ed. She was beginning to wonder if he had a secret twin going around pretending to be him. A very miserable, serious twin.

From the stage, the warbling notes of musicians warming up reached her. 'Thanks for phoning,' she said, aware that the concert was about to begin. The deep *parp* of a trombone followed and a titter of laughter rippled through the crowd as the trombone player stood at the front of the stage and took a bow for his accidental performance.

'Where on earth are you?' Ed asked. 'Sounds like you're at the Albert Hall or something.'

'Not quite. A bit closer to home and less glamorous. I'm at the Lower Gardens.'

'I had no idea plants could be so noisy.'

Dodie couldn't help a smile this time. She liked this funny Ed. 'It's an outdoor brass band concert. For Christmas.'

'Oh, sorry… I didn't meant to interrupt a night out with your friends…'

'Don't worry – it's just me, so don't think you're interrupting anything.'

'You're there on your own?'

'Yes.'

'Oh.' He paused. 'Were you let down by someone?'

'No. I don't mind going out on my own.'

'Well, I suppose I'll let you go and enjoy your concert.'

'Thanks… And Ed… thanks for coming door-knocking with me too. I really did appreciate the company.'

'No problem. I guess this is it then. Merry Christmas, Dodie Bright.'

'You too, Ed. Thanks again.'

The screen went black and Dodie turned her attention to the stage. The more she heard from Ed Willoughby, the more she was intrigued and confused by him. Her phone rang again and she frowned as she saw Ed's number a second time.

'Have you tried social media?' he asked before she'd had time to speak.

'For the letter?'

'Yes. I was just thinking about it… Have you tried putting something on Facebook asking for help? Just a thought.'

'I'm not much of a Facebook user to be honest.'

'It's the best way to reach a lot of people.'

'I realise that, but I… well, I just didn't go down that route because I was going to try to see what I could turn up myself first. And it seemed a bit random… Who on Facebook now is going to know anything about a couple from 1944?'

'It's about as likely as the person living in their house, and yet you still knocked on my door that night.'

'Well, yes, but…'

'It's up to you really, but it seems daft not to try it. I could—'

The rest of his sentence was drowned out by the band beginning to play 'White Christmas'.

'I'll have to call you back!' Dodie yelled into the phone, unable to hear his reply and hoping that he wouldn't be too offended that she was about to hang up on him. 'But thanks for the tip and I'll definitely think about it!'

Shoving her phone back into her bag, she sipped at her chocolate as she turned to watch the stage. The strains of a brass band would normally have her smiling as she became six years old again, sitting in between her grandparents as they ate ice cream on the grass. But her attention wasn't quite as devoted to the concert as it would normally have been. Ed Willoughby was on her mind, and she was beginning to wish he'd get off it.

As the band took their applause before launching into 'Rockin' Around the Christmas Tree', Dodie forced the enigmatic Ed from her thoughts. She'd come out to enjoy a brass band, not to fret about some hot-and-cold man she barely knew, and that was just what she intended to do.

When she'd first arrived at the concert, Dodie had been warm enough in her coat with her hot chocolate. But pretty soon, as the cup was emptied and the night drew its icy cloak around the gardens, her feet began to feel numb, then the end of her nose, and the rest of her body quickly followed. After an hour she felt bitterly cold, and though she was enjoying herself, she wished desperately that she was the kind of girl who favoured jeans and walking boots with thermal socks instead of sixties twinsets and Mary Jane shoes. A freezing fog had dropped over the grass, swallowing shrubs and frosting the lamps with dewy halos. The crowd thinned as people wandered away to warm themselves at the faux log cabin or simply decided they'd had enough of being cold and went home. Despite the tempting idea of her own cosy flat not far away, this was the most festive she'd felt so far this year, and Dodie was determined to stick it out until the end. As the strains of 'I Saw Mommy Kissing Santa Claus' rang out over the park, a light tap on her shoulder had her spinning around. When she saw who it was, her exclamation was almost louder than the band.

'What are *you* doing here?'

Ed grinned. 'Charming. I decided to check the concert out. It's ages since I've seen a brass band in action. Actually, I've even marched to one or two in my time.'

'But…'

'You don't mind, do you?' he asked, his grin fading. 'Only I thought…'

'It's a public performance. I couldn't mind if I wanted to… I'm just surprised. It's not everyone's cup of tea. In fact, it's almost nobody's cup of tea.'

Ed glanced around. 'Looks popular enough to me.'

'I just didn't expect you to like this sort of thing.'

'I thought it might be fun, that's all. I've hardly seen anything of Bournemouth since I arrived so I thought it was about time I got involved.'

The band stopped playing and a ripple of polite applause spread through the crowd. Dodie turned and added her own, though she hadn't been listening to the last song at all. When she looked back, Ed was watching the stage expectantly, hands in his pockets and beanie hat pulled down over his ears. Wearing the hat that way, he looked a little like a Christmas elf himself. A rather muscular, chisel-jawed Christmas elf who could knock you down with a well-aimed punch but would wish you compliments of the season as he did it. Dodie didn't know whether to laugh at the image or be alarmed by it.

'Ladies and gentlemen, you've been a wonderful crowd and we could play all night,' the conductor announced, 'but I'm afraid this is our last song, so let's make it a good, rousing one, eh?'

There were cheers and Dodie couldn't decide whether people were cheering because they'd enjoyed the show or whether they were happy they could finally go somewhere to get warm. The first notes of 'Here

Comes Santa Claus' rang out. She turned to Ed, unable to hold back the broad smile that lit her face.

'This is one of my favourite Christmas songs!'

'It is a good one,' he agreed. Probably to be polite but she was impressed by his tact. Ryan would have laughed right out and told her she was sad. 'Shame I missed most of the show,' he added. 'I didn't know anything about it until you mentioned it on the phone.'

'Would you have come for all of it if you'd known?'

Ed nodded slowly, as if giving the matter a great deal of consideration. Something about it looked endearingly comical and it was hard to imagine him in combats with a gun at his side. 'I might have done,' he said.

'Next time I know who to ask when I can't get anyone else to come,' Dodie smiled. 'They have concerts here all the time in the summer but I usually end up watching them alone these days.'

'I thought you didn't mind going out alone?' he said, cocking an eyebrow.

'I don't,' she laughed, recalling their recent conversation. 'But sometimes it's fun to have a friend along. If you ever fancied being that friend…'

He smiled. 'I'd like that.'

They listened in silence for the rest of the song. After brief applause, the band took their bows and began to pack away, the crowd dispersing to find other things to do.

'Have you got to go home now?' Dodie asked. 'You said you hadn't seen much of Bournemouth yet… maybe I could show you some places. Have you checked out the Christmas markets yet?'

'Not yet. To be honest, I'm starving. Must be the cold working up an appetite.'

'There's plenty of street food – noodles, hog roast, kebabs, bratwurst… take your pick.'

'I could eat all of it. What do you think? Hungry? Want to choose?'

'I suppose I *could* eat something. And noodles might be good as long as I don't get them down my chin, which I usually do. Even worse, I might get them on my coat and this coat is…' She paused, somehow feeling guilty she was wearing Margaret's coat in front of Ed but not knowing why. 'Come to think of it,' she continued, collecting her thoughts, 'there's potential for any of it to get all over me. I think street food was invented to make a mess.'

'Noodles it is, and I won't comment if I see any of it go down your chin.'

They began to walk towards the log cabins that lined the main shopping street outside the park. Fog clung to the glow of the streetlamps like cobwebs, shrouding the pavements in ochre mist. Crowds spilled out from various eateries and temporary bars, music blasting out while security guards looked on, expressions stony, though Dodie often liked to think that when they knocked off their shift they'd be in the bar sipping mulled cider too. Then Dodie stopped at a queue for a noodle stand.

'Can you believe that even though I practically live in town I haven't even tried any of these food stands yet?' she said, turning to him.

'I can, because I haven't either.'

'But you live further out so you have an excuse.'

'Not that much further.'

'Still more of an excuse than me.'

'I expect your shop takes a lot of your time?' he asked. 'Must be hard to run it alone.'

'It does…' Dodie replied absently as a figure huddled in the doorway of the now closed bank caught her attention. She shook her head. 'Sorry… I mean, it does but that's because I'm still getting it off the ground. Maybe I'll be able to get help when I'm turning a healthier profit.'

The couple in front moved away and the proprietor of the stall smiled. 'Yes please?'

'Chicken noodles for me,' Ed said. He looked at Dodie. 'This is on me,' he added. 'Fire away.'

'Can I have two portions of chicken noodles?' Dodie asked the stallholder, and Ed raised his eyebrows.

'How hungry *are* you?'

Dodie laughed. 'It's not all for me. And I can't expect you to pay for it either.'

'It's not that I mind paying… If not for you then who's joining us?'

'Nobody,' Dodie said as she took two of the cartons from the stall and watched as Ed paid. 'I've just seen someone I know who will appreciate a hot meal; that's all. As soon as I can get a hand free I'll pay you back for this one.'

'I don't want you to pay me back,' Ed said as he followed Dodie, who was already striding across to the bank.

'Hey, Nick!' she called, and he looked up from the cigarette he was rolling with a bright smile.

'Alright, sweetheart! I must have been a good boy to keep running into you like this!'

She stepped forward and handed him a box of noodles. 'I hope you like Chinese. I took a punt on the fact that you would.'

He put the cigarette to one side and dug the provided plastic fork into the box, yanking out a gooey tangle of noodles and sauce. 'Lucky you didn't get chopsticks with it,' he said, looking delighted as he shoved them into his mouth. 'Just the job!' he added with a thumbs up. At least it might have been that, but it was hard to tell through a mouthful of chow mein.

'You watch yourself out tonight,' Dodie said. 'I know you don't like them but you ought to get into a shelter tonight; it's going to be cold.'

'You know me,' Nick said with a quick grin. 'I've slept through worse than this and lived to tell the tale.'

'Even so.' Dodie smiled as she watched him dig into his noodle box again. 'I'd feel better if you did.'

'Maybe I will then,' Nick said, but Dodie knew he wouldn't. But at least she'd said it and she could be happy that she'd done as much as she could do. For what little it was worth, constant nagging was the only weapon she had in the war to keep him safe. She often wondered if he had anyone else to nag him.

'See you around then,' she said.

'Goodnight, sweetheart!' Nick called as she turned to go, aiming a nod at Ed as they began to walk back down into the main thoroughfare.

'Do you do that often?' Ed asked, throwing her a sideways look.

'What?'

'Feed homeless people?'

'Not really. Sometimes. I mean, you can't help everyone but I try to do what I can. I like Nick – he's really interesting. Has a lot to say if you get time to listen to him.' She handed Ed her noodle pot for a moment and pulled her purse from her bag.

'God, no!' Ed exclaimed. 'What sort of bastard would I be if I watched you hand a meal to a homeless guy and then let you pay me for it!'

'But you offered to buy me dinner and not Nick too. That was my choice.'

'Well, Nick can have this one on me. Please put your money away.'

Dodie hesitated, poised to offer some argument. But then she smiled and did as he asked before taking her noodles back. 'Thank you,' she said.

'Thank *you*!' Ed returned.

'For what?'

'For making me come out of my house.'

Dodie laughed. 'I don't recall making you come out of your house. How did I do that?'

'By turning up at my house that night when you came asking about the letter.'

Dodie was silent for a moment as they walked, hands cradled around the warmth of her noodle pot. 'Did you have a very bad time in the army? In action, I mean? Was it horrible?'

'I try not to think about it. I keep telling myself not to think about it. It's not so easy when you go to sleep to tell your brain not to dream about it, though.'

'Sorry… I didn't mean to dredge up bad memories.'

'I probably need to talk about it. I had a counsellor when I was first discharged from the army… back home in Blackpool. Didn't see the point in keeping it up but that's the first thing she said to me when I started.'

'What made you move to Bournemouth?'

'I needed a fresh start. I stuck a pin in a map and… here I am.'

'A pin in a map? Sounds a bit drastic – whatever made you do that must have been a bit intense.'

He stared out over the knots of people crowded around bright timber-clad stalls, seeming to consider his answer. But as Dodie waited and none came, she felt she'd hit a nerve he would rather have kept safe.

'I didn't mean to pry,' she said awkwardly. 'I suppose you might have been up for a bit of adventure or something, eh? That's why you went so random over it.'

But there was continued, unbearable silence as they walked, and Dodie sensed that taciturn, closed version of him she was beginning to recognise coming to the fore again. She didn't know what to make of it – she knew only that it was frustrating. One or the other she could deal with, but this sea change of moods… it was all too much.

'I don't mean to be funny,' she said slowly, 'but do you consider us to be friends now? I mean, we're spending time together as friends and I didn't ask you to come tonight so I got the impression that's what you wanted. Only, every time I think I have that figured out you go all secret squirrel on me and then I don't know what the hell is going on. Have I said something to piss you off?'

'Of course you haven't.' He stood the fork in his pot and finally turned to face her. 'And yes, I think we're friends now. It's just… I had a bad time in Blackpool when I came back from duty and I suppose it's made me a bit slow to trust.'

'I've never asked for your trust. We've just met. It's only brass bands and noodles. And if it helps, I had to have counselling once so I'm pretty familiar with how this works.'

'I know… I'm sorry.' He let out a sigh. Then he threw her a sideways look. 'You had counselling? You seem so… together.'

'Maybe that's because it worked.' Dodie shrugged. 'It got dark for a while, but things are much better now. I'm sure it'll get better for you too.'

He was silent for a moment, as if weighing up his options, how much of himself he wanted to give away. When he spoke again it wasn't what Dodie had been expecting.

'I had a girlfriend… was engaged actually. And then when I got back home to Blackpool she told me it was over. I found out she'd been seeing my best friend – cliché or what? But it broke my heart. When I needed her most, when I was already screwed up from my time in the army, she let me down. I thought I could trust her to the ends of the earth but I was wrong. And I thought, if I'm wrong about her, I can't be sure of anyone ever again.'

'I'm sorry; that sounds like it was hard.'

'So, you see, if I'm struggling in your company that's the reason why.'

'But we're just hanging out so there's no reason to feel scared. I'd like to think we're friends now and that shouldn't need to stress you out; it's just friends.'

'It doesn't… the friendship, I mean.'

'So you know when you go into your man zone you can share it with me? You don't have to drift off into an enigmatic silence… you can actually talk about it?'

He gave her a slight smile. 'You have a way with words, don't you? My *man zone*? *Enigmatic silence*? Honestly, though, there's nothing to say about it. She ripped my heart out and stamped on it and sometimes I'm still pissed off – end of story. I'm moving on.'

Dodie didn't think that was true at all. Perhaps now wasn't the time to say it; she felt she might have already pushed him on the subject as far as he could go, and the whole evening was getting a bit too serious. She had enough on her plate worrying about Ryan without worrying about a man she wasn't even dating.

'So in your capacity as my new friend,' she said, steering the subject of his heartbreak away from the point of no return, 'tell me more about your genius social media plan to find my letter writer.'

'I'd hardly call it genius,' he said with a smile, seemingly happy to change the subject too. 'A simple plea on Facebook or whatever platform you use might get some interest. Ask people to share it , that sort of thing. It might yield nothing – in fact it probably will yield nothing – but you never know.'

'I suppose it's got to be worth a try. The one problem is my friends list is pretty small and select.'

'And you call me a miserable sod.'

Dodie flicked him a grin, feeling as though they were back on safe emotional ground once more. 'I'm introspective. There's a difference.'

'I always thought that was just another name for miserable sod.'

'No; I'm afraid you're very much mistaken there. It's another name for anti-social sod and that's quite different.'

'Right!' Ed laughed. 'So, what do you think? Worth a try?'

'Will you help? Post something on your wall for me?'

'I don't have a Facebook account.'

'And you call me miserable!' Dodie exclaimed. 'The cheek of it!'

'I did have one but I closed it down when…' He stopped, forced away a frown and pushed a smile onto his face. 'It doesn't matter. It's better off posted on your wall anyway as you live locally so there's more chance of you getting a response. Everyone I know is in Blackpool or still away on duty abroad, so there's not much point in me asking them about a couple who lived in Bournemouth in 1944.'

'I suppose you might have a point there,' Dodie conceded. 'I'll give it a go when I get back later.' She retrieved her fork from the noodle box and began to eat again. 'So, this tour of Bournemouth – where do you want to start?'

He nodded his head at a mulled wine vendor they were passing. 'How about there?'

Dodie grinned. 'Looks good to me.'

On reflection, it had been a weird and slightly awkward night so far, but it looked as if it was about to get a whole lot better as she led him over. A bit of her wondered whether, if she could get enough drinks into him, she might hear more about this girl who'd broken his heart. As usual, no matter what her rational brain told her about staying out of things that would only complicate her life, she couldn't help but get involved. She could feel herself getting drawn into Ed's world now, despite saying she didn't want to. But if she could understand what had happened, learn a bit more of his past, then perhaps she'd be able to help him, and that had to be a good thing.

Nine

Dodie had the distinct feeling that her cunning plan had backfired. The thudding headache of a hangover as her alarm woke her that morning told her as much, and if she'd drank too much God only knew what inappropriate information she'd ended up sharing with Ed. But mulled wine was a sneaky devil and she should have known better; it didn't taste like ordinary wine and it was easy to underestimate its potency. It was too late for regrets now because she had a shop to open. For once, she prayed for a slow day – or at least a slow morning – so she could pull herself together. Being a Wednesday, she thought she might just be in luck…

But, of course, a freak alignment of the stars meant a steady stream of customers through the morning. She was thrilled, of course, but she couldn't help but wish she could leave an honesty box on the counter and let them all get on with it while she went back to bed.

Drastic times called for drastic measures, and by lunchtime her usual rule of no smelly food in the shop had gone out of the window; a quick phone call to the lovely owner of the delicatessen a few doors down and one of his teenage daughters had run down to deliver a bacon sandwich, which Dodie devoured in the back room next to a wide-open window in a bid to keep the smell from clinging to the clothes in the shop. When she'd finished, she was freezing, but at least she felt more human again. The chill was nothing that a good hot coffee wouldn't sort.

Settling back at her seat behind the counter and jotting some expenses into her ledger, she smiled to see a text arrive from Ed.

I had a good time last night. Think I'm going to like Bournemouth.

Me too. I'm glad you like Bournemouth.

And she wasn't just saying this in response to his compliment – she'd had a great time in his company once they'd cleared the air. He was witty, well-read and chivalrous. She couldn't get him remotely interested in her extensive library of black-and-white movies but she supposed you couldn't have everything. She was interested, however, in his thoughts on philosophy and politics. Most people would yawn at the mere mention of politics as a general rule, but he'd managed to make it sound interesting and they'd talked all the way back to the shop as he walked her home.

What else had they discussed? Her gran had made it into the conversation and stories from her childhood. He'd told her about practical jokes in the barracks and the gruelling training sessions during his time in the army. He'd told her he was looking for work but he still had some money from the army to keep him going until he decided what he wanted to do. She'd told him about opening the business and her passion for upcycling and recycling. Had they discussed Ryan? They'd skirted around the issue of the ex who'd sent him running from Blackpool, but had Ryan cropped up? She couldn't remember. And why did the idea bother her so much?

In the time it had taken to process these thoughts another text had arrived.

Have you put out your Facebook plea?

Not yet, busy in shop but will do it later.

You're busy? Sorry, hadn't realised. Sorry for texting.

Don't be daft! Texts won't distract me that much! Thanks for asking, I'm going to give it a go as soon as I have a minute to think about what to say.

Good, I'm glad. I'll let you get on.

Don't be a stranger.

What does that even mean?

I don't know!

Dodie waited for a response, but when none came she stashed her phone in the drawer of the counter with a smile. 'Here Comes Santa Claus' was playing on the radio and her smile broadened at the memory of the last song played at the brass band concert. It had been a great evening in the end, and she couldn't honestly recall having such a good time on a night out in a long time. Granted, it was hardly debauched nightclub antics or pub crawling until the early hours, but that was also why she'd loved it so much. It was just two friends, getting to know one another in a lovely, convivial atmosphere. As she'd showed him some of the sights, it had felt almost as if she was discovering her town for the first time herself, seeing it the way he saw it. They'd popped in and out of various mulled wine establishments with the excuse that they were keeping warm but had become so tipsy that soon they were unable to resist one, regardless of whether they needed warming. And as there weren't that many, there was also a strange feeling of déjà vu as they returned to the same ones with alarming regularity but couldn't quite remember how many times they'd been back.

The shop door tinkled and two teenage girls wearing school uniforms came in. Dodie checked her watch and was shocked to see it was half past three. The day had somehow escaped her and she still had so much to do in the shop. She gave the girls an encouraging smile and turned her attention back to her ledger so they'd be able to browse without feeling awkward, looking up every now and again just to check they were OK. She smiled to herself as their initial shy awkwardness gave way to noisier enthusiasm as they giggled and pulled items from the rail, egging each other on to try them. There probably wouldn't be a sale in it, but who was Dodie to complain when they sounded so happy?

When the shop had been locked, Dodie checked her phone again. There were no new texts from Ed, but there was a message from Isla saying she'd made up her mind, and one from Ryan asking if she fancied getting together on Saturday night. More to the point, he wanted to get together at the flat on Saturday night, and Dodie couldn't help thinking that their conversation would inevitably lead to him pushing to move in earlier than they'd agreed, because once Ryan got an idea into his head, there was no waiting. It was immediate with him or not at all. She quite liked the idea of the not at all, although not at all would probably signal the end of their relationship.

Ignoring that text for the time being, she turned her attention to the one from Isla. That was easier to deal with and Dodie was anxious to hear what her friend had decided to do about her long-lost dad.

'Hey.' Isla picked up the call on the second ring.

'Wow, that was fast!'

'I was just about to phone you actually. The shop's closed now?'

'Yep, thank goodness – it's been a hell of a day.'

'Busy? But that's good, isn't it?'

'It would be if I hadn't started off with such a hangover and in desperate need of my bed. It got a bit better by this afternoon but now

I think I'm just running on the after-effects of the caffeine I've poured down my throat all day.'

'Where did you get a hangover from on a school night? Ryan leading you astray again? It's alright for him – he can take a day off, but you can't.'

'Nah, this time I can't blame Ryan. I went to see a concert in the gardens and stayed out late.'

'And you got drunk? In the gardens? What sort of concert was it?'

'A brass band.'

'Jeez, Dodie!' Isla laughed. 'A: What the hell are you doing going to a brass band concert? And B: How did you manage to get drunk at one? Is this like an old person's rave? Were you just rolling around the park on your own necking cheap cider and swearing at passers-by?'

Dodie chuckled. 'Not quite. I was in the park watching the concert and that guy from Wessex Road just happened to turn up.'

'What guy?'

'The one I told you about – Ed. He lives at number eleven now and promised to help me find information about where Margaret's family is.'

'And he just happened to be at the same brass band concert as you?'

'Well, yeah…' Dodie lied. Even as she said it she wasn't sure why she felt the need to keep the truth from her best friend. It wasn't that she had anything to hide or that Isla would judge her. Would she? There was nothing to judge her for. So why did Dodie suddenly feel guilty about her evening with Ed? 'We ran into each other and decided to get some mulled wine. Quite a lot of mulled wine, as it happens.'

Isla was silent for a moment. 'That's so weird. You both turned up at the same brass band concert. Considering you're both under the age of eighty I don't think you can fully appreciate the levels of weird that is. I think you may have just found your perfect man.'

'And I think you may be forgetting that I already have my perfect man. Never mind that, what's this decision you've made?'

'I'm going.'

Dodie gave a small smile. 'I thought you might.'

'Do you think it's the right decision, though?'

'If it's right for you, it doesn't matter what I think.'

'So you don't?'

'Yes, I do. Because it's right for you, so it doesn't matter whether it's right for anyone else. What did your mum say? You've told her?'

'Pretty much what you'd expect her to say. Threatened to disown me, begged me not to, told me I'd regret it, then hoped I'd get what I deserved by finding out his whole family were hideous… more or less the seven stages of grief.'

'Wow… So how have you left it with her?'

'She's sulking right now, but at the end of the day even she can see that I'm an adult and I have to make my own decisions, much as some of them might pain her.'

'Just for the record, I'm glad you stuck to your guns. Although I'm not sure I'd have been brave enough in your shoes.'

'I haven't gone yet so there's still time for me to stop being brave. But thanks.'

'When are you going?'

'I'm going to book flights today and hopefully go early next week. No point in putting it off, and if I want to be back for Christmas I need to get a move on.'

'Fancy a quick get-together before you go? If you have time, that is.'

'Aren't you fully booked with all your men?'

'Ha ha, funny. I only have one man and we could always include him in the plans. I know you're not his biggest fan, but…'

'I don't think he's mine either. Let me know when you're next seeing him and we'll work around it. Otherwise, it's not like I'll be gone for a hundred years – I can see you when I get back from France and, to be honest, I'll probably have a lot more to tell you then.'

'I'm sure you will. I'll text you later.'

'Brilliant! Take care.'

'You too.'

Dodie ended the call. Isla sounded so calm, but they both knew something big, something life-changing, was brewing. A flight to France was just the start, and Dodie could only hope that it was the start of something good, and not something disastrous.

As Dodie was eating beans on burnt toast that she couldn't bear to throw away, *It's a Wonderful Life* in the DVD player, her phone bleeped the arrival of a second text from Ryan.

What are you up to?

She was going to have to reply to the first one soon or he'd get the hump.

Not much, watching TV.

Did you get my text?

Dodie's finger hovered over the keyboard for a moment. Then she began to type.

Text? You mean just now?

Earlier.

Haven't seen anything from you today but this one I've just replied to. Sorry.

Thought it was funny you didn't reply. Wanted to know if you want to do something this weekend. Cheap, because it's nearly Christmas and I have to buy you a present, lol.
That is weird. Don't know why I didn't get the text. Must be a problem on the network or something.

She paused. He would expect to see her, and she couldn't quite understand what was stopping her from just making arrangements. She shook herself and continued.

This weekend good. Saturday night?
Saturday good. Will be at your place at 8.

She finished by sending him a single kiss, just so he'd know she'd received the last message and that it was OK. She'd wanted to see Isla too but wasn't sure now whether it was a good idea to have her and Ryan in the same room after all, especially with Isla having so much else on her mind. Maybe she'd try to see her friend on Sunday instead.

Finishing her supper and pushing the plate to one side, Dodie turned off the TV. She couldn't concentrate on the film now, even if Jimmy Stewart was just about to snog Donna Reed before emphatically stating that he never wanted to get married, while simultaneously proving that he was hopelessly in love and wanted nothing more than to marry her. Instead, she dragged her laptop across the dining table and logged into her long-neglected Facebook account.

Ninety-seven notifications were more than she could be bothered to deal with. Most of them were invites to join some event or game or other, and most people who knew Dodie knew that she didn't often venture onto social media anyway, preferring to do her socialising in a much more personal way. But others did, and despite her initial doubts she could see the logic in Ed's suggestion that she use it to get help with her quest to find Margaret and George. In her status box she began to type:

Can you help? I need to track down someone named Margaret (surname begins with a V) who lived on Wessex Road in Bournemouth in 1944 or her family. I would also like to find someone named George who was engaged to Margaret and was fighting in France in 1944. A bit vague, I know, but I have something that I'd like to return to them or their families, if I can find them. I'd be grateful for information or shares. I can't offer a reward, but you will experience the warming glow of a good deed if you can help!

Dodie checked the post over and then clicked submit. It might do no good at all, but Ed was right, it had to be worth a try.

For the next hour she refreshed her page every so often, but apart from exclamations of shock at seeing her online, and jokes about her having been replaced by an alien doppelganger, there was no new information about Margaret or George. Dodie supposed she couldn't really expect things to happen that fast, and with an impatient sigh, decided that the old adage about a watched pot never boiling was probably a good one to take heed of right now as she shut the laptop down and got ready for bed. It had been a long day, and there was plenty more to do before the week was over.

Ten

It wasn't often that the main phone in the shop rang. So the sound of it almost had Dodie leaving her seat as she sat behind the counter on Friday morning, staring dreamily out of the window, thinking of nothing in particular. The fact was that despite her early night she was still tired, and she began to wonder whether it wasn't all these extra responsibilities she was piling on herself that were the cause rather than a single night out with one too many mulled wines.

'Forget-Me-Not Vintage...'

'Can I speak to Dodie please? Dodie Bright, that is.'

'Gran?' Dodie frowned. 'Gran, is that you?'

'Oh, it is. Hello, Dodie! I didn't recognise your voice.'

As she worked in the shop alone, it was hardly going to be anyone else answering the phone, but it was easier to let it pass than try and explain that to her gran.

'Is everything OK? Did you need me for something?'

'Oh, I'm absolutely fine; I've got woodworking in half an hour... I just wanted to tell you about your lady.'

'Woodworking...?' Dodie shook her head. 'Never mind. What lady?'

'Your Margaret from Wessex Road. Gloria popped over for a cup of tea and she said she'd asked her relatives and her aunt thought the name was Vincent... Margaret Vincent. She says she can't be sure because her aunt's memory isn't what it used to be, and sometimes she can't even remember that she's not married to Bruce Forsyth when she sees him on the television, but that's what she thinks. Is that any good?'

'It's something,' Dodie smiled. 'Thanks, Gran. And thanks for phoning me with it.'

'I didn't want to wait until I saw you next in case you needed it sooner.'

'That's brilliant.'

'Right...' Gran said briskly. 'I'll pop in next week, shall I? See about that coat you're getting for me...'

'I haven't actually found one for you yet.'

'But you might have one by next week.'

'It doesn't work quite like that but maybe if something comes my way. But come in anyway for a chat – you know you're always welcome.'

'Alright then. Bye bye for now.'

'Bye, Gran.'

Dodie put the phone down and grabbed her laptop from the drawer beneath the desk where it lived when she was working. The easiest thing would be to edit her original Facebook post to add in the surname as a possible rather than write the whole thing again. It was then that she noticed the private message waiting to be read.

Hi Dodie,

My name is Sally Chandra and I'm a journalist for the Echo. A friend forwarded your Facebook message to me regarding your attempts to find a lady who lived on Wessex Road in 1944. Do you mind me asking what it is you want her for? I'm intrigued, and I think our readers would be too. They might also be able to help.

If you can spare a moment I'd like very much to have a chat with you about it and perhaps feature your story in the paper. Let me know your thoughts.
Regards, Sally

'That didn't take long,' Dodie murmured as she clicked Sally's photo to get more information about her. It seemed that whoever had once said that news never sleeps was speaking quite literally. Her profile seemed genuine enough and a story in the paper would be a great idea. Once again, Dodie was annoyed that she hadn't thought of it herself, but then she probably wouldn't have considered it likely that any newspaper reporter would be interested.

Hi Sally,
I'm trying to track either of them, or their relatives, because I have a love letter from George to Margaret written while he was serving in France during the war. I run a vintage shop in town and I found the letter in a second-hand coat I got at auction (I'm guessing the coat belonged to Margaret, but I don't know for sure). I'd like to return the letter to Margaret herself if I can as I now think George is dead, or their relatives if I can't. I think a newspaper story would be very helpful and I'd be happy to talk to you. I would struggle coming to your offices as I run the shop alone and I have to be here during working hours, but you're welcome to come and see me at my premises whenever you like.
Dodie

Dodie closed the message window and went on to alter her status so that it now contained the new information about Margaret's surname possibly being Vincent. Then she dialled Ed's number. He'd be pleased, she was sure, by the contact from the newspaper, and if he hadn't suggested social media it would never have happened.

'You'll never believe it!' Dodie squeaked as he picked up. 'We've got newspaper interest!'

'Dodie... what...?' Ed sounded dazed. Dodie faltered.

'Oh... did I ring you at a bad time? You sound—'

'No. No, it's fine. I had a bad night... Was just getting a bit of catch-up shut-eye. Of course, it's fine, you wouldn't have known.'

'I'm so sorry; I didn't mean to wake you. I could call you later... it's no problem.'

'Yeah... that would be good. Speak to me later...'

He ended the call before Dodie had the chance to say goodbye. She raked her teeth over her bottom lip thoughtfully as she put her phone away. She hadn't been expecting quite such a brusque dismissal. Was that his way of saying sod off, or was he genuinely half asleep? The day she could read that man would be the day she'd keel over from the shock. More perplexing still, why did she keep trying, and why did it matter so much?

She was spared any further ruminating on the subject by the sound of the bell over the door announcing the arrival of customers. Painting on a smile, she put her mind to her job and pushed Ed Willoughby and his funny moods firmly from it.

Late-afternoon drizzle had done a good job of keeping customers out of the town for the rest of the day, and so Dodie's afternoon had been quiet. It had given her plenty of time to get small jobs done around the shop, but days like this had her on edge, worrying about takings and anxious for a busier than usual end to the week to make the money up. She'd spent the previous hour staring out of the window as the odd shopper hurried by, fighting with umbrellas or huddled in hooded coats, and cars hissed through the spray on the road. The one highlight of the afternoon was another message from her journalist, followed by a phone call. Sally Chandra sounded amiable and very interested, and they arranged to meet in Dodie's shop so Sally could get more information and some photos. When Dodie had briefly outlined her efforts so far, Ed's name had come up along with a brief explanation of his involvement. Sally sounded keen to involve him too, for a bit of colour, and although Dodie said tentatively that she'd ask him, there was no way of telling what his reaction might be. It all depended on which Ed she got at the time, but as he'd told her to phone him later to fill him in on the latest developments, she'd do just that and ask; for better or worse.

At five to five she'd had enough of staring out of the window and if she missed a vintage-hungry horde of customers by closing five minutes early, then so be it. It was as she turned the shop sign from open to closed that she saw a man running across the road towards the door. Raising her eyebrows in surprise, she opened up to him.

'I didn't know if I'd catch you,' Ed panted. 'I must have got some right looks running through town. And I'd forgotten where the street was because… well, we were a bit drunk last time I was up here.'

'Is everything OK?'

'Huh? Oh yeah… I just wanted to say I'm sorry. You know, for being so rude on the phone earlier. I didn't mean anything by it.'

'I know – I didn't think you did.' Dodie closed the door behind him and locked it. 'Just in case any customers decide to come in,' she replied to his silent question. 'I was about to close up anyway.'

There was an awkward pause. Dodie wondered why Ed had felt the need to come all this way to apologise when a text or phone call would have done just as well. 'Do you want a drink?' she asked, not knowing what else she was supposed to say and feeling obliged to offer something in return for his trek over.

He nodded. 'I'd like that.'

'Is tea OK?' she said, beckoning him to take a spare chair behind the counter. It was strange, but she wasn't quite sure how an invitation up to the flat would look and it felt somehow safer to offer him a seat in the shop, in full view of the windows. Not that she was afraid of him, though when she really thought about it she wasn't quite sure what she was afraid of. Perhaps she was more afraid of some new feeling lurking inside her, something she couldn't yet identify but felt the presence of just the same. 'I don't have any coffee, I'm afraid.'

'I'm northern – tea is always OK,' he said as he took a seat. 'I like your shop,' he added, looking around with interest. 'Last time I was up here it was dark and we were a bit worse for wear. And, as I recall, you didn't let me in.'

'I didn't *not* let you in,' Dodie laughed. 'You just didn't come in. I expect you were being gentlemanly or something.'

'That's deeply out of character,' he said. 'Are you sure that was me?'

Dodie grinned. 'Give me a minute and I'll get those teas.'

He nodded and Dodie headed up to make their drinks. As she waited for the kettle to boil she could hear his footsteps downstairs. He must have been inspecting the shop. Perhaps it was a bit too trusting to leave him alone down there but she guessed she could be fairly confident by now that he wasn't planning to run out with armfuls of psychedelic shirts. At least he was here, so she could tell him about Sally Chandra's proposition properly. A face-to-face conversation might have a much better chance of success than a short, easily refused text request. She'd even break out the biscuits too, and that way he couldn't possibly say no.

'Sorry, Dodie, it's just not going to happen.' Ed shook his head vehemently, just to emphasise exactly how unlikely the happening was. She could understand why he wouldn't want to, but she'd hoped for a different answer.

'I thought you might say that. I asked only because the journalist said it would be a great angle, to see how we'd met while I was on the hunt for my letter writer and we'd teamed up. She probably thought it made us sound like Scooby Doo's gang or something.'

'I get where she's coming from, but I'd really rather avoid my mug being in the paper.'

'But you've done so much towards it; I think it would be nice for you to take some credit. Can she at least print your name and say you've helped?'

He was thoughtful for a moment, his gaze trained on a cinema poster for *Casablanca* hanging over a rack of shirts. 'Do you think that's a good idea?' he asked finally.

'Why wouldn't it be?'

He turned to her. 'I bet you haven't told your boyfriend about us spending Wednesday evening together, have you?'

Dodie frowned. 'What's that got to do with anything?'

'That means you haven't. I bet you haven't said a single word about me.'

'Well, no, I haven't, but—'

'Did you ever intend to?'

'I don't see that I need to. Quite frankly I don't see how it's relevant either.'

'So the first he'll hear of it is to see my name mentioned in the paper and to read how we've been doing our Scooby Doo detecting together, and he'll be pretty pissed off, won't he?'

'Well…' Dodie said, exasperation creeping into her tone, 'I'll tell him first, before the paper is out.'

'But he'll still wonder why you didn't tell him straightaway. And believe me from someone who knows, it'll look bad.'

Dodie opened her mouth to argue, but then clamped it shut again. He was right, and she could see how right he was now that he'd said it. Every word of Ed's reasoning made perfect sense. She should have been straight with Ryan from the start – transparent and frank – given him a reason to trust instead of reasons to suspect. She didn't even know why she had been so reluctant to tell him about Ed, because Ryan wasn't usually the jealous type and she had nothing to hide. Unless she did have something to hide, a budding sense of guilt about something that she didn't even know herself yet. None of it made any sense.

'Ryan's not like that,' she said stubbornly.

'Every man's like that. It might have escaped your attention, but I'm one, so I should know.'

She gave a vague shrug. 'To be honest I haven't even told him about the letter yet, so it will all be a surprise.'

'You haven't?' Ed stared at her.

'I know; I don't know why either. He thinks my vintage obsessions are silly and I knew he'd think this was silly. I suppose I felt stupid explaining it to him.'

'You should never have to feel stupid sharing the things that matter to you with the people you love. And you should never have to apologise for them. I don't see how he can think your love of vintage is silly when you've built a business from it.'

'I know that.' Dodie forced a smile. 'And it's probably just me; I expect he'd be more tolerant than I give him credit for. But really, he doesn't even read the paper apart from the sports pages so I doubt he'll see this story whatever. He probably wouldn't even see if I was topless on page three.'

'Bloody hell!' Ed laughed. 'I think someone might point it out to him, though!'

Dodie giggled, the tension building between them dissipated by their laughter. 'After they'd finished burning all the copies they could find.'

'Oh, I don't think so,' Ed smiled, the laughter subsiding.

And suddenly Dodie was aware of something shifting between them, something imperceptible and yet seismic.

'You make me laugh,' he said, but he wasn't laughing at all as he held her in a gaze that seemed to appraise her soul. He wanted to say something and he was holding back, she could tell. Did she want to hear it anyway? She wasn't sure she did at all.

Heat rising to her face, for the first time she wondered whether she ought to be sitting alone with him like this.

'Without meaning to, I expect,' she mumbled, downing the last of her drink and making a fuss of collecting their mugs so she wouldn't have to look at him. Bustling up to the flat to dump them in the sink, she returned a moment later to see he'd got his coat on.

'I should go,' he said. 'Thanks for the drink, and sorry I can't help with the newspaper thing.'

'It's OK.' Dodie forced what she hoped was a carefree smile. 'You've done so much to help already.'

'But you'll let me know what happens?' he asked, edging towards the door. She nodded.

'Of course I will. Will you pop back in some time? To the shop, I mean? Stay for a cuppa?'

'If I'm passing,' he said. Was he suddenly feeling as awkward as she was? Aware of something in the air between them so tangible she could almost grab it? 'See you around,' he added as Dodie unlocked the door to let him step out onto the street. She smiled hesitantly and nodded, locking the door and watching through the glass as he walked away.

She had no idea what she thought of Ed Willoughby, but she was beginning to recognise that she missed him whenever he wasn't there.

It wasn't often Dodie met someone smaller than herself, but Sally Chandra made her feel positively titanic. What the reporter lacked in stature, however, she more than made up for in presence. Her personality seemed to fill the shop from the moment she walked in that Saturday afternoon, having phoned ahead during the morning to say she was free and asking if she could pop by. Apparently, Sally was still as keen as her lightning-fast Facebook response suggested, explaining that she was supposed to be off work but found herself at a loose end and wanted to get the story into the paper by the following Wednesday if she could. She'd breezed into Forget-Me-Not Vintage, run an approving gaze over the interior of the shop and announced in a loud voice how quaint and charming it was before grasping Dodie firmly by the shoulders and kissing her lightly on both cheeks. Dodie had never been greeted quite so informally on a first meeting and had been slightly taken aback. It was hard not to get swept up in her enthusiasm, though, and she found herself taking an instant liking to the reporter.

'So…' Sally said as Dodie pulled out the spare seat for her. 'Let's hear all about your mysterious letter.'

'Would you like to see it?' Dodie asked. She didn't particularly like sharing its contents but as Sally was very likely to ask, it seemed sensible to put her strange possessiveness firmly out of her mind and show her straight off.

'I'd love to!' Sally beamed. 'I love a story with a romantic angle and we don't get nearly enough.'

'It *is* romantic,' Dodie said, going to the drawer where she'd put the letter in readiness for Sally's visit. 'A little sad too, especially if I don't manage to track anyone down. It doesn't seem right that it sits in my flat and never gets back to people who might treasure it more than me. That's really what this search is about.'

'True love.' Sally nodded. 'A worthy cause. The one thing we're all searching for.' She eyed Dodie keenly. 'Are you truly in love, Dodie? Or are you still searching for it?'

'I… I have a boyfriend,' Dodie replied hesitantly.

'Well, I'm sure that's yours all sorted then,' Sally said briskly, but something about her manner threw Dodie momentarily. Instead of trying to find a reply, she removed the letter from the envelope and handed it to the reporter, who cast her eyes over it, a smile stretching her lips as she read.

'How sweet,' she said finally as she looked up and handed the letter back to Dodie. 'Bittersweet. What an absolutely lovely bit of history. I can see why you were so beguiled by the idea of finding Margaret. And you say you haven't managed to get any leads from social media yet?'

'Not from there, but my gran knows someone who knows someone who thinks Margaret's surname might be Vincent. We're not entirely sure but I think it might be a lead worth following up. I'm still hoping that more information will come from social media – there's been a lot of sharing so it's reaching more and more people.'

'It's just the sort of thing to go viral; people love a personal interest story. What about this man who lives at the property now…' She looked down at a spiral-bound notepad she'd just pulled from a magenta satchel. 'Edward Willoughby. Rather a romantic name in itself, isn't it? Like a Jane Austen hero. What about him? Is he still involved in your search?'

Dodie almost reminded her that Mr Willoughby wasn't quite one of Austen's heroes, but she didn't. The way she felt about Ed these days she didn't want to dwell on the possibility he might not be one of the good guys, either.

'He has been. But as I said on the phone, he's not so keen to be in the paper… I did try to talk him round but…' She shrugged. 'Sorry.'

Sally waved away the apology. 'Do you think he'd object to me popping round to see him? Just to ask a few questions. I wouldn't feature him in any way he wasn't happy with, of course, but it would be another angle to the story and I do rather like the idea of him being in it.'

'I suppose anything that makes people take interest has to be good,' Dodie said, though she was doubtful about asking Ed again. He'd been most emphatic in his refusal of any kind of publicity the night before, although perhaps he'd be more amenable if Sally promised to leave his personal details out of the article. 'I could ask him again I suppose.'

'Could you ask him now, darling? I could whizz over there this afternoon. You have a phone number for him, I take it?'

Dodie nodded as she went behind the counter and pulled her phone from the drawer. As she dialled Ed's number, the door tinkled to announce the arrival of a customer, and while she waited for him to answer, she smiled and nodded at the newcomer, who glanced between Dodie with her phone to her ear and Sally with her pen poised over her notebook, probably wondering just what on earth she'd walked into. The woman took herself over to a wooden chest stuffed with belts, ties, scarves and handbags and began to rummage as Dodie paced the floor, to be met, eventually, by Ed's answerphone message.

'Hi, Ed, it's Dodie. I've got Sally with me… the reporter from the *Echo.* She wants to know if she could possibly have five minutes with you. I know you didn't particularly want to get involved, but she says it's just for another angle to the story. She says you don't have to be in it but she'd like to talk to you if possible anyway. So… if you get this message any time soon… well, if you can let me know either way that would be brilliant… OK… so, bye…'

Sally shot Dodie a coquettish sort of smile as she sat down again. 'Is he handsome?' she asked.

Dodie blinked. 'I hadn't really thought about it. I suppose so.'

'I thought he might be…'

Sally's smile was still in place as she clicked her pen on. Dodie held back a frown as she watched her begin to write. What did she mean by her question? What did it matter if Ed was handsome or not? And what made Sally so sure he would be? Dodie's attention was diverted momentarily by the customer leaving the shop. It was frustrating to lose a potential sale but perhaps the woman never intended to spend much anyway judging by her beeline for the bargain basement stuff in the chest.

'So,' Sally said brightly, 'tell me a little about yourself – background for the story. I won't include it all but it's good to know, helps me give some context.'

Dodie shrugged. 'There's not much to tell. I lived in Dorchester for most of my life and moved to Bournemouth six months ago to open this shop.'

'What made you want to open the shop?'

'I've always been interested in design, fashion and history. A vintage shop seemed like the perfect marriage of the three. I studied fashion and dress history at university… actually, I dropped out of fashion and dress history at university, but I might go back and finish my degree one day. If I have time, of course.'

'I don't suppose you get much time now running a shop six days a week.'

'It tends towards seven, really, by the time I've done all the odds and ends I can't get done in the week while the shop is open.'

'What made you drop out of university?'

Dodie paused.

'If you don't want to tell me then of course, that's fine,' Sally added.

Did it matter if Dodie told her? It was nothing to be ashamed of, despite Dodie feeling like a failure at the time.

'It's complicated,' she said. 'I had some issues with anxiety and depression and I couldn't concentrate. I'm fine now,' she added quickly. 'But at the time I struggled to cope and it seemed sensible to take a breather. I hunkered down with my mum for a year. Strangely, it was the death of my grandad that finally pulled me out of the hole, which most people would think would make things worse still. But it made me realise that life is short and precious and I didn't want to waste mine any longer.'

'You've certainly turned things around,' Sally said with an approving glance around the shop. 'You should be proud of yourself.'

'It's nothing to make a fuss about,' Dodie replied. 'I'm doing something I love.'

Sally scribbled a series of indecipherable squiggles into her notebook. Dodie supposed it was shorthand, though she'd never seen it in use before. 'How did you come by this letter?'

Dodie opened her mouth to reply when the sound of her phone ringing came from the desk drawer.

'Do you want to get that?' Sally asked.

'They'll probably leave an answerphone message if it's important.'

'But it might be Mr Willoughby,' Sally reminded her. 'In which case it would be helpful for me to know before I leave you today.'

'Oh… of course.' Dodie leapt up and dashed to retrieve the phone before it rang off. When she'd left the message for him earlier, she hadn't really expected Ed to call back given her request and his previous refusals. But it was him on the line.

'Hey, Dodie… Sorry about before, my phone was out of charge. What is it you need from me? The reporter wants to come and see me? Did you tell her I didn't want to be in the paper?'

'Yeah, I did. But she thinks it would be a good angle to include your involvement – make the story more appealing.' Dodie glanced up, feeling awkward about having this conversation with Sally present. Though the journalist was busy checking emails on her own phone as Dodie talked, it was obvious she was listening to Dodie's end of the discussion. 'She's here now… I suppose you could have a quick word on the phone? I mean, say no if you really don't want to but it might be enough for now…?'

There was a heavy sigh of resignation on the line. 'OK. A quick word on the phone but nothing more – no photos, no namecheck, no visiting me here. And I'm only doing this much because I know it's important to you.'

Dodie nodded, even though he couldn't see it. 'I'll put her on the line now,' she said, handing her mobile to Sally.

Whatever powers Sally Chandra had, Dodie was convinced she could make a lot more money bottling it for sale than she could as a journalist. After a ten-minute chat with Ed, he'd agreed to let her go to his house for a quick interview and, after she'd collected Dodie's story, she hopped into her car and went straight over. How Sally had managed to change his mind was a mystery when he'd been so adamant with Dodie that he would not get involved in any publicity. In fact, when he sent Dodie a text just after closing time to let her know he'd spoken to Sally and allowed his name to go into the article, Dodie was shocked to learn that he'd eventually relented and given Sally permission to get a photo of him standing outside his house too.

Confused as Dodie was by this change of heart, she was hopeful too that the story would reach further than her own efforts in tracking down Margaret or George now that the local paper was involved. She was excited by the prospect, though a little part of her was sad too that the adventure might soon be over. Because, strangely, while she had more than enough to fill her every waking hour, she'd rather enjoyed the quest and it had taken up so much of her time lately it had become a huge part of her life, something that would leave a hole when she didn't have it any more.

Ryan was due at the flat in less than twenty minutes, but Dodie was still pottering around in the shop cleaning shelving that contained a selection of old vinyl and eight-tracks. A departure from her usual stock, it had been part of the auction that had also brought the letter into her life and when the lot had come up she hadn't been able to resist making a bid, fuelled in part by a desire to own the entire collection of Monkees albums contained in it. After winning it and taking delivery, she'd gone through the rest and sorted others she wanted to keep, including the best of Manfred Mann, a Bing Crosby Christmas collection and two Dusty Springfield albums, until there was barely anything left. What *was* left was now out on display in the shop, though there hadn't been much customer interest in it as yet.

Sometimes, Dodie had to wonder at her own business acumen. If she was going to buy in stock based purely on her desire to listen to cheesy old records, she'd be out of business by the end of the year. She'd also have to buy an actual record player to listen to the ones she'd got, but that was a problem for another day. Ryan would roll his eyes and tell her it was all shit, of course, before trying to explain why she ought to be listening to 50 Cent or Puff Daddy or P Diddy or whatever. It was just one of the many glaringly obvious differences in their personalities, and though people always said opposites attract, they probably didn't mean a couple whose oppositeness was so apparent that they might as well be different species. Still, Dodie reminded herself as she slapped the cleaning cloth onto the shelf and scrubbed vigorously, Ryan had a lot of qualities that made the awful rap music and the disparaging remarks about her taste worth putting up with. He was decent looking, had a steady job, was good at DIY, sensible with money... And her mum liked him a lot, and that was not to be sniffed at because her mum hardly ever liked anyone.

A tap at the shop window interrupted her musings. Her head flicked up and her hand flew to her chest, sending water sloshing over the side of the bucket as she dropped her cloth in fright. It was Ryan, grinning at her. Drying her hands and trying to get her breathing back to normal, she went to unlock the door.

'You're early,' she said as he stepped in. 'I'm not ready yet.'

'Ready for what?' he asked.

'For anything. I'm not changed, not freshened up, not done my hair...'

'You're fine as you are,' he said. 'We don't have to go far anyway, so I wouldn't worry about getting changed. Especially as I'll only be taking your clothes off again in about half an hour...'

'It's good to see romance isn't dead,' she replied, arching an eyebrow.

'You want me to serenade you first? *Dodie, Dodie, how I love your bountiful, bootylicious booty…*'

'Yeah, enough thanks,' Dodie interrupted. 'And are you saying my butt is big?'

'No, it's just the right size for my hands,' he said, grabbing her behind as he followed her to the shelving. Dodie slapped him away.

'Sod off, Ryan!' she squeaked. 'If you want something to fit in your hands you can grab hold of this cleaning cloth and help me!'

His disapproving gaze went to the bucket. 'You're kidding me, right? I've done a day at work already.'

'So have I, but I still have to do this.'

'This is *your* job, though.'

'And if you want to spend any time with me then you'll either help or let me get on so I can finish. Can't you make yourself useful in the flat… get some supper on the go or something? There's pizza in the fridge; you could put that in the oven?'

'I suppose I ought to get used to your kitchen,' he said slowly. 'As I'm going to be living here after Christmas. One pizza, coming up!'

Dodie watched him go through to the back, suddenly feeling as if someone had just pushed her from a plane with a cocktail umbrella for a parachute. She'd tried not to think about their impending cohabitation agreement but there was no getting around it – he was moving into the flat in a matter of weeks and there would be a lot more of this. She was about to retrieve her cloth and finish up when her phone bleeped the arrival of a message. It was Ed.

Having second thoughts about the newspaper interview. Don't know if I want to be mentioned and I don't want my photo in there.

Dodie held in a groan and turned her phone off. One irritating man was enough to deal with for now.

Ryan had managed to burn the pizza, the only job she'd left him in charge of. But they scraped off the worst of it and ate what they could salvage, filling up on bags of crisps and a giant Dairy Milk bar afterwards. There was no point in being annoyed about it so Dodie grabbed a couple of beers from the fridge for him, opened a bottle of wine for herself and decided that the best thing to take her mind off things was to get tipsy. Perhaps then she'd also be happier broaching the subject of the impending newspaper article. She'd decided that Ed, apart from being annoying as hell, had made a very good point: Ryan did need to know, and if he found out any other way he'd be hurt.

'So what's new?' Ryan asked as he sipped at a can of beer on the sofa, Dodie sitting on the chair across from him. Some game show was on the TV, the newest lottery quiz extravaganza, though they changed so often she could barely keep up with them, and the rules seemed to get more and more elaborate with each new incarnation.

'Nothing much. Work, work and more work. There's no time for anything else.'

She put a glass of wine to her lips and turned her gaze back to the television. A couple were leaping around on a bouncy castle trying to snatch travel tickets from a wire suspended above their heads while a gleeful presenter shrieked with fake laughter and the audience egged them on. This would be as good a time as any to mention the newspaper, wouldn't it? But then she opened her mouth to say something and couldn't.

'What exactly is going on here?' she asked, nodding at the TV.

'Beats me.'

'Well, how do they win the prizes?'

'I think they have to grab them.'

'They've already got loads. Surely that's it now?'

He shrugged and took a sip of his beer. Dodie couldn't have cared less one way or the other whether the contestants on the television had won their prizes, so why was she talking about it? Why couldn't she bring herself to tell Ryan about the letter? About George and Margaret V? About Sally Chandra and the newspaper? About Ed? What was stopping her?

'So your mate is off to France then?' Ryan said into her thoughts, his gaze trained on the TV screen.

'Yeah.'

'I bet her mum's impressed.'

'That's what I said. She knows what she's doing, though.'

'Expect so,' Ryan said. He pushed himself up from the sofa. 'Going for a slash. And then maybe we could turn this show off. As you don't seem that keen on it then perhaps we can do something else…'

Dodie looked up at him and he waggled his eyebrows suggestively.

'There's a film on BBC Two I wanted to watch,' she said.

'God, don't tell me it's black and white.'

'It's colour.'

'Are any of the actors still alive?'

Dodie frowned. 'I know you don't like old stuff, but I do.'

'It's Saturday night! Come on, Dodie, this is our night – I don't get to see you much in the week. Why can't you record your film and watch it on a night I'm not here?'

She could, and it wouldn't make a scrap of difference. If anything she'd probably enjoy the film more without Ryan there. But a stubbornness had taken hold and she pursed her lips as she turned away.

'I've been looking forward to it. And I don't have time to watch stuff in the week.'

'You just said you don't do anything all week!' Ryan snapped. Without waiting for a reply, he left the room, and Dodie could hear him muttering, something about him wondering why he bothered to come and visit at all and that it was like she didn't want him there. And she had to wonder whether he had a point.

Eleven

Dodie was still in her pyjamas with her nose in a book about interior design, despite the fact it was gone midday, when the out-of-hours doorbell rang in the shop below. Ryan looked across at her as he lounged in his boxers and a sweatshirt watching catch-up TV.

'Are you expecting someone?'

'No,' Dodie said, feeling vaguely alarmed. Her phone had been switched off for the remainder of the previous evening and she hadn't turned it on this morning either. Partly because she was just sick of dealing with Ed's tidal moods, and partly because she was terrified that Ryan would notice the texts coming in. But what if it was Ed at the door? It wouldn't be the first time he'd turned up unannounced. 'I'd better check the closed sign is actually up at the door,' she added, vaulting from the sofa, 'just in case it's someone thinking we're open.'

'Why would they think that if the door's locked?' Ryan called after her, but Dodie had already crossed into the bedroom to pull a long coat over her pyjamas before she went downstairs.

Down in the shop, she frowned slightly as she hurried to let her gran in.

'Everything OK?' she asked, fear clenching her gut. Her phone had been off – what if something terrible had happened, an emergency, and she hadn't been there to respond to it?

'Oh yes,' Gran said cheerfully. 'I was just passing, you know, and I thought I'd pop by.'

'But you rang the shop bell?'

'I thought it was about time you were open; it's ever so late, you know.' Gran stepped in and Dodie locked the door again.

'It's Sunday. I'm not open on Sunday.'

Gran blinked at her. 'Is it? I hadn't realised. You do lose track of the days when you retire, you know, and with all the other shops open in the town it felt like Saturday…'

'They're open because the Christmas markets are on.'

'Perhaps you ought to be open too?'

'I don't think I'd get enough business to warrant it and I already do six days,' Dodie replied, suddenly wondering how on earth she'd come to be discussing her business strategy with her gran on a Sunday standing in the middle of her shop in her pyjamas.

Gran looked confused for a moment, but then she shook her head. 'Oh, don't mind me, I have some news for you.'

'What's that?' Dodie asked, her vexation at her gran's appearance suddenly lifted. 'Something more about Margaret?'

'Margaret?' Gran shook her head. 'No idea who you're… Oh! You mean that woman who wrote the letter?'

'She didn't write the letter; George did…' Dodie began, but then she stopped herself. 'Never mind. What's your news?'

Gran broke into a broad grin but didn't reply. Dodie waited as Gran continued to grin like a loon.

'Ryan's here, Gran, so if you've got something to tell me you'd better—'

'I'm getting married!' Gran squeaked.

It was Dodie's turn to stare like a loon, but she wasn't grinning. 'What!' she spluttered.

'I'm getting married!' Gran repeated. 'Isn't it exciting? Bernard Truman asked me and I said yes!'

'Who the hell is Bernard Truman?'

'I met him at darts… remember?'

'No, I bloody don't! I'm pretty sure I'd recall if you told me about potential marriage material! And since when did you play darts?'

Gran looked troubled. 'I'm sure I did mention it. Are you upset? It means I might have to bring Bernard when I come to visit you…' She lowered her voice as if Bernard might be hiding around the corner eavesdropping. 'He gets very anxious when he's left alone.'

'What is he, a bloody labradoodle?'

'Oh, don't be cross, Dodie. I'm old I know, but I'm entitled to a bit of happiness. And he really is no trouble. He's got his own bungalow in Moordown and five thousand pounds saved up. Gets free sausages from the butcher's on account of his cat helping keep the mice down.'

'Of course you're entitled to be happy,' Dodie said, trying to level her voice. 'I'm just surprised, that's all. Very surprised. What's Mum said?'

'Well… you know how protective she is… I was hoping you'd tell her.'

'Holy Mary! You want me to tell her? I don't sell bulletproof vests here you know!'

'But she'll take it so much better coming from you.'

'I doubt it.'

'And you can persuade her it's a good idea.'

'I doubt that as well. Besides, I don't think it's a good idea. You've hardly known him for five minutes.'

'At my age you don't mess about,' Gran said. 'Never know how long you've got left.'

Dodie tugged a hand through hair that still needed combing from bed. There was no argument against her gran's statement, even though the whole idea was madness.

'Have you set a date?'

Gran looked sheepish. 'Don't be angry…'

'I'm going to get angry? Like, you're going to tell me something even worse than what you've told me already?'

'You might. Because we can't see any point in a long engagement. Like I said, not at our age because you never know…'

'Go on…'

'So we thought Christmas Eve.'

Dodie had run out of exclamations. She stared at her gran, hoping she'd wake any minute to find this had all been a cheese dream.

'What about your other boyfriends?' she asked, not knowing what else to say, despite how weird her question was when looked at in context and how ridiculously imminent the wedding date was.

'Oh they won't mind. He does have his own bungalow, after all, so how can they compete with that?'

'How indeed…' Dodie let out a sigh. 'What are you going to wear?'

'I don't know. Will you come shopping with me?'

'What about Mum? Surely she'll want to go shopping with you, and I don't have time with my own shop to run.'

'Oh, your mother won't want to come.'

'Anything to do with the fact that she won't approve of this shotgun marriage?'

'I'm not pregnant!' Gran said indignantly, and Dodie held in a scream.

'I mean it's sudden!' She took a deep breath and tried to level her voice. 'Gran... you're going to have to talk to Mum about this. She won't be happy hearing it from me. Ideally, Bernard should talk to Mum with you, seeing as he's about to become her stepfather. Have they even met?'

'I doubt it; I only met him two weeks ago and that's hardly time. Unless they've run into each other in town before now.'

'Hardly likely as Mum is in Dorchester and Bernard, as you just mentioned, has a lovely bungalow in Moordown.'

'Oh yes,' Gran said. 'I'd forgotten about that. In that case they won't have met.'

Dodie was about to sit her gran down and explain her reservations about the whole marriage business, which mainly boiled down to the fact that she'd only known Bernard for two weeks, and that, regardless of his bungalow and his five thousand pounds and excellent mouse-hunting cat, perhaps she ought to get to know him a little better before she committed in a legal capacity, but then Ryan appeared at the doorway.

'I wondered...' he began but stopped when he realised what he'd walked into. He was already backing away from the door when Gran threw him a bright smile.

'Oh, hello, Brian!' she said.

Neither Ryan nor Dodie bothered to correct her because, no matter how many times they'd done so in the past, he'd always been Brian in Gran's mind and probably always would be. It had got to the point now where it was easier to live with and sometimes Ryan even thought it was funny. Not today, though. Today he just looked terrified as he clocked Dodie's thunderous expression.

'Everything OK?' he asked tentatively, looking from one woman to the other.

'I came to tell Dodie about my engagement,' Gran said. 'You'll come to the wedding, won't you?'

Dodie could tell Ryan didn't know whether to laugh or scarper. After a moment of indecision he opted for the latter and disappeared at a speed that would have made Usain Bolt proud, mumbling something about waiting upstairs until they were finished. Dodie turned to Gran.

'Sit down; I'll put the kettle on and we'll sort this out.'

Gran had left with a promise to phone Dodie's mum as soon as she got home. Ryan had left shortly afterwards when Dodie explained to him what her gran had done, and that it looked as though she had a lot of smoothing over to do with her mum. Dodie figured he was probably terrified he might somehow end up involved and thought it was better to be out of the way entirely. She couldn't blame him for that, though she would have appreciated the support.

A bit of Dodie could understand why her gran had rushed into an engagement, but she couldn't fight the constant weight of her need to protect her. They didn't know the first thing about Bernard, and every time Dodie's objections to the wedding had brought them round to that fact, Gran had an answer that did nothing to lessen Dodie's fears. The fact was that Grandad had provided well for Gran in the event of his demise, so she was a relatively wealthy woman these days. Dodie felt sure that this fact wouldn't have escaped the attention of many of the so-called friends she'd made here and there since Grandad had died.

When Dodie phoned her mother later, she got the answering service, which meant her mum was either out or already embroiled in a heated debate with Gran and blocking the line. Whichever it was, Dodie needed some air. She was juggling so many balls right now that it was beginning to feel as if she'd have to grow extra arms to keep them up. Very soon, she was going to drop them and everyone who was relying on her to keep them whizzing around and around was going to be let down and it would all be her fault. She could feel her anxiety levels zipping through the roof as she thought more and more about all the things demanding her time and this was the kind of stress that a glass of wine or an old film couldn't fix. At times like these, there was only one place she wanted to be – a place where the only thing that mattered was the feel of sand beneath her feet and the steady rhythm of an ever-dependable tide.

The sun was already dipping below a shell-pink horizon as she stepped out onto the street and locked the door behind her. December was racing by, bringing not only Christmas but also the shortest day of the year. Her breath rolled into the frosty air as she took the road into town. The evening was clear and crisp – a good night for stargazing on the beach. This was one of her favourite things to do since she'd arrived in Bournemouth to live. She didn't manage it as often as she'd have liked to, but sometimes she'd take herself along the promenade, walk for miles along the tarmac that hugged the softest sand, all the way along the coast to the outskirts of town at Boscombe. Somewhere in between, the lights of Bournemouth faded and the ones of its coastal neighbour were still too far away to reach into the dusk, and the stars would burn brighter. Dodie would sit huddled on the sand and look up at the pinpricks of light for a while and feel like a comfortingly tiny part of creation. Nobody ventured this far out from either resort apart from the odd jogger or cyclist, and so it was like a little no-man's land, and Dodie loved the peace and calm of it.

One day, she'd think as she passed the pastel beach huts that flanked the promenade, she'd get herself one of those beach huts and she'd stay out all night, every night, as long as she wanted, looking up at the stars that were as numerous as the grains of sand on her beloved beach.

But the prospect of that life was distant and muddied as she walked through town tonight. Not only did she have Gran and the shop to worry about, but there was also Ryan. Once he moved in, nights like this, where she was free to come and go as she pleased, would be gone. He'd never forbid her, of course, but he'd frown and roll his eyes and complain and make snarky comments and eventually it just wouldn't be worth the hassle. They'd settle down to nights in front of the telly with game shows, take-outs and sex on a Saturday, and the months and years would roll by until she'd quite forgotten who she used to be before he'd moved in. Perhaps it was all a normal part of growing up and growing older, but if it was, Dodie wasn't sure she was ready to grow up just yet. What if she was never ready?

The lights of the Christmas markets greeted her as she reached the town centre, along with the sights and smells of the season that had been so welcoming the last time she was here with Ed. Now it filled her with an odd sort of melancholy that she couldn't explain. Leaving the markets behind, she crossed down into the gardens and past the now dark and silent bandstand, down the path and out the other side to the promenade. As she crossed under the road bridge that straddled the space, she heard her name echoing across the tarmac and turned to see Nick leaning against a wall, sleeping bag scrunched on the floor at his side, nursing a Starbucks.

'Looking for your boyfriend?' he asked as Dodie made her way over.

'Ryan?' Dodie asked, trying to pinpoint an occasion where Nick had met Ryan. She was pretty sure it had never happened while she'd been with him, and if it had Ryan wouldn't have given Nick the time of day.

'Is that his name? Decent bloke. He was down here earlier today. Gave me a tenner so I got myself a nice cinnamon latte.'

'Ryan gave you a tenner? Earlier today?' Dodie repeated, realising even as she did that she probably sounded like a mentally subnormal parrot.

'Not long ago, actually,' Nick continued. 'An hour, tops. Stopped for a chat. Asked about you; I said you were a good 'un, a real keeper, and that any man worth his salt ought to treat you nice.'

Dodie frowned. Ryan had left her two hours ago, but it was likely he'd have headed straight back to Dorchester. But then the lightbulb finally popped.

'Ed?' she asked. 'Ed was down here earlier?'

'That geezer you were with the other night,' Nick said. 'Ed, is it? Top bloke.'

'He's not my boyfriend,' Dodie said.

'Pity. I reckon you two would go well together.' Nick sniffed. 'Who's this Ryan then?'

'My actual boyfriend.'

'He treats you nice? Takes you out and stuff?'

'Sometimes,' Dodie said.

'Good,' Nick said, nodding sagely. 'Good.'

'Are you OK?' Dodie asked. 'You need anything? Supper? Some money?'

'Ah, well, I'm flush tonight on account of Ed.'

'But you won't be tomorrow,' Dodie smiled.

'Love, you keep your money. You do enough for me as it is and I'm not taking it when I have plenty to keep me going for now.'

Dodie forced a smile and put her purse away. 'Do you know where Ed went?' she asked.

'Said he was going to walk along the beach. Must be a fair distance by now though.'

'Which way – left or right?'

'Left… up towards Boscombe.'

'Thanks, Nick. See you later,' she said, starting to walk in the direction of the beach. 'And watch yourself tonight – it's going to be freezing!'

Striding past the pier entrance towards the sand, Dodie fished her phone from her bag. In all the excitement of the day she'd clean forgotten to switch it on. She wasn't quite sure how she felt to see that there was no further message from Ed apart from the one expressing his uncertainty over the decision to let Sally Chandra from the *Echo* interview him. With her non-reply, she'd wondered if he'd send another one asking again, or even articulating annoyance at her lack of response, but this apparent indifference was strangely disappointing. She wasn't sure what she wanted from Ed, but it wasn't indifference. It didn't really matter, though, she decided, because perhaps indifference was for the best – she was hardly going to be able to hang out with him when Ryan moved in anyway.

Still having no more of a clue how to reply than she did before, she closed the original message again. There was also a missed call from her mum, obviously returning Dodie's from earlier, and there was a text from Isla saying she'd pop over on Monday evening before she left for France.

Stuffing the phone back in her bag, Dodie pulled her collar around her chin and picked up the pace along the seafront. The sea was calm and very still, a gently undulating mass of black stretching as far as she could see, but the air was already bitterly cold, the beginnings of frost glinting on the tarmac as she passed under the sodium pools of streetlights. Before she'd left she'd pulled on her thermal undies. Ryan would have died laughing to see her in them so it was lucky he hadn't been there, but at least she'd be warm on the beach as she stargazed. Although that was something else he'd have died laughing at.

There were more people around than Dodie had expected to find, and she passed joggers, cyclists, dog walkers, even the odd brave family, kids armed with beach toys and wellies on their way home. But as she moved further from the town, further than the beach huts and showers, the walk became more solitary. Once the sounds of the town had faded, she found a spot under the shadow of the gorse-speckled cliffs and sat down on a bench, looking out to sea. Pinpoints of light bobbed around on the blackness and she watched, trying to imagine just how much better the light from the stars would be if she was aboard one of those boats now, out on the open sea. They'd be scattered across the sky in vast swathes, like dust in the sunlight. She'd only ever seen them look like that once before, during a power cut on holiday in a remote villa in Spain with her parents when she was fourteen, but she'd never forgotten it. She'd probably never see them like that again.

Her thoughts were interrupted by laughter coming from close by, high-pitched giggles followed by the voices of two, maybe three young men, and then a couple of different girls. She turned to see a group of teenagers making their way towards her seat. But then they veered off onto the sand, pots clanging in bags and blankets under their arms. It was a bit cold for a beach party, but Dodie had learned that in Bournemouth nobody cared about such trivialities; if you had a beach this good on your doorstep, why not have beach parties, even in the winter?

Time to move on for Dodie, though. Much as she didn't blame them for wanting to enjoy the seafront, she didn't want to listen to them. She'd come for peace and solitude, and it looked as though she'd have to find that further down the beach.

She walked for perhaps ten minutes more, moving away from the sounds of the town, passers-by getting less and less frequent. Her shadow lengthened and shrank as she passed from lamp to lamp, her breath curling into the frosted air. Then she spotted a figure, sitting alone on the sand, just visible in the darkness. They had the posture of someone who'd spent a lot of time having to think about it, and that was one thing she'd always noticed about Ed – his proud bearing. She often wondered whether that had come from his time in the army, but it was just another question she had been too afraid to ask.

Making her way cautiously across the sand, the figure became clearer and she saw that it *was* Ed, just as she'd guessed. He'd been motionless, straight-backed as he stared out to sea, but suddenly whipped around at her approach.

'Sorry!' she said. 'I didn't mean to startle you…'

'Dodie?'

'Hey.'

'What are you doing here?'

'I could ask you the same thing. We seem to be making a habit of being in the same place at the same time. I come down here a lot to sit and think. Didn't expect to find you doing the same.'

'I used to do it at home,' he said. 'Blackpool, I mean. I used to go down to the beach at night. The tide used to come in a lot further than it does here, so sometimes you had to scarper pretty quick if you didn't want to get wet…'

Dodie laughed. 'I'll remember that if I ever go there.'

'It's the first time I've been down here though. After you brought me down here the other night I wanted to get a better look.'

'Mind if I sit with you?' she asked, already settling on the sand beside him.

'Help yourself.'

It was then that she noticed he had a blanket over his knees. Unfolding it, he spread it so that it covered hers too. It was warm and smelled like his house, bringing sharply to her mind the memory of that first meeting in his hallway.

'Thanks,' she said.

'It can get a bit parky out here.'

'Wimp.'

'I know,' he chuckled. 'So much for being a hardened soldier.' He looked across at her. 'So, does it help?'

'What?'

'Coming down here to think? Do you find the answers?'

'That all sounds very grasshopper.' She put on a spooky voice. 'Do I find the answers I seek on my path to spiritual enlightenment…?'

'I wouldn't go that far,' he said with a wry smile. 'Did anyone ever tell you you're daft?'

'Weird is the word they usually use.'

'I wouldn't; I'd use daft. A good kind of daft though.'

'I think that's a compliment.'

'It is. I like daft.'

'Have you found your answers?'

He shook his head. 'I'm not sure I even know what the questions are yet.'

'That does rather put you at a disadvantage to begin with. Something you want to talk through? I'm a good listener.'

'I don't doubt it.' There was a faint sigh, like he was trying to contain it. 'I wouldn't know where to begin.'

A wind came from nowhere, picking up sand as it swept over the beach and making Dodie shiver slightly. Ed pulled the blanket further around her. She could feel the heat of his thigh as he pressed in.

'I'm OK,' she said, suddenly conscious of a new emotion at the edges of her awareness, of a sensation she hadn't expected from his proximity. It would have been better to move away, but something was stopping her.

'No, you're not,' he said, putting an arm around her and rubbing her shoulder, which only made the sensation more acute and more confusing, filling her with a strange mix of guilt and desire and anger at her weakness. 'I'm only trying to keep you warm because I don't want to administer first aid later.'

'I'm warm,' she said. 'Can you even do first aid?'

'Of course. What do you think they teach in the army?'

'How to shoot guns and get shouted at?'

'That, yes… And sometimes other stuff. I learned to cook too, and to speak French.'

'In the army?'

He nodded.

'Wow. I had no idea. I wouldn't have thought you'd have time with all that fighting.'

'A lot of time we sat around waiting for the fighting. You needed as much as you could find to take your mind off the prospect of your last day lurking around every corner.'

'Oh, God… I didn't mean… I'm so sorry, that was a stupid joke, so insensitive—'

'Forget about it,' he said. 'That's what I'm trying to do.'

'It was that bad?'

'Not all the time. In fact, hardly ever because you got used to it. But this one day…' He shifted position, the movement releasing the scent of his cologne from beneath the blanket. 'Well, it changed everything.'

There was silence for a moment. Dodie wanted to ask what that day had brought, what could have been so bad that it had changed his life. Putting the pieces together, there were only a few conclusions she could possibly draw from his statement, and that was he'd killed someone, or witnessed someone close to him being killed. Part of her wasn't sure she wanted to know, but her curiosity wouldn't leave her alone.

'Are you allowed to talk about it? To people who aren't in the army, I mean?'

'I am, but I don't know that I want to. I'm trying to put that and lots of other things behind me. That's why I came to live here.'

'On the whim of a pin in a map?' Dodie raised her eyebrows.

He hesitated before replying. It was a split second but it wasn't lost on Dodie.

'Exactly,' he said. 'It didn't turn out too badly, on reflection. For a start, I got to meet you.'

'I'd hardly call that a result.'

'I would…' He turned to her, and though his face was in shadow, Dodie could see that his expression was suddenly earnest.

'I'm sorry about your text,' she said.

'What?'

'Your text from earlier. I'm sorry I didn't reply, but I had some stuff going on with my gran and—'

'It doesn't matter now. I phoned Sally and she just managed to pull it in time.'

'So you won't be in the write-up?'

'No.' He was still holding her in that earnest gaze, as though she was a complex puzzle he was trying to work out. Or perhaps he was the puzzle and he was trying to work himself out. But then he spoke again, and it was not what she'd been expecting.

'Dodie Bright… what would you do if I said I wanted to kiss you?'

Instinctively, she backed away an inch so they were no longer touching. 'I'd say you can't. I mean, I have a boyfriend…'

Ed couldn't have looked more wounded if Dodie had stuck a knife in his chest. Instantly she regretted her response. He'd probably agonised over that sentence, struggled with the need to say it, and she'd cut him down without so much as a second thought for his fragile heart. Why the hell had she issued such a terse reply? It was even partly her fault – she'd seen it coming, unconsciously almost willed it – and now he was paying the price. This had been coming, and she hadn't done a thing to stop it. But she wasn't free to kiss him, and that was all there was to it.

'You're right,' he said quietly, his gaze cast onto the ground. 'It's a dirty trick and your boyfriend doesn't deserve it.'

'Oh, Ed, I didn't mean…'

He got up and brushed the sand from his trousers. 'You'll be alright getting back? You won't stay out too late by yourself?'

Dodie jumped to her feet too. 'Why, where are you going?'

'I have to go home.'

'Why?'

He caught her in a pained gaze. 'Do I really have to spell it out? Please… just leave me alone. Don't call, don't come to my house. I wish you all the luck in the world, I really do, but just please stay away.'

'As I recall…' she called stubbornly after him as he began to walk away, 'it was you hassling me! *You* came to *my* shop! And *you* came to the brass band concert! *You* stay away from *me*!'

He didn't look round, just carried on walking, head down. Dodie dropped to the sand, overwhelmed by tears of rage and frustration. How dare he blame her? How dare he make her out to be the villain of the piece? How dare he try to steal her from Ryan when he knew from bitter experience how hurtful that was? How dare he be so... so... so *gorgeous*... Lovely and kind, chivalrous and considerate, deep and interesting and everything she'd ever wanted in a man. Her very own Jimmy Stewart. *That's a mean trick, fate.* How cruel to throw him to her now, when it was too late, when she'd have to break more than one heart to act on her desires. Ryan didn't deserve that kind of treatment, and it wouldn't happen, not by her hand, not ever.

When she looked up again she couldn't see Ed, his figure already swallowed by the dark. She sat for a moment, the waves rolling in a gentle rhythm like a baby's sleeping breaths, the sand soft beneath her, the sky sparkling above her, and the world should have been perfect. But suddenly it felt very big, and very empty, and the truth knocked the wind from her like plunging into freezing water. With the *Echo*'s involvement she'd been ready for the possibility that her search for George and Margaret would soon come to an end, and she'd been strangely sad about that. But it wasn't simply about the hole the end of the quest would leave in her life, but about the hole not having a reason to see Ed any more would leave. Only now, as he walked away from her, could she see it clearly. From the moment they'd walked the street together knocking on the doors of Wessex Road, she'd been falling, and she'd been too stupid and too stubborn to see it. He'd blown hot and cold and he'd muddled the truth of her emotions, and now she saw that it was because he'd been falling for her too. He'd fought it, knowing that she wasn't free to love him back, knowing that it was wrong, not wanting to be the man who inflicted the same pain he'd felt when his ex-girlfriend ran off with his friend. It only went to dig the knife in further, because it proved just what an incredible man she'd lost. The fact that he was never hers to lose in the first place did nothing to make her feel better, though she tried to focus on that now as she dried her eyes on her sleeve and tipped her face to the stars.

One thing was certain as she pulled herself together, it had been one hell of a day. Had it really only been twelve hours ago since she'd sat in her pyjamas on the sofa with her nose in a book, thinking she was about to spend her Sunday in slobby boredom?

It might have been ten minutes she'd been sitting alone on the beach, or it might have been an hour. Suddenly, time had stopped making sense, but she'd grown cold as she'd sat there. It was then that she noticed Ed's blanket on the sand. He was long gone so there was no point trying to find him. Pulling it around her shoulders, she breathed in the scent and fresh tears blurred her vision. *Stupid, stupid girl*, she told herself, *you get what you deserve*. But if she was feeling this wretched, how bad would Ed be feeling right now? Hadn't he already been through enough without her making things worse?

Twelve

In any other job, Dodie could have feigned sickness and had a day under the blankets at home, hiding from life until it stopped screwing her over. But there was only her to open the shop, and the moment she started to take unscheduled days off she'd be on the slippery slope to failure. She'd messed enough things up, and her business was not going to go the same way. So, despite very little sleep and the fact that her face looked as if it had been mistaken for some dough pummelled into a bread tin, it was business as usual – smiling and small talk for the customers. And as usual, when she felt least able to cope with a busy shop, she got one.

At lunchtime her mother had called, incandescent with rage over Gran's plans to marry a virtual stranger, and with all her other drama, Dodie hadn't even had time to give that particular situation any more thought. All she could do was listen and make noises of agreement, but when her mum decided that they'd have to do something to stop it, Dodie gently reminded her that Gran was about as adult as it got and as such she was perfectly entitled to marry whoever she liked, regardless of their disapproval. Dodie was very much of the opinion that things would work themselves out, and if they didn't, then everyone would just have to live with it. Her mum said that Dodie ought to care more, but the fact was that Dodie was clean out of caring these days, and what she really wanted was for everything to just go away so she could get on with the business of being happy again. Fat chance with a text from Ryan asking her whether she'd got room for his entire collection of sporting DVDs at her place, another from Sally Chandra telling her that the story was going to feature in the following night's edition of the *Echo* and reminding her forcefully about Ed by mentioning how lovely he was despite his reluctance to be in the paper, and then another from Isla letting her know that she'd be over at eight and was really scared about her decision. For now, Dodie would have to be all things to all people, when all she really wanted was to be a nobody for a while until she fitted all the pieces of her own life back together again. And she had a feeling that when the chips were down the only person who really needed her was Ed – the one person she couldn't help and definitely shouldn't see.

Isla arrived bang on time, a bunch of flowers and a bottle of wine in her arms as Dodie let her in.

'For you,' she said.

'Me?'

'You've been such a rock over the last week or so. It's to say thank you.'

'I haven't really done anything,' Dodie replied, taking them from her. 'But thank you.'

She led the way up to the flat and Isla followed.

'I'll get these in some water,' Dodie said, veering off into the tiny kitchen. Isla sat at the table and watched her closely as she rummaged in the cupboards for a suitable vase.

'Is everything OK?' Isla said after a few silent moments.

Dodie nodded shortly. 'Why shouldn't it be?'

'I don't know. Why don't you tell me?'

'Everything's fine. I'm tired, that's all.'

'I've seen you tired plenty of times. I've seen you after all-night parties and you haven't looked like this.'

Dodie threw her a tight smile. 'It's been a long time since we went to an all-night party and I'm older now – I can't cope with a lack of sleep the way I used to.'

'Bollocks!' Isla patted the chair beside her. 'Sit down. I know when there's something wrong and you're going to spill. I can't go off to France knowing things aren't right here.'

'Honestly,' Dodie said, taking the wine to the fridge, 'there's nothing to worry about. You came to get things off your chest – remember? Let's focus here.'

'I came to see my best friend before I went,' Isla said. 'The getting-things-off-my-chest bit is just a distraction from the main event. Anyway, it's only me complaining about the fact that I'm shitting myself. I was never going to change my mind about going.'

'You're bound to be nervous,' Dodie said briskly, pulling a stack of takeaway menus from a drawer and dumping them in front of Isla. 'It's only natural. It's not every day you get to hook up with your long-lost father.' She nodded at the menus. 'What are we having?'

'Chinese?' Isla said, flicking a menu at Dodie as she took a seat alongside her.

'We always have Chinese.'

'That's because we like it.'

'Don't you want something different?'

'I'm going to have enough different tomorrow. Today I need comforting routine. Please indulge me and let me be *not* different.'

Dodie smiled briefly. 'Chinese it is then,' she said, opening the menu and then closing it again. 'I suppose you're going to have your usual too and I probably don't even need to bother reading this.'

'Why waste time reading when we can order and then you can tell me what's eating you?'

Dodie dropped the menu back onto the pile and looked up at her friend. 'It would be easier to tell you what's not eating me. I sound like a pointless, whining bag, though, and when I put it all into context and remember that other people have actual real problems, I realise I have nothing to complain about so I'm not going to.'

'Pretend for a minute that nobody else has actual real problems, and pretend for a minute that I'm entertained by pointless whining, and tell me anyway.'

'I don't know if I want Ryan to move in.'

'Well, that's not completely unexpected.'

'It isn't?'

'Anyone with eyes could have seen that coming. Casual sex and nights in front of the telly are one thing, but making a commitment like that… Dodie, you already know what I think. I've never made any secret of the fact that I think you're about as well matched as Lady Gaga and Pope Francis.'

'So what do I do? If he doesn't move in then that's the end of the line, isn't it? For us as a couple, I mean. Moving in would be the next logical step in our relationship, and if we don't make it then, effectively, there is no relationship. At least not one that's going anywhere.'

'It sounds like you've already decided that.'

'I haven't, though. I don't want him to move in, but I do like him. I don't want to dump him.'

'Is that true love talking or guilt? Because I know you do guilt rather well.'

'And then there's my gran, who's suddenly decided she's getting married to a man she met about two weeks ago at darts… Don't even ask what she was doing at darts because I have no idea. The point is, it's mental!'

'Well, it does explain a lot…' Isla arched an eyebrow.

'What?'

'She's eccentric. And, well, you're a bit eccentric…'

'I'm not!' Dodie squeaked.

'What are you going to do?' Isla asked, ignoring Dodie's expression of outrage.

'There's not a lot we can do, is there? I mean, she's bloody seventy whatever she is… she might even be eighty. I forget. The point is we can hardly stop her.'

'Then you can't worry about it. Move on, concentrate on what you can fix – what's next?'

'That's it,' Dodie said.

'I thought you said there was a huge pile of things? It would be easier to tell me what's not wrong? I counted just two there, and one of those is only half a thing when you really look at it. Quit holding out on me.'

Dodie let out a heavy sigh. 'There's Ed.'

'Ed? Who the hell is Ed?'

'You know – Wessex Road Ed. Letter Ed. Helping me look for George and Margaret Ed.'

'Oh… Ed. OK, so what's he done?'

'It might be more about what I've done.'

'Please don't tell me you've shagged him.'

'God, no! Of course I haven't!'

'Heavy petting? Nearly there? Snogged him?'

'No, but I wanted to.'

'Which one?'

'All of them.'

'But you haven't done any of it?'

Dodie shook her head.

'Not quite sure I see your problem then.'

'I *want* to; that's the problem. I shouldn't want to, should I?'

'Because you're seeing Ryan you should never fancy anyone else? Now who's being mental?'

'I don't fancy him…' Dodie squeezed her eyes shut, tried to focus her thoughts. How could she say this? How could she speak this truth – and she knew now it was truth – without acting on it? But to act on it would be wrong, wouldn't it? 'I think it's gone way beyond fancying.'

She opened her eyes to find Isla staring at her. 'Does he feel the same way? Have you been seeing each other?'

'As friends, that's all.'

'That's all! Why didn't you tell me this was going on?'

'I did… sometimes anyway. I don't know, it felt like it was happening more than it should and I thought you would disapprove.'

'You mean you thought I'd try to talk some sense into you? Too bloody right. You don't want Ryan to move in and you have feelings for someone else? Come on, Dodie, even you can fit those pieces together and see the big picture.'

'Maybe. I've probably blown it anyway so I don't suppose it matters now.'

'How?'

'He asked if he could kiss me.'

'When?' Isla leaned forward.

'Last night.'

'He was here last night? You've been sneaking him in?'

'No – at the beach.'

Isla shook her head slowly. 'So you *did* kiss him?'

'No. I told him I couldn't kiss him because I already had a boyfriend. And then he went. I suppose he was embarrassed or ashamed. He told me to stay away from him.'

'You don't do things by half. What now?'

'Nothing. I have no right to, but I can't stop thinking about him.'

'And you're still going to let Ryan move in?'

Dodie gave a vague shrug, and Isla simply rolled her eyes in reply.

'I know what you're thinking,' Dodie said quietly. 'And you're right – I'm an idiot. I can't tell Ryan, though. And there's no point now that Ed has made it clear he doesn't want anything more to do with me.'

'He's only saying that because he thinks you don't want him. Surely you can see that it's self-defence. You can't blame him for rejecting that which rejects him.'

Dodie gave a faint smile. 'Now you sound like a psychology student.'

'That might be because I am one. Come here.' Isla leaned across to pull Dodie into a hug. 'You may be an idiot,' she said. 'But you're my idiot.'

The photo wasn't as flattering as Dodie would have hoped for, but at least the shop sign was clearly visible as she posed outside it and that had to be a bonus. If nothing else, it was a little subtle advertising for the shop. Sally Chandra's article took up a quarter of a page – a good result Dodie thought, or perhaps a slow news day in the town. Dodie read quickly through it, noting that her quotes had been tweaked slightly to make them just that little bit more sensational, but she supposed that came with the territory too. There was an inset photo of the letter below her version of how George's letter came to light and, though there was mention of a Wessex Road resident who'd been intrigued enough by the story to get involved in helping Dodie on her quest, Ed's name hadn't been divulged.

Dodie tossed the newspaper onto the counter and turned her gaze to the sludge of the streets beyond the shop window, where drizzle and fog had reduced visibility so much she could barely see the estate agent's office across the road. The weather seemed to mirror her mood a bit too perfectly. If it hadn't been for that stupid letter, there wouldn't have been any knocking on Ed's door. There would have been no friendship, no turbulent emotions running hot beneath the surface, no confusion, no angst and no heartache. Her life would have continued on its original course in blissful ignorance of any alternative, and while she might not have been wildly fulfilled, she'd have been content. Part of her still couldn't really understand why the letter had impacted on her thoughts and emotions in the way it had, ruling her decisions and actions.

Rifling in the drawer beneath the counter, she pulled it out and read it again. Apart from the story it told, it shouldn't have any bearing on her life at all, should it? It should have been like watching a film or reading a good book that you loved and remembered long after you'd closed it but it shouldn't have been taking over her life. It had to mean something but she wished she knew what.

With a sigh she folded the paper back into the envelope and made it safe in the drawer again.

Her phone sat on the counter beside her, showing the same unopened text message from Ryan that had come through over an hour ago. Just the thought of reading it made her skin crawl with guilt, about the lies she might have to tell or the omissions she'd have to make. He at least ought to know about the letter – even Ed had said so. But still

Dodie couldn't bring herself to discuss it with him and she couldn't understand why. Perhaps because now it had turned into a connection to Ed, and something about it felt wrong and duplicitous. But if she didn't reply to Ryan soon he'd call and he'd be pissed off. With a sigh, she dragged the phone across the counter and swiped to unlock.

Can I buy this for the flat? Will it fit?

Dodie scrolled down to the photo he'd attached. It looked as if he'd been in a furniture shop, and he'd snapped a monstrosity of a TV chair – chestnut padded leather, reclining seats, wide enough for at least two people or one enormous couch potato, complete with cup holder and headrest. Dodie sucked in a breath and pushed the phone away again. This was like being on a bus on a mountain road with no brakes, the driver collapsed at the wheel and Dodie not knowing how to drive. If she didn't do something to stop it, disaster waited at the end of the road, but the options looked hopeless, even if she'd known where to begin.

She looked up as the shop door tinkled to see a young woman walk in. Dodie forced a smile.

'Do you have any eighties denim?' the woman asked.

'A few pieces,' Dodie said, folding the paper up and stowing her phone in the drawer of the counter. 'Just over on that rack next to the coats.'

While the woman went to take a look, Dodie switched on the CD player. The atmosphere of the shop was as dismal as the weather outside and even Dodie in her current mood could see that was hardly conducive to a pleasant customer experience.

She turned to the customer. 'Anything in particular you're looking for? I've got some cute dungarees, very Dexy's Midnight Runners.'

The woman chuckled. 'My mum still plays them all the time. She'd be stealing those dungarees off me if I took them home!'

While the customer turned her attention back to the rack, Dodie pulled out her ledger and began to list some new stock. Whatever else was going on, she still had a shop to run and, right now, it seemed like the only thing she knew how to do without making a mess of it.

The weather struggled to improve and it felt as if the sun had hardly risen at all that day. Dodie ploughed on, determined to put her maudlin thoughts firmly out of her mind and concentrate on work. Then, late in the afternoon, Gran came into the shop waving a copy of the *Echo*.

'Ooooh, Dodie! Everyone at woodwork class has seen you in the paper! Isn't it a lovely photo of you!'

Dodie looked up from her bookkeeping with a faint smile. 'Woodwork today? I can't keep up with your clubs.'

'Hmm,' Gran replied, as if suddenly giving the matter a great deal of thought. 'I'll probably give woodwork up anyway – keep getting splinters and that lathe is so loud I can barely hear myself think!' But then her expression brightened again and she rushed over to the counter, putting down the paper. 'Who's this young man who helped you? I'm surprised you didn't tell me about him.'

'There wasn't anything to tell,' Dodie said in a dull voice. Try as she might to forget him, Ed kept haunting her in one way or another.

'Is he handsome?' Gran asked, poring over the story again.

'I really couldn't say,' Dodie replied. 'How's Bernard?'

'Oh, he's fine,' Gran said.

'Good. Um… you want a cup of tea?'

'Oh I'd love one but I'm in a rush. Bernard wants me to choose a wedding ring with him.'

Dodie tried not to grimace. 'Well, it was good of you to bring me the paper.'

'Gloria says she's got her hands on some photos that might help.'

Dodie felt her whole body lighten, that frisson of excitement suddenly banishing all misery. 'Of George and Margaret?' she asked keenly.

'Yes. So I thought we might pop over together. She'd love to meet you.'

'Fantastic!' Dodie beamed. 'When can she fit me in?'

For some reason Dodie had been expecting a statuesque, immaculately groomed blonde to open the front door; a perfectly preserved specimen of womanhood, pickled and surgically enhanced into a wax model of her former self. She couldn't even say why she'd built this picture of Gran's friend in her head, but the Gloria that greeted them on the doorstep, the odour of burning incense wafting around them, was about as far away from that image as you could get. She was, in fact, a frail-looking woman, her wrists jangling with bangles and bracelets and her feet bare beneath huge skirts, like a little Woodstock reject left behind to wither in the sun. She had to be the most unlikely acquaintance her gran could have had. But what she lacked in stature and presence she more than made up for in warmth and Dodie instantly liked her as she beckoned them in with a broad smile.

'I don't have any shop tea I'm afraid, but I can offer you a cup of camomile,' Gloria said as they followed her down the hallway. 'I dried the flowers last summer from my own garden.'

'That would be lovely, thank you,' Dodie said.

'You know I can't stand that rubbish,' Gran said. 'Lucky for you I have my own teabags with me. I expect Dodie will have one of these too,' Gran added, handing a little plastic bag over.

'Oh…' Gloria stared at the tea with an expression that suggested she was just about to announce the end of the world. 'I only have almond milk, you know.'

'It'll have to do,' Gran said briskly. 'I might have known to bring milk as well.'

'Almond milk is just fine with me,' Dodie said. 'I've often thought about trying it anyway. You know, it's supposed to be good for you, isn't it?'

'Much gentler on your digestive system,' Gloria said. 'I can take milk up to a point but too much and my bowels… well, you get the picture.'

Dodie got the picture only too well. In fact, she fervently wished the picture would go away.

Gloria showed them to a living room that looked exactly like it would belong to her; eclectic furnishings in ethnic patterns and full of knick-knacks picked up from all over the world.

'You've travelled a lot?' Dodie said, taking a seat.

'Oh, when I was younger,' Gloria said. 'Couldn't stay still. My health was the only thing that tied me down in the end.' She gave a thin smile. 'Be back in a tick – just getting those drinks.'

'Mastectomy,' Gran whispered as Gloria left them. 'Double. Poor thing.'

'But she's OK now?' Dodie asked.

'Oh yes, *now* she's OK,' Gran said. 'Shook her confidence though. Never was the same afterwards.'

Dodie took a moment to take in her surroundings as Gran checked her lipstick in a compact mirror whipped from her handbag. There were elephants carved from stone, people carved from wood, models of landmarks and photos of a younger Gloria standing at various iconic sites – sometimes alone and sometimes with companions – but always smiling.

'Is she on her own now?'

'Who?' Gran snapped the mirror shut and dropped it into her handbag.

'Gloria…' Dodie replied, lowering her voice. 'Does she have a partner?'

'She did, but the relationship broke down. Lives alone now.'

'That's a shame.'

'Only like me,' Gran said. 'And I get on with it. You don't feel sorry for me, and I don't need you to.'

Dodie shot her a sideways look. That wasn't exactly true, but there was no point in arguing about it now. There wasn't time anyway as Gloria appeared with a tray of drinks. As Dodie and Gran helped themselves to a mug each, Gloria went to a cabinet and pulled out a box.

'These were cleared out of my uncle's house when he died,' she said as she brought the box to the coffee table and set it down. She removed the lid to reveal a stack of dog-eared photos inside and handed the top one to Dodie.

'What's this?' Dodie asked, taking it.

'A photo,' Gran said, rolling her eyes.

'Yes, I can see that. What's it a photo of? Who are these people?'

'It's a VE Day party,' Gran said, as if it was the most obvious thing in the world.

Dodie frowned. But then the cloud lifted from her expression. 'So this photo… my couple is in it? George and Margaret?'

'Just Margaret…' Gloria tapped at a figure in the photograph. Dodie peered more closely at the woman she'd indicated. It was difficult to make out much about her – her image was a tiny one in the periphery of the action – but she didn't look like someone who was celebrating, despite the revelry elsewhere in the picture. In fact, clinging onto a chair back and staring mournfully at the camera, she looked like she'd rather be anywhere other than where she was.

'So this is Margaret Vincent?' Dodie murmured, studying her face. She looked up at Gran and Gloria in turn. 'And George isn't here because…'

'He didn't come home from the war,' Gloria said. 'Lost in action, nobody knows what happened to him. Poor fella.'

'Poor Margaret, too,' Dodie said, looking at the image again. No wonder she looked so lost and lonely.

'There is a story… but this is just hearsay…' Gran gave Dodie a peculiar look.

'Yes?'

'Margaret had a baby by George,' Gloria cut in. 'Out of wedlock, but the baby died at birth. At least that's the story.'

Dodie clapped a hand to her mouth. 'Oh, that's so sad!' While she'd half-guessed there was an illegitimate pregnancy somewhere in the story, she had never considered the child might not have survived.

Gran shrugged. 'The way it was viewed back then, perhaps it was a good thing she didn't end up as an unmarried mother. It wasn't like it is now when you can have babies with any passing man who takes your fancy and everyone's just la-di-da about it.'

'But you can understand why they did what they did,' Dodie said. 'Imagine thinking that he might never come back from the war… It's no wonder they wanted a little intimacy before he went if they thought they might never have the chance.'

'It's a shame they didn't just go out for a nice meal and a dance,' Gran said briskly. 'Lots of people went off to war but they didn't all make babies first.'

'But she lost the baby after all that,' Dodie said, studying the photo again. 'Not only did she lose George and live with the shame of being pregnant without him by her side, but then the baby died. Poor Margaret. No wonder she never married.' She looked up at Gloria. 'Do you know where she ended up living? From what I can tell the family hasn't been at Wessex Road for a long time.'

'No idea. I don't think they've been there since at least the sixties but nobody I've spoken to is sure.'

'Well,' Dodie said, handing the photo back to Gloria, 'while this is very interesting, it doesn't really tell me much more about where to get hold of Margaret. Or anyone else who might be interested for that matter.'

'I thought you'd like to see it, though,' Gran said.

'Oh, of course! I'm really grateful for the help and for another piece of the puzzle, I just wish it had more clues in it to find the rest of the pieces.'

'I suppose I could ask if there are any more photos,' Gloria said. 'But that's the only one I can see in the box from this party and the rest are mostly my family.' She nudged the box towards Dodie. 'You're more than welcome to go through it yourself just in case you pick out something I've missed.'

'I'm sure you've looked through just as well as I would have done,' Dodie replied, feeling that to go through Gloria's treasured family photos would be a little invasive. 'But if you can find out if there are any more lying around that'd be brilliant.'

Gloria nodded, and as she slurped at her tea, Gran and Dodie did the same, the conversation dying for a moment as everyone seemed to be lost in their own thoughts. Dodie was pondering on Margaret's loss and she wondered if perhaps the story of the photo had put the other two women in mind of their own losses. It was odd, but hearing the tragedy of Margaret's life suddenly made her own woes seem silly and insignificant. Margaret and George had lived and loved in the shadow of real hardship, not the trite, meaningless worries that Dodie routinely concerned herself with, and so many others did too. She might have felt like running away and never coming back from time to time, but as her mind went back to her little shop, her brilliant friends and a family who cared deeply about her, she realised that, compared to some, she had a lot to be thankful for.

But then Gran broke the silence. Looking at her watch she frowned slightly. 'Ballroom classes in an hour, and I need to go and fetch my dancing shoes.'

'Oh,' Dodie said. 'Do you need me to take you?'

'You're a love,' Gran said. 'That would make life a lot easier for me if you could.'

Gloria looked disappointed at their sudden retreat, but Gran promised to visit again the next day and she seemed happier as they drained their teacups and made their goodbyes. It had been good to finally see Margaret, to put a face to the name, but as they got into Dodie's car and pulled away from the kerbside, Dodie didn't really see how much help it would ultimately be. Not wanting to take Gloria's photo with her, Dodie had been content with a promise that Gloria would get a copy for her as soon as she was able. At least it might be something to post on Facebook in the hope somebody might be able to shed more light on the life of the mysterious woman who was increasingly in danger of taking over Dodie's every waking thought.

Thirteen

Although Dodie had been hopeful for a response from the newspaper story, its swiftness took her completely by surprise. When she really thought about it, being hopeful for a response hadn't meant she'd necessarily been expecting one. It had always been a long shot as far as she was concerned, a last-ditch attempt to solve the mystery of Margaret and George before she gave in and went to plan B with the letter, whatever plan B ended up being. So when Sally Chandra called her that Wednesday morning with news that someone had contacted the paper, Dodie didn't quite know how to feel.

'It's all very exciting,' Sally said, as if to signpost to Dodie exactly how she *ought* to feel. Dodie listened, phone clamped to her ear, gaze trained on the street outside where two motorists were arguing over a parking space. 'We couldn't have hoped for a better result!'

'But I was told the baby died,' Dodie replied doubtfully. 'My gran's friend said Margaret's baby died at birth.'

'Do you know for sure the baby died?'

'Well, no, but…'

'Perhaps Margaret's family spread that rumour to cover up what they'd done. They could have even told Margaret that before they sent the baby away. It wasn't unheard of in those days. Who knows what happened, but we might soon find out.'

'I just don't know.'

'Isn't this what you wanted? I thought the object of this exercise was to find the family.'

'Yes, but I was thinking cousins, nephews, nieces, that sort of thing. Not secretly disposed of children who may or may not be who they say they are. How do we know this woman is telling the truth?'

'Her story does add up,' Sally said. 'I don't really see what she has to gain by lying.'

'She might be a bit…' Dodie's gaze went to the window again as she searched for the most delicate way to express her thoughts. 'A bit of a fantasist,' she said. 'Perhaps a bit taken with the story and wants to play a role in it by saying she's someone she's not.'

'A nutter, you mean?'

'Not quite how I would have put it but, yes.'

'But our newspaper story has been passed to her from someone who knows she has a legitimate interest, don't forget. She hasn't just randomly come across it; she's living out of the area and the details have been deliberately sent to her. She says she has legal proof, too. I think it would be very interesting to meet with her and see her documentation.'

'Where did you say she's from?'

'Some little place up north. Never heard of it… Cleveleys or something like that.'

'Can't say I know it either,' Dodie said. 'I'd expected to find someone a bit closer to home, if I'm honest, so this has thrown me… but I suppose the adoption might explain how she ended up moving so far away.'

'Well,' Sally said briskly, 'it's not that unheard of for people to move around the country of their own accord.'

'Yes, I know. I just wasn't expecting to find someone so far out of the area.' Dodie paused, weighing up the new developments. She'd expected perhaps a name, an address to send her letter on to, at best a little family history from the newspaper story. But a woman claiming to be Margaret Vincent's supposedly dead child? Of course, family was what Dodie had hoped to find, right at the start, but something about the circumstances of Julia Fleet's birth, the woman who had contacted Sally off the back of the newspaper story, made her feel uneasy. A cosy family with fond memories of their ancestor, that was fine. But a woman with a fractured past and unanswered questions about her heritage? Did she expect Dodie to have the answers with one old, faded letter? It felt like a situation she would do well to steer clear of.

'I think you should meet her,' Sally said into the pause. 'It would make fantastic copy. And of course, I'll sit in with you so there's no need to worry about being alone with her.'

'Oh, it wasn't that. I'm not worried, it's just…' Dodie sighed. Obviously Sally wanted Dodie to meet Julia considering the trouble everyone had gone to in order to make the story public. She'd most likely want to cover the result of the meeting too. Dodie just hoped that Ed wouldn't get dragged into the proceedings as well, because she knew for a fact that he'd be desperately unhappy about that. On balance, the only way to stop Ed getting dragged into it was probably to go and meet Julia herself, to save Sally having to get another angle on the story and falling back on Ed's connection. 'Of course I'll meet with her. It's just difficult, with the shop and everything.'

'I thought you'd say that, and I told Julia as much. She's happy to drive down in the next couple of days and I'm completely flexible so I can bring her to see you at a neutral venue one evening if that helps.'

Dodie drew a deep breath. She wasn't getting out of this now. 'OK,' she said. 'Let's fix something up.'

Her finger hovered over the send button. Ed had told her to stay away, but surely this wasn't overstepping the boundaries, was it? He'd want to know that there'd been developments in the story of George's letter when he'd been so deeply involved. And she wasn't exactly hassling him; she'd done him a favour by keeping him off Sally's radar and this was just a short, friendly text to tell him there might be developments. Shaking her doubts away, she jabbed her finger on the screen and the text whooshed off.

Putting her phone on the kitchen table, she turned back to the pan of tomato soup she'd been heating for supper. Ryan had wanted to come over this evening, but she'd made excuses about feeling unwell and put him off. His message in reply sounded far from happy or sympathetic. True, it was a made-up illness, but the fact that he hadn't even asked after her welfare had made her bristle. This meant she hadn't felt the need to apologise in the slightest, something she would have done at any other time, real or fake illness. Besides, it was Wednesday night and Ryan being over on a weeknight always left her groggy and irritable in the shop the next day because he insisted on keeping her up so late – hardly conducive to a great customer experience. Ryan knew this only too well because she'd complained about it enough. Despite her reservations about him moving in, at least that was one upside she'd hoped would come from it – that them being together would become so commonplace the novelty of staying over would wear off and they'd start going to bed at a proper time, like normal people. Whenever Dodie thought about it that way, she realised it sounded boring, but then, life was often only small bursts of excitement breaking up the boring. Boring meant the shop opened on time and she was bright enough to run it efficiently.

The sound of a message hitting her phone broke into her thoughts, and she rushed to the table to check it. But it was Isla, letting her know that she'd arrived in France after an uneventful flight and was on her way to the hotel. Happy as Dodie was that everything was going smoothly there, she couldn't help but be disappointed that it wasn't a message from Ed. But then, did she even want a reply from him? Perhaps it was easier not to get one – not having to deal with whatever he wrote would lead to? Perhaps it was enough to know he'd seen the message and her obligation to keep him updated on a chain of events he was invested in had been fulfilled.

Sally had arranged a meeting at a quiet coffee shop in town for Friday evening after Dodie had closed Forget-Me-Not Vintage. All Dodie had so far was a name: Julia Fleet. A woman from a little place up north, claiming to be the baby Margaret had supposedly lost, not dead at all, but put up for adoption instead. It was all at once exciting and terrifying to think of meeting her; after having this tiny keyhole view into Margaret's life for so long, it felt like the door was about to be opened at last. But if Dodie's stomach did somersaults at the thought of the meeting, she had to wonder what poor Julia was feeling.

The vague, perhaps misplaced, hope that she'd still get a reply from Ed refused to leave her, and Dodie checked her phone once again before settling down to eat her soup. But there was nothing. For better or for worse, it looked as though he was gone from her life and she'd just have to get used to it.

The following evening Ryan wasn't taking no for an answer and Dodie relented. On reflection, it was the least he deserved and perhaps she was being too hard on him. Moving in together was a huge commitment and, despite her doubts, it was one they'd both agreed to embark on. Recently, her time had been so filled with other things and other people that perhaps she couldn't really blame him for feeling neglected. And Christmas was coming, so things would only get more hectic before they got quieter again.

She had, however, stressed that they were going out, not sitting in front of the TV while their brain cells quietly died. Perhaps her reservations about Ryan, about their ultimate compatibility, needn't exist. Perhaps, if she introduced him to the things she liked with a little more conviction, he might discover they weren't so bad after all? Even if he didn't love what she loved, if he could like it enough to tolerate it then maybe sharing more would bring them closer together.

He arrived at seven, and Dodie was already in her coat.

'One of your second-hand jobs?' Ryan asked.

Dodie looked up from fastening the buttons on Margaret's green coat and blushed, though she couldn't say why. 'This, you mean?' she asked as she unconsciously smoothed a hand over it.

'Yeah, I haven't seen you wear that before.'

'I'm pretty sure you have seen me wear it actually.'

He shrugged. 'Don't recall.'

'Do you like it?'

He paused for a moment, as if weighing up what response he was expected to give rather than the one he wanted to give. 'It's nice, yeah. Old fashioned, but you like old fashioned, don't you?'

She plunged her hands into the pockets and instinctively her fingers searched for the soft, weathered parchment of George's letter. It wasn't there, of course, it was safe in a locked drawer, but somehow her brain was wired to search every time she wore the coat, as if remembering the moment she found it and yearning to repeat it. It was the moment when her life began to change into something she was hard pressed to recognise these days, a moment that felt huge for reasons she still couldn't fully identify yet.

'Where are we supposed to be going?' Ryan asked as they stepped out onto the pavement and Dodie locked the door behind her.

'Pub, restaurant, gardens, Christmas markets… anywhere as long as we're not vegging on the sofa while our brain cells slowly abandon the will to live. Honestly, if I have to watch one more person throw a dinner party while their guests score them, or video clips of people falling off boats on holiday, I think I'll go into a coma.'

Ryan dug his hands into his pockets and sniffed. 'Right then. It's just background noise, though, isn't it? While we have tea and talk and stuff.'

They didn't talk, and what was supposed to be background noise usually became the main attraction. But Dodie didn't say a word about that; she just began to walk.

'I haven't got much money on me,' he said as he fell into step beside her.

'That's OK. Looks like the food stalls at the market then, nothing swanky. And then we could go to the seafront, see what's going on down there.'

'It'll be freezing.'

'It won't be that bad if we keep moving. And we can always get a hot chocolate if we get too cold.'

'Hmm.'

'I can buy you a hot chocolate if things are that bad!'

'I'd rather be drinking a can or two by the fire.'

'You can do that at the weekend. Come on, where's your sense of adventure?'

'I'll have a sense of adventure in the summer when it's warm, thanks.'

Dodie reached for his hand. 'Well then, do it for me?'

'Only because I won't hear the end of it if I don't,' he said, sounding like a child who'd just been told meals didn't start with pudding.

'Right then, so let's see what goodies are on offer at the market stalls.'

As their footsteps echoed over the frozen street, Dodie babbled about customers in the shop, about the mouse problem in the restaurant down the road, about the newsagent's daughter having a new baby… about anything except what really mattered. Because if she spoke about the things that really mattered, she couldn't be sure that her relationship with Ryan wouldn't be in tatters by the end of the night. So the letter, Ed, Sally and Julia; she kept it all in. Most of it would go over Ryan's head anyway. Practical Ryan, who wouldn't know a flight of fancy if it slapped him in the face. He wouldn't understand why Dodie was getting so involved in a quest that made no difference to her life, and she'd get frustrated trying to explain it to him. A million times she'd meant to tell him and she knew she ought to. But the way she felt right now, it was best to leave it alone and concentrate on things they could see eye to eye on.

They were at the bratwurst stall, its fulsome aromas of meat and spice clinging to the smoke rising from the griddle, when Dodie heard her name being called. She turned to see Nick give her a wave from the steps of a nearby shop.

'Alright, sweetheart?' he called.

'Hey, Nick!' Dodie replied with a broad smile. She pointed to the stall then pointed at him and mimed eating a hot dog. He nodded eagerly.

He grinned. 'If you're offering!'

'Who's that?' Ryan asked, sending a look of deepest distrust in Nick's direction.

'Oh, that's Nick,' Dodie said amiably. 'Lives around here. I have told you about him before.'

'Have you?'

Dodie nodded while Ryan clamped his mouth shut. Clearly there was something he wanted to say but Dodie pretended she hadn't noticed. They shuffled forwards and took their turn in the queue to be served. Dodie ordered three and paid, and as Ryan began to unwrap his to eat, he followed in silence as she took the spare over to Nick.

'You're a star!' Nick said, taking it with a grateful smile. 'Just what the doctor ordered.'

She smiled. 'Enjoy!'

'I'm sure I will!'

They turned to go, but then Nick spoke again. 'You've got a good girl there, Ed! Make sure you look after her!'

Dodie froze, a terrified smile fixed to her face as she turned back to Nick. 'It's Ryan,' she said, the calm of her voice hiding the sudden disquiet inside.

'Oh, sorry, love,' he said cheerfully. 'Must have got mixed up—'

'That's OK,' Dodie replied carefully. 'See you later.' She began to walk again, heart beating wildly as she shot Ryan a furtive glance. He didn't seem perturbed, more interested in his hot dog. Perhaps she'd got away with it. But after a couple of minutes he spoke, the words he'd so clearly been trying to hold back now tumbling out.

'Is he homeless?'

'Yes.' She wanted to add how obvious that should have been but it didn't seem wise to antagonise him right now.

'You shouldn't keep giving people all your stuff,' he said.

'It's not like that. Sometimes I share my dinner with Nick or I give him something I have left over. It's either that or the poor bloke's fishing things out of bins.'

'You just bought him a hot dog.'

'He doesn't get much hot food. It didn't cost a lot.'

'That's not the point; people will take you for a soft touch.'

Dodie was silent for a moment. 'Well, maybe I like being a soft touch,' she said. 'There are worse things to be.'

'They'll screw you for every penny.'

'I hardly think a hot dog is screwing me for every penny.'

Ryan shook his head. 'I don't like it, that's all. I don't want you talking to every Tom, Dick and Harry around town.'

'I don't.'

'You even know that guy by name. And he knows yours.'

'I don't see why that's an issue. We chat occasionally and actually he's very sweet. Just because he's homeless doesn't mean he should be nameless and identity-less as well.'

'Is Ed one of your homeless mates, too?'

Dodie's bratwurst halted halfway to her mouth. She paused. 'No,' she said finally, wishing her breaths would steady and hoping he wouldn't notice how shallow they were. 'I don't know who that is.' And even as she said it, she couldn't understand why she'd felt the need to lie. She had nothing to hide, but the longer she continued the more it would look to everyone else like she did.

'I don't like it,' Ryan repeated. 'I don't think you should be so friendly with them.'

She rammed her hot dog into her mouth and chewed like a robot. She wasn't hungry any more, but it would stop her having to say anything else.

'Ooooh, look!' Dodie squeaked as they walked past the old art-deco cinema. 'A special Christmas showing of *It's a Wonderful Life*!'

'What's that then?' Ryan asked, glancing over at the posters at the entrance. Dodie watched as his expression changed from one of curiosity to one of recognition and vague disappointment. 'Oh. Black and white. And that bloke's in it.'

'I wonder if Gran wants to come and see it with me – before they take it off,' Dodie said, if only to reassure him that she wasn't going to subject him to the torture of a showing. 'Do you mind if I go and check the dates it's on?'

He followed as she made her way across the road and peered up at the posters. 'It's only on until tomorrow night,' she said. She'd agreed to meet Julia and Sally then. It didn't matter, she had the film on DVD anyway, but she loved this little cinema and it would have been fun to see it here.

Ryan looked at the poster. Then he looked at his watch. He let out a sigh. 'You want to go in?'

'Well, yes, but I don't know about tomorrow—'

'Tonight? We've got time.'

Dodie stared at him. 'But you'll hate it!'

'Probably. I can always get a quick nap while you watch.'

'Oi!' Dodie slapped him but she wore a grin.

'I won't snore. Not loudly anyway,' he added with a smile of his own.

'Are you sure?'

'Yeah, why not? If it means so much to you then I'll give it a go. But you have to learn the offside rule in return.'

'I already know the offside rule, I just pretend I don't so you won't go on about football all the time.'

It was Ryan's turn to stare. 'Is that true? Cheeky little mare!'

She let out a raucous giggle. It was nice; it felt like they hadn't laughed properly in ages.

'So are we going in or what?' Ryan asked.

Dodie nodded eagerly. If there was a chance she might persuade Ryan there was some value in the old films she loved then she didn't need asking twice.

Dodie had been in the cinema before though not as often as she'd have liked. It was a tiny place, almost like a living room, showing mostly art-house and independent films that rarely made it onto the screens of the bigger chains. The seats were wide and squishy like armchairs, and in the winter there was a faint smell of damp in the worn red carpets, but she loved the atmosphere of the place, how the staff had extensive and intimate knowledge of films and always had time to share recommendations and opinions. She loved how the popcorn was handmade and they had snacks made out of proper deli food prepared by an actual kitchen, and how the manager was sometimes also the projectionist. In any other town it would have closed down years ago, but somehow it had survived here, ploughing its own furrow, refusing to bow under the pressure of the mainstream film market.

'When was the last time it was decorated in here?' Ryan said, looking around the foyer, covered in flock wallpaper like some maiden aunt's living room, framed film prints of classics in regimented lines along the walls. '1950?'

'Quite possibly.' Dodie nodded, taking her mittens off and stuffing them into her coat pockets. 'I absolutely love this place and they show the best films.'

'By best films you mean films that only ten people in the world have ever seen?'

'No!' Dodie laughed. 'I mean classic pieces of cinematic history. Films that make you lose yourself, films that make you think and laugh and cry and feel that all is right with the world when you step out into it again. That sort of film.'

'Like *Terminator 2*?'

'As I've never seen any of the *Terminator* films I'll have to trust your judgement on that.'

There was a handful of people at the ticket booth ahead of them, two couples waiting on sofas outside the screen to go in, and a lady who looked close to retirement age dressed in a striped uniform taking tickets, and that was about it.

'They know how to party around here,' Ryan whispered.

Dodie giggled. 'Don't be so mean. It was your idea to come in.'

'I'm just saying. And I didn't want to come in, you did.'

'You offered.'

'I'm beginning to wish I hadn't.'

Dodie turned to the front as the knot of customers ahead of them cleared away and Ryan stood with his hands in his pockets as she bought the tickets. Then he followed her to the screen doors, head down as he tapped on his phone.

'I'm afraid you'll have to turn that off when you go in.' The woman at the doors nodded towards Ryan as she ripped their tickets and handed the stubs back to Dodie.

'Right,' he said, but he threw Dodie a look that told her he was less than amused at being chastised. 'I'll put it on silent,' he added.

'We prefer it to be off,' the usherette said. 'It's the screens, you see. When they light up it can be distracting for other viewers.'

'Whatever,' Ryan sighed, shoving it in his pocket.

Dodie smiled brightly at the woman. 'Don't worry, everything will be turned off once the film starts.'

'I'm not being funny,' she said. 'Just rules. And common courtesy, you know?'

'Absolutely.'

The woman seemed happy with Dodie's response, though she still eyed Ryan with the deepest suspicion. Then she turned to Dodie again. 'Beautiful coat, by the way. Really suits you. Where did you get it?'

'Oh, this?' Dodie ran a hand down the heavy fabric. 'It's actually vintage. I have a shop nearby.'

'It's gorgeous. You can tell it's quality, not like the tat you get in the shops nowadays.'

'It's definitely well made,' Dodie agreed.

'Where did you say your shop was?'

'I didn't,' Dodie smiled. 'But I can do better than that… here's my card. The address is on there and if you pop in I'll do you a discount.'

'I might just do that!' the woman said, looking at the card before throwing Dodie a grateful smile. 'I'll have to set a good hour aside for a rummage.'

'You do that. And I'll even have the kettle on for you.'

'Lovely!' the woman said. 'I'll see you soon then. Enjoy the film!'

'Thank you, we will,' Dodie said.

'Well played,' Ryan said as they left her to deal with the next customer. 'Now that's how you do business. I knew you'd get there in the end.'

'That's just chatting,' Dodie said.

'Networking. It's all about the charm offensive. It's how I get most of my work.'

Dodie could well imagine him charming the pants off bored housewives and lonely old ladies – he'd got more than a bit of the loveable rogue about him. He did have a good point, though; it was easy for her to wax lyrical about vintage clothes but perhaps she ought to blow her own trumpet a little more, or at least her shop's trumpet. Ryan threw her a wink and she couldn't help but smile, a new hope beginning to grow that perhaps their relationship was going somewhere after all. Perhaps this would be the night she'd look back on as the turning point, when they finally began to function as a couple who gave and took, who tried to understand each other even if they failed. A couple who respected each other's differences and celebrated what set them apart even if they didn't love it, who toiled as a team and supported each other in their bids to make a success of their lives. Perhaps this would be the night that changed everything.

'I must look a mess,' Dodie said, dragging a hand across her eyes. Lost in a fantasy land of monochrome celluloid, it hadn't concerned her all that much that Ryan had fallen asleep shortly after the opening credits had rolled, although she should have expected it. He'd offered to take her in, though, and she had to keep remembering how important that part was.

'Nah, you look alright,' Ryan said. 'You need a minute to go and fix your make-up before we head off?'

'I suppose I should,' she replied uncertainly. Was she supposed to take his suggestion as a kindness or a strong hint that she did, indeed, look a mess and he wasn't prepared to walk the streets in her company until she tidied herself up? She paused. 'So, did you see any of the film?'

'Yeah,' he said, but Dodie knew he was lying. Did it matter? He'd gone in and sat down with the intention of watching and that was progress, she supposed. He looked at his watch. 'Not too late either. If we're quick we'll be able to fit a couple of cans in and a roll in the hay before bedtime.' Nudging her, he gave a wide grin. 'My reward for being a good boyfriend and taking you to see your favourite film, eh?'

Dodie nodded slowly but despite everything she still wasn't convinced. Was that how it was supposed to work? What happened to getting to know each other better? Had tonight been simply about brownie points for sex? She wanted to believe it was more than that, but he wasn't helping. And as for taking her to see her favourite film, they'd just happened to be passing and she'd paid for the tickets; it was hardly the most romantic gesture ever witnessed. But she forced a smile. 'I'll just pop to the loo then and we'll go.'

Fourteen

Julia Fleet was tall and slender, but not the type of slenderness that comes from a natural tendency to keep off weight, rather from often refusing food. Brown hair with grey roots, nails bitten down to the quick, she was grasping her portly husband's hand as if her very life depended on it as she entered the coffee shop where Dodie waited with Sally. She looked older than Dodie had been expecting, closer to her gran's age than her actual seventy-three years. The first thing she did as she settled down at the table was to pull on an inhaler. Sally seemed not to notice the obvious distress the woman was in, while Julia's husband patted her hand reassuringly and Dodie, not knowing what else to do, tried to give a bright smile.

Sally stuck her hand out. 'Sally Chandra, from the *Echo*; we've been chatting on the phone. Lovely to meet you both at last. Did you have a good journey down?'

'Not too bad,' the man said, shaking her hand. Sally held it out for Julia, who took it limply and barely moved hers in reply.

'And this is Dodie Bright, who found the letter,' Sally added, while Dodie put her hand out to greet them both.

'It's good of you to come,' the man replied, giving Dodie an amiable nod. 'We weren't sure you'd want to.'

'I had wondered the same about you,' Dodie said. 'I imagine it was a nerve-wracking decision.'

'Well,' he said, shooting a glance at Julia, 'we wanted to find out as much as we could about her real mum. We haven't been married all that long but I know it hasn't been easy for her to come to terms with her adoption, especially when her mother didn't want to know her at all.'

'You made contact in the past then?' Sally asked, flipping her notebook open and beginning to scribble in it. Dodie wondered whether it was a trifle insensitive to launch straight into an interrogation but then, she supposed, that was the reason she was there. Julia's husband, at least, seemed perfectly happy to volunteer the information.

'About twenty years ago,' Julia put in, her voice wavering. 'I traced her through government documents and asked if we could meet, but she refused. She said she didn't want to be reminded of old wounds.'

'So you didn't get to meet her?'

Julia shook her head. 'She didn't want me anywhere near her.'

'I would have pushed it but I wasn't on the scene back then,' Julia's husband said.

'Trevor and I only got married two years ago,' Julia explained, looking fondly at him. 'My previous husband died… cancer. He always said if my mum didn't care about me then I shouldn't waste my time caring about her. He said I'd got a good adoptive mother who'd brought me up and loved me and that ought to be enough even if she wasn't flesh and blood. I suppose he was right, but you can't help but wonder, can you?'

'And you had no idea about your father?' Sally asked. 'Who he was?'

'There were no details of the father on the birth certificate the adoption services sent to me. Apparently it wasn't allowed if the couple were unmarried and the father wasn't present at the registration of the birth. Since my mother wouldn't talk to me I didn't know where to start searching for him, and… honestly, I didn't know if I wanted to find him; I wasn't sure what sort of man he might be to abandon me and my mother like that. I never thought…' She pulled a tissue from her handbag and dabbed beneath her eyes.

Trevor patted her hand as the waitress came to take coffee orders from them.

'How does it feel to discover he was a brave man who died for his country?' Sally asked. The question was almost too eager, the hint of glee a little too obvious. She was in this for the story and she was getting one hell of a scoop, so it was no wonder she was pleased. She was probably already picturing the sensational headline, perhaps a journalism award or commendation – almost certainly a pat on the back from a grateful editor. She'd helped Dodie get a result and she was about to help Julia get answers, and although it was all good, none of it was out of the goodness of her heart.

'I'm still getting over the shock,' Julia said. 'I don't know whether to feel proud or sad for all the years I was robbed of, all the years I could have been getting to know him. My adopted father was a lovely man, but he was quiet and sensible and somehow we never really clicked. Growing up, I always felt there was a difference, something between us that we couldn't quite bridge. I got the impression that my mother had wanted to adopt more than he did, and that he'd have been happy enough without kids. I used to wonder about my real dad all the time… When I say real dad, I mean my birth dad. Of course, my dad was my real dad, but…'

Dodie tried to give her an encouraging smile, but all she wanted to do was reach over and hug this poor woman, who had been through so much. And even at the end of it all, she still didn't really have any answers apart from a weathered old scrap of paper marked with words of love from a father she'd never be able to meet and a mother who had abandoned her. Dodie almost wished she'd never started this, as if she was somehow responsible for Julia's heartache. If not responsible, then she'd almost certainly helped rake up feelings that perhaps had been better off buried.

'Would you like to see the letter?' she asked, wondering if it was the best idea after all. Julia seemed so emotionally brittle that the letter might just break her. But the woman nodded and Dodie pulled the envelope from her bag. Julia's eyes widened as Dodie handed it over.

'Want me to open it, love?' Trevor said, his gaze flicking to Julia's shaking hands.

Julia nodded weakly and he took it from her. His eyes moved across the page as he removed the letter from the envelope and Dodie was tempted to snatch it from him and give it back to Julia. It was *her* father and *she* ought to be reading it first. But she resisted the urge and breathed a silent sigh as Trevor gave it back to his wife.

Julia began to tremble as she read, her eyes misting. After a moment she folded it carefully and pushed it across the table to Dodie.

'It's yours.' Dodie frowned. 'That's what I wanted… to return it to its rightful owner. That's you.'

'Oh…' Julia's gaze went down to the letter, and although she stared at it she didn't make a move to reclaim it.

Trevor reached out. 'I'll put it safe,' he said, tucking it back into the envelope and placing it on the table in front of him.

There was a sense of almost palpable relief as Dodie watched the letter disappear from her life. It was odd, how it had become such a huge part of it since she'd made the discovery in the pocket of her green coat, how its contents had lodged in her thoughts so completely that there was barely a day she wasn't occupied with it. But now she could get back to normal, whatever that was. She half wondered if she might wake up tomorrow morning and miss not having to think about George's words of love.

'Is there anything you want to ask me?' Dodie offered, not knowing how else to break the strange, loaded silence that had descended over the table. Even Sally seemed subdued as they watched Julia wrestle emotions that looked set to overwhelm her. Julia gave her head a stiff shake.

'Sally said you found it in a coat,' Trevor said. 'Margaret's coat?'

'I can only assume it was Margaret's coat but I bought it in a job lot at auction so I have no way of knowing exactly where it came from.' Dodie's gaze flicked to the red coat she'd come in, relieved beyond measure that she'd had the foresight not to wear Julia's mother's coat to the meeting. 'I mean, I could let you have the coat if you'd like it? If you wanted to have something of hers… Not that we'd know for certain, of course…'

Julia, thin-lipped, shook her head again. 'No… thank you.'

'Was there anything else?' Trevor asked. 'Any other personal effects?'

'Just the letter. I went through all the things in the lot carefully.'

Trevor nodded before reaching for Julia's hand again. 'Are you alright, love? It's a big shock, isn't it?'

'He was a soldier,' she said quietly. 'How about that?'

'Do you have a family of your own?' Sally asked.

If possible, Julia suddenly seemed more agitated than before.

'She has a son, but we don't see him much,' Trevor cut in. 'It's… complicated.'

'We should be helping him,' Julia said.

'We can't help someone who doesn't want to be helped…' Trevor's voice rose slightly, and from the exasperation creeping into his tone,

Dodie guessed this was a conversation they'd had frequently. He shot a quick, anxious glance at her and Sally and then smoothed his features again.

'You have just the one child?' Sally asked.

'I thought I couldn't have babies,' Julia said. 'It was so ironic that I'd been an unwanted pregnancy myself but the baby I wanted so badly wouldn't come. I'd all but given up when it happened. I was thirty-nine; they told me I was an old mother but I didn't care, I'd have still had him at forty-nine or fifty-nine. I was just happy to be a mother at last.'

'It's about time you forgot all that and started to put yourself and your needs first,' Trevor cut in. 'It was his decision to leave.' He turned to Sally. 'In the two years we've been together it's always been about everyone else and never Julia.'

'These things are never that simple, are they?' Julia said, and she shot the briefest glance at Trevor that told Dodie more than a thousand words of explanation could. It was clear this was a line of enquiry that shouldn't be followed, even to Sally whose next question returned to the letter.

'What will you do now you know a little more about your parents?' she asked. 'Will you make an effort to trace more family? Perhaps try to find George's?'

'I wonder if they won't want me to find them, just like my mother didn't want to be found. I don't know if I could stand it. What if my mother married another man? Her children won't want to know about me and I don't know if I could take the rejection again.'

'I don't think she ever married after George,' Dodie said. 'My gran knows someone who knows someone who knows… well, you get the picture. But they think Margaret stayed single her whole life; she never got over losing George.'

'Then there's nobody to find,' Julia said.

'There's plenty of digging still to do,' Sally put in brightly. 'There must be cousins and nieces and nephews and all sorts from both Margaret and George's side.'

The waitress returned to the table with a tray of drinks, Sally offering a nod of thanks as she placed them on the table.

'I don't know,' Julia said as the waitress left them again. 'I'd need time to think about it.'

'Let me follow up the original story with one about our meeting today and let's see what comes of it,' Sally suggested. 'We might get more information and more family members coming forward. After all, wouldn't it be lovely to meet them?'

Julia stirred her tea silently for a moment. But then she looked up and gave a small nod. 'Alright,' she said. 'Let's see what happens.'

'Why didn't you tell me you were in the paper?' Ryan pulled a rolled-up newspaper from the pocket of the coat he'd just hung on the back of a chair. He opened it out on the kitchen table to a dog-eared page stained with a coffee ring, where Dodie's first article about finding the letter was printed.

Dodie stopped stirring the pasta sauce she had on the hob and glanced over, her cheeks flushing. Ryan had been odd when he'd first arrived, and she should have seen this coming. He'd clearly been stewing on his discovery, trying to figure out how to tackle it and wondering what she was keeping from him – she'd have done the same in his place. She wanted to pre-empt the argument they looked set to have, to tell him that he had no need to tackle anything, but doing that would admit she'd been in the wrong. Her silence probably made it look as though she had something to hide, but that couldn't be further from the truth. Making Ryan understand that, however, could be a problem.

She tried to make her shrug seem nonchalant. 'I didn't think you'd be interested.'

'Not interested?' He slapped the back of his hand on the photo. 'You're in the paper and you think I wouldn't be interested?'

'It's only a little write-up. Not like I'm on the evening news or anything.'

'I still ought to know about it. How do you think it makes it look that I don't? What do you think my mum makes of it when she's the one to show me and she can't understand why *I* haven't told *her* about it?'

Dodie paused for a moment before stirring the sauce again. 'I suppose you've read the story?' she asked, not looking up from the pan.

'Sort of… well, no. But my mum told me what was in it. Lucky she hadn't got rid of the recycling already when she remembered to mention it to me.'

'So you know it was about a letter. I just didn't think you'd be interested in it… you'd think it was a waste of time. You're always saying how you don't get my fascination with old things and I thought you'd say it was silly chasing around after the owner.'

'And who's this guy it mentions? You went to his house?'

'Only because I thought Margaret's family might still live there.'

'Who's Margaret?'

Dodie held in a sigh. 'The woman the letter was addressed to: Margaret Vincent. I thought she might still live there but Ed lives there now.'

She glanced up to see Ryan frowning and she knew the look. The cogs were creaking in his brain, trying to place something that should have been significant but as yet not quite knowing how it fitted.

'Ed?'

'*Edward*,' Dodie said quickly. 'Edward Willoughby. The man in the article. We found the family, actually,' she added, realising that her best option now was to come clean. Sally was planning another story and Ryan would think it really weird if Dodie didn't tell him about it. 'I met up with Margaret and George's daughter yesterday. She was given up for adoption as a baby so she never knew either of them.'

'Yesterday?'

'At a coffee shop in town. I handed the letter over to her and she's going to see if she can track down some more of her family with it.'

'You met this woman? And you didn't think to tell me?'

'Like I said, I didn't think you'd be interested. It's old stuff, and you hate old stuff.'

'So you wouldn't have mentioned it if I hadn't found out?'

'I wasn't hiding anything. How could I be when the world could read the story in the newspaper? I'm sorry if you thought so and from now on I'll run everything by you.' Dodie gave the sauce a brisk stir, causing it to spray from the pan. She frowned, wiping it from her apron.

'There's no need to be sarky,' Ryan said, throwing a dark look that she caught as she glanced up.

'I'm not. There's going to be another story about Julia in the paper.'

'Who the hell is Julia?'

'Margaret's daughter. The lady who was adopted. It's very sad, actually.'

'And you'll be in the story?'

'I might be, but it will only be a little mention. Maybe a photo of us together. Nothing huge though.'

Ryan was silent for a moment. Dodie glanced up again. A silent, thoughtful Ryan was never a good thing.

'I don't suppose you could open the wine?' she asked, hoping to distract him. 'And get some plates out because this will be ready in a minute. There's parmesan in the fridge if you want to get that out too.'

The ruse seemed to work, because Ryan's expression cleared and he dug into the kitchen drawer for a corkscrew. 'Nice wine,' he said, peering at the label as he collected it and the parmesan from the fridge. 'Good week in the shop?'

'Good offer on at the supermarket,' Dodie said, forcing a careless chuckle.

But when she looked around again, the troubled expression was back on his face. 'It's weird,' he said slowly.

'What is?'

'That you need to have this whole other life without me. It's so secret you can't even tell me about it.'

'Do we have to be joined at the hip?' Dodie turned the heat off and took the pan from the stove. 'Being a couple doesn't mean we have to be interested in the same things. I understand you don't get excited by the same stuff as me and that's why I try not to force it on you. We aren't the same, never have been, and it's never been an issue before.'

'I still talk to you about my interests even though you don't like them.'

'Yep, and it doesn't make me any more interested, no matter how many times you tell me about the best goal you've ever seen.' She spooned pasta into two dishes. 'Look, I just feel sometimes like it's a burden to you, or it's boring, and so I don't always tell you about stuff I'm up to. There's no secret, no other life you're not allowed to know about, it's just that. But if you want me to start telling you everything then I will.'

'Now you make me sound like a control freak,' he said, and the warning signs of a sulk were in his tone. They were signs Dodie knew only too well. It wouldn't make for much of a night in, but part of her was just too tired to care, too fed up of pandering to his moods. Yes, she'd been out of order hiding the letter and the newspaper article from him, but he made it so difficult to discuss anything that it was no wonder she'd felt the need to.

'That's not what I'm trying to do. We live apart and so there's going to be a degree of separation in our lives, and that's just how it is. There's no reason it should affect the time we spend together, though.'

Ryan was silent again as he poured the wine. 'I suppose,' he said finally. 'But we're not going to be living apart for much longer now,' he added. 'After Christmas I'll be here all the time. Maybe it won't be such a big deal then.'

'No,' Dodie said. 'Maybe it won't.'

At this he seemed to cheer, and he smiled slightly as he handed her a drink. But while he visibly brightened, the conversation had the opposite effect on her. Far from being cheered by the prospect of him moving in, Dodie now felt more miserable than ever.

It was Saturday night so everything stopped for *Match of the Day*. Ryan had even been known to plan sex around it. This Saturday had been no different – they'd eaten their pasta, drunk a good quantity of white wine and settled down to a slew of game shows, celebrity panel quizzes and finally the footballing TV highlight of Ryan's week. At this point Dodie, woozy from her alcohol intake, tired from her week in the shop, and just plain bored, fell asleep leaning against him on the sofa.

She was woken by the sound of the end credits and Ryan nudging her. She opened her eyes, about to give him a groggy mouthful for being just a little too rough, but was startled into sudden wakefulness by the thunderous expression on his face.

She sat up and rubbed her eyes, instantly sober and awake. 'What's the matter?'

'You got a text.' Ryan held the phone up to Dodie's face. She squinted at the message that he'd already opened. It was from Ed, and her blood turned to ice as she read it.

Hey, thanks for letting me know. Who's come forward? And I'm sorry about the things I said to you on the beach, but I hope you'll understand why I said them. I know I asked you to stay away, and I stand by that, but I hope if we see each other on the street we can still say hello as old friends.

She looked at Ryan, whose features had never shown such naked anger in all the years she'd known him. Of all the times for Ed to reply to her message about Julia coming forward, it had to be now. Of all the times he could have chosen to apologise for the beach, it had to be now. It looked bad, and even Ryan couldn't fail to add up the twos and get four. Half an hour either way and she'd have been able to intercept the message and all would be well, but now the situation looked set to blow.

'Who's this bloke?' he asked, his tone cold. 'Who the hell is this Ed? This isn't the first time I've heard his name, is it? First the newspaper story, and now this? Why all the secrets, Dodie? What are you hiding?'

'I'm not hiding anything. Ed's just a friend. He's—'

'He's sorry about the things he said to you on the beach? Come on, Dodie, you think I'm stupid? He's apologising for things he said on the beach and there's nothing in it? Please, I know I'm not the sharpest tool in the shed but even I can recognise an affair when I see it!'

'There's no affair!' Dodie sat up, heat rushing to her face. There was no affair, but the awareness of how much she'd wanted one made her burn with shame. 'He was helping me with the letter, that's all.'

'Oh, the letter you couldn't even tell me about? *That* letter… the *secret* letter… the Ryan's-too-dumb-to-understand letter? I would have helped you!'

'You would have laughed; told me I was stupid. You've always thought my ideas are stupid.'

'When have I ever said that?'

'You've never had to! It's in everything you do. When you look at me with that contemptuous smile, when your eyes glaze over as I tell you about something… You don't need to tell me I'm stupid because I know, but I can't help it if I see the world differently than you do.'

'If I've been such a terrible boyfriend then why have you put up with me all this time? Made me believe we had a future… let me *move in*, for God's sake!'

'You pushed to move in!' Dodie yelled. 'I never wanted you to move in!'

She stopped, her eyes widening as she saw his reaction.

'I'm sorry,' she added, 'I didn't mean that, I—'

'Oh, I think you did,' he said, his tone granite. 'Now it all makes sense: the unanswered text messages, keeping me away from the flat, secrets and lies… it all makes so much sense. And where does Ed fit in all of this? Is he the reason you don't want me to move in?'

'Of course not! There's nothing going on between me and Ed!'

'Not what this text message is telling me.' Ryan unlocked the phone again and as Dodie launched at him to reclaim it, he lifted it out of her way and held her at bay with a hand against her chest. 'Interesting message thread you've got here,' he said coldly. 'Looks like you've been having a ball with Ed while I was stuck out at Dorchester.'

'We're just friends!' Dodie cried, weaving around and snatching the phone from his grip. 'And you have no right to read my messages!'

'It wouldn't matter if you had nothing to hide.'

'It would always matter, and that's just what's wrong with you! Private is private and what I choose to keep to myself about my life is my business, boyfriend or no.'

'So now there's something wrong with me? In that case I'll take myself out of your way.'

'Stop twisting things so that it's always my fault!' Dodie shouted.

'I'm not the one having an affair.'

'I'm not having an affair!'

'I don't believe you!'

Her defiant gaze never left his face as they squared up, the next salvo hanging in the air between them, waiting to be fired. In the past they'd argued, of course, but Dodie – peaceful, tolerant, lover of harmony – had always backed down. But something had changed, and if Ryan was waiting for the moment where she apologised and begged for his forgiveness, he was going to be waiting for a long time.

'I suppose,' she began, the steadiness of her tone now belying the tumult of emotions that made her hands shake, 'this is the moment where we admit things aren't working. You want to believe I'm having an affair then I can't change that no matter what I say. So believe what you like, and leave me if you like. I'm past caring what you think or do.'

His expression flicked from anger to incredulity in an instant. 'What are you saying?'

'Do I really have to explain it again? We're done. You're wrong about the affair but you were right about one thing: we're going nowhere, have been for a long time, and I'm only sorry we kept things going this long when we should have just admitted it.'

'You're dumping me?'

'No, I'm telling you that we should split up – there's a world of difference.'

'Look, I'm pissed off, granted, but I don't want us to split up.'

'You do,' Dodie said. 'You just can't admit it to yourself yet. I'm only a comfort blanket to you, an old pair of slippers, and that's no basis for a life together. You don't love me—'

'I do!'

'You don't. And even if you did, I don't love you. I'm sorry, Ryan, it's been fun, but I don't love you enough to build a life with you.'

'Then why would you let me move in?'

She shook her head. 'I don't even know. Guilt. Pretence. Hope that the affection I had for you would turn into love. But all those things were ridiculous. You have every right to be angry at me for not being straight with you about it, if nothing else.'

His mouth hung open. 'So that's it?'

'I suppose it is.'

'And what does it mean? You're going off with this Ed bloke?'

'It has nothing to do with Ed and quite frankly I wish you'd stop blaming him. I'm sorry it's come to an end like this, but perhaps coming to an end now is the kindest thing before you moved in and things got really complicated.'

He was silent for a moment. 'You're saying you want me to go?'

'You've had a drink. I don't suppose you can go anywhere until the morning.'

'But you want me to?'

'That's not the point. I'd prefer it if we didn't share a bed tonight, though.'

'You want me to sleep on the sofa?'

She shook her head. 'I'll take the sofa and you have the bed.'

He didn't argue. Without another word he took himself through to the bedroom and slammed the door shut. Dodie curled into a ball on the sofa, silent tears streaming down her face.

When Dodie woke from a night of fitful sleep and crept, almost fearfully, into her bedroom, the bed was empty. Despite the gnawing guilt that wouldn't leave her, and the fact that it would have been healthier for them to talk when they'd had time to sober up, she heaved a silent sigh of relief. Ryan had collected his things and left before the sun was up. Perhaps it was for the best, because in the cold light of day she might have been convinced to give him another chance if he'd asked for it. But another chance would simply have been another lie and it would have made things worse when they split up again, something that, with hindsight, had been inevitable all along.

Her first instinct was to phone Isla, but her friend had enough of her own worries without Dodie adding to them. She could phone her mum but couldn't face explaining that it didn't mean she needed to come home to Dorchester. Gran wouldn't understand, or if she did her response would make little sense. Which left Ed, but why on earth he registered as a potential confidante at a time like this was as unclear to Dodie as it would undoubtedly be to him. Besides, things in that quarter were complicated enough.

So this was it, the first day of her new life as a single woman. When she thought about it that way, an empty future seemed to stretch out before her, featureless and vast. She and Ryan had hardly lived in each other's pockets but what plans they'd made had included each other. She'd simply assumed that one day they'd be married and buy a house and have kids. And now there was just her and the shop. What did that mean for her life from this day forward?

She pushed away her melancholy thoughts. It was for the best, wasn't it? That life was a lie and no matter how good everything looked on the surface, the fabric of a lie would never stand enough pressure to prevent it from crumbling in the end. Better to build her future on truth, and the only truth she had right now was that she was alone. Holding on to that thought, she began to clear away the mess they'd left from dinner the night before, and it felt like clearing the mess of an old life to make way for the new.

As she rushed around, determined not to dwell on the conversations of the previous night, her gaze fell on Margaret's green coat, the thing that had started it all, hanging on the door of the wardrobe. Right now she couldn't decide whether it coming to her had been a blessing or a curse. She stood and stared at it, almost in a trance. But then she shook herself, dumped the blankets she'd used on the sofa the previous night and pulled the coat on. Fresh air – that was what she needed. A walk on the beach always made everything seem better.

Fifteen

Mondays were hard enough as it was, but if ever there had been a reason for closing the shop for the day, Dodie's current situation was it. But her current situation was also the strongest motivation she could have had for keeping the shop open and carrying on as normal. It was only by carrying on that she'd get her life back on track, and as she kept reminding herself, the shop meant everything now. So at nine, despite her low mood and the flurries of powdery snow stuttering in windswept eddies around her door, she pulled up the shutters and painted a smile on her face ready for the first customers.

As she stood warming herself with a little oil-fired heater behind the counter, the door tinkled. But the first body through the door wasn't a customer at all – it was her gran.

'You're out early,' Dodie said, forcing a cheery tone. The last thing she needed was Gran getting any sort of clue that things were amiss. She'd tell her about Ryan, of course, but in her own time, when she was quite sure what it all meant herself. 'It's a bit cold for you to be wandering around too.'

'Oh, the cold doesn't bother me,' Gran said, cupping her hands and blowing into them just to demonstrate the fact that the cold clearly did bother her but she was perfectly entitled at her age to be rather martyred about it. 'I've got this new tai chi class that Lesley down the road has persuaded me to try out starting at eleven so I thought I'd better bring your tea bags over first. In case you run out.'

'Gran, I keep telling you I can afford a few tea bags.' Dodie took the cloth bag Gran had just handed over and peered inside, not even commenting on the tai chi. Nothing that Gran did surprised her any more. Some days, like today, Dodie was even a little jealous of her grandmother's social life. The bag held two boxes of Dorset tea, various packs of biscuits and some instant lattes. 'And what's all this other stuff? Is this for me?'

'Well, I drink so much when I come I thought it only fair to help out.'

'You don't, and you didn't need to, but thanks.' She put the bag on the counter and pulled out the spare chair for Gran to sit. But Gran shook her head.

'I won't take a seat – if I get settled I'll be late for tai chi.'

'I can remind you when it's time.'

'Have you had any camel coats in yet?' Gran asked, wandering over to the rails.

'Not yet, but I keep looking.' Dodie followed her gran to the rail, absently straightening the row of hangers as her gran flicked through them one by one. 'How's Bernard, by the way? Shouldn't you be arranging a wedding instead of bringing teabags and worrying about camel coats?'

'Oh, that,' Gran said, her expression darkening. 'It's all off, I'm afraid.'

'What happened?' Dodie asked, trying hard to keep her tone neutral. But she couldn't deny her immense relief at the news. Nobody but Gran had been happy about the wedding, and although she felt guilty that Gran was clearly bothered, no wedding would certainly make life less complicated than it already was.

Gran folded her arms tight across her chest. 'Astrid told me that he's asked at least two other women to marry him this year.'

'Oh.'

'As if that wasn't bad enough he was trying to marry all of us at the same time!' Gran pursed her lips so tightly Dodie was afraid they might disappear into her face. 'Imagine that!'

'I'd rather not. How was he planning to make this work?'

'I have no idea but I'm not going to be one of his concubines, not for anything. If he's one of those Mormons or something he should have said before he popped the question.'

'Perhaps he thought you'd say no.'

'Of course I would have said no! Your grandad would be spinning in his grave to think of it, God rest his soul! And just imagine the bedroom arrangements!'

'Again, I'd rather not.'

'It's terrible! Would you let your Brian have another girlfriend as well as you?'

Dodie's gaze went to the window. 'Have you told Mum about this yet?'

Gran waved a vague hand. 'I expect I'll give her a call later. She'll be over the moon. Annoying really.'

'I think she'll just be relieved.'

'I'm all alone in that big house. If she visited more often then I wouldn't have to think about marrying people.'

Dodie forced a smile. 'She does her best, but she works and it's hard to fit things in. We only see each other so often now because I live close, but it would have been like that for me if I still lived in Dorchester.'

'Before I forget,' Gran added, instantly seeming to forget her vexation about Bernard and his serial proposing, or Dodie's mum and her apparent reluctance to visit, 'there's a carol concert in the gardens tonight. They're lighting candles of remembrance too. I thought I might go to light one for your grandad, God rest his soul. I know you like that sort of thing.'

'That sounds lovely. Want me to come and pick you up in the car?'

'Oh, could you? You are a love. My legs aren't what they used to be. And they used to be good, you know. I won Butlins' Miss Lovely Legs in Minehead. Beat women half my age. They had a curtain over our top halves, so they didn't know who was who. Your grandad said, go on, go up, I bet they never guess you've got a few years in the tank with your legs. And the judge said we could have knocked him down with a feather when the curtain came back – he could have sworn he was looking at the legs of a 25-year-old. And I hadn't been twenty-five for a long time by then.'

'I know,' Dodie said, her smile more genuine now. 'I've seen the photos. I don't mind picking you up one bit – it might help to take your mind off Bernard to go out for an hour.'

'Bernard?' Gran frowned. 'Oh, yes! Bernard! What a good idea!'

Dodie smiled faintly. Gran might be as flaky as the topping of a steak pie, but an evening in her company would help take her mind off her own problems too and she didn't take her out nearly as much as she ought to.

'Thanks for asking me,' she said. She clapped her hands together and nodded towards the seat. 'Come on, you can spare ten minutes for a cup of tea, surely? Especially as you've bought a year's supply of tea bags. I promise I won't let you be late for your class.'

Gran hesitated, and then she toddled over to sit down. 'I suppose I could take the weight off for a bit. And a cup of tea does sound nice.'

'Right then,' Dodie said. 'You watch the shop for a minute and I'll get sorted.'

That evening, Gran stood next to her on the path, her arm looped through Dodie's. Though they'd had plenty of cold days recently, this evening was possibly the coldest they'd had this year, and the crisp air held the promise of snow, which had stopped and started all day but never really got going. The crowds hemming them in on all sides as they gathered in front of the old bandstand helped a little to keep the cold at bay, but underfloor heating on the pathways of the gardens would have been very much appreciated right now. Glass lanterns hung from the trees, tea lights tucked inside them and handwritten messages attached by paper tags. Dodie had wiped a tear away as she'd watched Gran write a dedication to her late husband before attaching it to a lantern of her own. Despite the busy schedule full of clubs and classes for things Dodie had never even heard of, and the flirting with pensioners and random acceptance of marriage proposals, Dodie was reminded that, above all, her grandmother battled with loneliness every single day. Her grandparents' marriage had been a love affair of epic proportions, like Liz Taylor and Richard Burton, like Lancelot and Guinevere, like the love stories you saw in films, unbreakable and everlasting, vital, touching, fiery and poignant. They'd loved each other until the end. Gran pretended that she was alright, but she'd never been alright, not since the day she'd found him on the chair in a sleep he'd never wake from.

Over at the bandstand harassed adults raced to and fro organising crowds of children wearing different school uniforms under huge coats, a sea of bobble hats of all shapes and colours ebbing and flowing like the tide as they fidgeted and chatted, the air alive with excitement and anticipation. The voices of teachers and assistants struggled above the noise, getting more and more hysterical the louder the children got. Many of the children waved manically at the crowds, where parents and grandparents, aunts and uncles and siblings waved back. Some picked their noses or twiddled with the ends of scarves, lost in worlds of their own making, while others whispered behind their hands and giggled at private jokes. From every tiny mouth rose hot plumes of breath curling into the icy air.

'Look at their little faces!' Gran cooed. 'It doesn't seem like five minutes since you were that age singing in the school choir.'

'Life was a lot simpler when I was that age,' Dodie replied, stamping her feet in a bid to bring some feeling back to them. Unconsciously, her gaze flicked over the crowds, as it had done at least five, maybe six times since they'd arrived. She wondered whether she'd see Ed. The last time she'd stood here watching a performance he'd been with her, the promise of a friendship blossoming. She'd toyed with the idea of texting him today, a casual mention of the fact she would be here with her gran and maybe he'd like to join them. The presence of her gran might make it less awkward for them to make small talk and he might enjoy the concert. But her mind had gone back to his words, how he'd made it clear she wasn't to contact him again, and she'd decided against it. Everything else he'd said might have been easier to forgive and forget, but that bit, the staying-away-from-him bit… It was difficult to interpret that as anything but stay away. She could tell him she wasn't with Ryan any more, but would that make a difference? What had he really meant by his warning? Perhaps it wouldn't change his mind even if she told him because she'd already rejected him and she knew it must have hurt.

'So is your friend away for Christmas then?' Gran asked.

Dodie shook herself. 'What's that?'

'Your friend. You were telling me about her being in the Alps.'

'Isla? Oh, yes. I don't know, her mum wouldn't be happy if she stayed away for Christmas.'

'But you said her mum didn't want her to go in the first place and I'm not surprised; I wouldn't like it if a no-good strip of a husband who'd abandoned me with the baby for all those years rang out of the blue and wanted to wander back into our lives again. Your grandad, God rest his soul, would never have done such an awful, mean thing. He knew his responsibilities.'

'I can understand what you're saying, but it's tough for Isla too and I understand why she'd be desperate to know more about her dad. I suppose you'd feel a bit incomplete in a way, not having that in your life. I do hope she makes it back though – it would be the first Christmas in years I wouldn't be seeing her. And she's supposed to do the White Christmas Dip with me this year too.'

'What on earth is that?'

'You know, the charity thing? Where we swim in the sea on Christmas morning.'

Gran rolled her eyes and tutted theatrically. 'Oh, that nonsense! She'll probably tell you she can't get home so she doesn't have to do that!'

'I doubt it!' Dodie laughed. 'We loved it last year.'

Gran shook her head. 'Silly idea – people charging about in the sea at this time of year. It's a wonder the hospital isn't full of people with flu after that business.'

'It's for a good cause.'

'Couldn't you do something a bit safer? I'm working at the Salvation Army soup kitchen on Christmas Eve – that's sensible and it's for a good cause.'

'I could do that too if you need an extra pair of hands then as well,' Dodie said cheerfully.

'Are you going to see your Brian after Christmas lunch?'

The smile faded from Dodie's face. 'I don't think that's happening now.'

Their conversation was cut short by the PA system blasting out a backing track that sounded like the tune to 'Jingle Bells', but was so distorted it was difficult to tell. Somebody went to fiddle with it, and eventually it settled into something recognisable. A hush fell over the crowd, and all eyes turned to the front as the children began to sing along while the conductor waved his baton with wild abandon. There was obviously a method in his madness, but to Dodie it looked as though he'd got some melted toffee stuck on the end of his pointer and he was trying to shake it off. Whatever he was doing, though, he was encouraging a wonderful sound and there was something angelic about the voices of the children as they lifted into the air, pure and clear. Many of them obviously couldn't sing a note and alone would have made a very strong case for handing out earplugs. But collectively there was nothing sweeter than the sound of a school choir and Dodie felt a very real sense of peace and happiness steal through her. She was arm in arm with the gran she adored in a crowd of people all moved by the spirit of Christmas, and whatever else was wrong in her life, just being here now could make it all seem right, if only for a little while.

Sally had emailed Dodie to tell her that the story would appear in the newspaper on Christmas Eve. So that morning Dodie had rushed across to the newsagents before she opened up her own shop, figuring that a couple of minutes either way wasn't going to lose her any customers. Not that she was exactly fighting them off most days, but Christmas Eve for most people was more likely to be about last-minute food shopping and token gifts than any serious vintage hunting. Back in the shop, as the kettle boiled for her first tea of the day, Dodie was looking forward to indulging in the biscuits her gran had brought over. She spread the newspaper out across the counter and started to flick through the pages until she found the story, just before the centre crease. Right-hand page – that was good, or so Sally had told her – and though it was further back in the paper than it had been last time, it was bigger.

Julia's Christmas Miracle

There was a large photo of Julia and Trevor holding hands, and a smaller inset of Dodie holding the letter up. The article opened with a recap of Dodie's finding of the letter, leading on to explain how Julia had heard about the story through the social media network of an adopted children's support group, which had led her to travel from her home in Lancashire to Bournemouth to meet Dodie and claim the letter. It appealed for more information about Margaret and George so that Julia could track down other members of her birth family and also said that, although the letter was written by George and they now knew quite a lot about Margaret, they still had no more information about Julia's father than what little was in that letter. Julia, it said, never knowing the identity of her father and having no name on the birth certificate, was desperate to find out who he was and about the rest of her paternal family. Sally went on to quote Julia saying that finding her father's family would change her life and answer many questions she'd pondered growing up. Dodie couldn't remember Julia putting it quite like that, but she supposed

Sally was doing her job, turning it into living, breathing prose rather than cold reporting. Sally ended the story by reiterating her plea for information and reassuring readers that the *Echo* would follow up on Julia's efforts.

Dodie closed the paper again and put it to one side. It was telling that there was no mention of Ed this time. Perhaps Sally had felt his part in the story redundant now that she had Julia's to tell. Even Dodie was hardly mentioned this time, not that she was sorry about it. When all was said and done, it was only right. Her and Ed's roles were over now, and it was all about Julia and her search for her birth family. If Dodie had played a part in making that possible – even a tiny one – then she was happy, content enough to step out of the limelight and wish Julia all the best.

The shop was quiet, but then so was the whole road by the looks of things. Everyone would be down in the main town or at the markets, racing around for last-minute items. Gazing sleepily out of the window as she mused on this, she jumped as the shrill ring of her phone cut through the silence of the shop.

'Hey!' Isla said. She sounded as if she was in the next room, not hundreds of miles away. At that moment, Dodie wished she could reach through the phone and pull her into a hug. 'How's everything? What's happening with your letter? The woman came to see you?'

Dodie had explained, as briefly as only texting would allow, that Julia had come forward and she was to meet with her. It was just like Isla to ask about Dodie's news first when she probably had a lot more earth-shattering news to tell herself.

'She did,' Dodie said. 'It looks as if it's all settled now… at least my part in it is.'

'What about Ed?' Isla asked.

Dodie shook her head. 'He's out of the picture.' She paused. She wanted to tell Isla about her bust-up with Ryan but it felt too complicated and messy to go into now when Isla was so far away. Her friend had enough to worry about for both of them. 'Have you seen your dad yet?' she asked.

'Yeah…'

'How did it go?'

'It's so much harder than I thought it would be.' There was a long sigh from the other end of the line.

'Oh, Isla!' Dodie said. 'I'm so sorry! I wish I could be there with you.'

'I'm being silly,' Isla said, seeming to rally. 'I'm going to see him again, and we'll keep going until we get somewhere because I've realised that I want to know him better. I've got a half brother and sister too and I want to get to know them more too.' She gave a nervous laugh. 'It's so weird saying that. I mean, I've got loads of family, of course, on Mum's side, but…'

'I know,' Dodie said. 'They're all strangers there, aren't they? It will be weird at first. But do you think you might like them?'

'Honestly? I don't know.' Another pause. 'Anyway, I just phoned really to say merry Christmas. I'm sorry but the weather has turned and I won't make it home after all, so it means I won't be able to do the sea dip with you this year but we'll definitely do it next year. Are you still going?'

'I think so. Unless we get blizzards here and then I might change my mind. There's one thing about being there – you're guaranteed a white Christmas.'

Isla laughed. 'There is that. Merry Christmas, Dodie.'

'Merry Christmas. Stay safe, won't you? And let me know how you're getting on – regular updates to stop me worrying.'

'You're not actually worrying about me, are you?' Isla laughed. 'That's ridiculous!'

'Of course I am. You know me better than that.' Dodie smiled.

'I do. I know that… I'm guessing you're just about to have a cup of tea.'

'I am!' Dodie laughed. 'It's early for you though, seeing as you're on holiday.'

'Couldn't sleep in and I wanted to catch you before the shop got busy.'

'Thanks. I appreciate it.'

'Right! Take care, and I'll see you soon.'

'Bye.' Dodie ended the call, sniffing hard. It wasn't until she'd spoken to Isla that she'd realised just how much she was missing her. There was so much she wanted to share and confide in her, and she guessed that Isla was feeling the same, but they were hundreds of miles and a blizzard apart.

Rubbing her eyes, she took a deep breath. There was no point in moping. A cup of Gran's lovely tea would make her feel better, and she'd just decided to nip upstairs to make one when the doorbell tinkled. Customers were like that – you could wait for hours and nobody would come in but the minute you wanted to do something you'd get one. Perhaps the best business strategy she could have was to stand by the kettle all day with the intention of making a drink and the shop would be heaving.

But when she turned back to greet them, she found it wasn't a customer. Unless Ed Willoughby had suddenly been struck by the urge to buy a pair of corduroy bell-bottoms. From the look on his face, and the way he wore his clothes as if he'd thrown them on in a rush, and his hair sticking up at odd angles, it didn't seem likely.

'Ed?' Dodie frowned. 'It's lovely to see you but—'

'I had to come,' he cut in, his voice urgent. He unfolded a copy of the *Echo*, opened at the page containing Sally's story about Julia. 'Dodie, I don't know how to tell you this and I should have come clean before but I haven't been completely truthful with you.'

'I don't understand.'

'The woman you met… The woman in the paper today…'

'You mean Julia?'

'She's my…' He cleared his throat and ran a shaky hand through his unruly hair.

'What's wrong?' Dodie asked. 'You want to sit down? Whatever it is you think you've done, it can't be that bad.'

He shook his head. 'You might think otherwise when I tell you. I've been an idiot to keep it a secret. I don't know why I just felt… I didn't even know if I wanted to find them myself but I ended up drawn into the search because it mattered to you and it sort of ended up mattering to me. I didn't think we'd actually find anything, so it was OK because I didn't know if I wanted to find anything… but of course, it must have mattered to me on some level. I suppose I wanted to find the answers if I ended up in Bournemouth on account of what little I knew—'

'Ed,' Dodie interrupted. 'Please… you're making no sense. What is it you need to tell me?'

He took a deep breath and held her in a steady gaze. 'Julia Fleet…' he said. 'She's my mother. The family you've been looking for all this time is *my* family.'

Sixteen

Dodie stared at him. 'I don't understand.'

Ed began to pace the floor of the shop, jacket open and flapping around him. 'I'm not sure I do either. I don't know what I was thinking. I don't even know why I'm here in Bournemouth, or in your shop right now. I don't know why I didn't send you away that first night on my doorstep. I don't know why I didn't come clean with you right from the start. I only know that what you were offering… it was like I couldn't resist, even though part of me didn't want to know. And I thought it would be OK to keep quiet because I never expected you to get as far as you did. And I liked spending time with you. And I thought if we weren't searching then we wouldn't have a reason to spend time together…'

'She said she hadn't seen her son for ages,' Dodie said in a dazed voice. 'She said… she said… So that's *you*? She was talking about you?'

At that moment, Dodie couldn't decide who had the right to look more confused – her or Ed. So the errant son Julia had been crying over was Ed? This was the craziest, most unlikely thing she'd ever heard, and yet she didn't doubt for a moment that he was telling the truth.

'What else did she tell you? That I was a selfish bastard? That I wallowed in self-pity and made her life a misery? That when she told me how the people I'd been calling Grandma and Grandad weren't that at all she'd been hoping for understanding and support and I hadn't even given her that much?'

'Well, no, but…'

'That's exactly what I did. And then I left and I didn't tell her where to find me. It meant she'd been abandoned twice in her life, and when I thought about it I couldn't breathe, I couldn't go back and face her knowing what I'd done, and time just went on and on and things got worse. And then you came and you were like an angel who could fix everything that was broken in me and…' He let out a sigh. 'Forgive me, Dodie. I don't even know what I'm saying any more. I'm so, so sorry I lied to you.'

Dodie raced over to the door and flipped the sign from open to closed before locking it. Closing on Christmas Eve hadn't featured in her plans but the situation called for radical measures. Ed was clearly distressed and he had a lot of challenging emotions to work through – the last thing they needed was a customer walking in on them.

'I'll make us a drink,' she said. 'We can go upstairs to talk where it's quiet.'

Without argument he followed her up to the flat. She made him sit at the table while she switched the kettle on to re-boil it.

'Start from the beginning,' she said, leaning against the worktop as she turned to face him. 'What happened?'

'When I was discharged from the army I was in a mess. I mean, unbearable to be around – I know that. Mum and Trevor struggled with me and things got even worse when I moved back in with them after splitting with my girlfriend. Mum wanted me at home with them, though. I suppose she was scared I'd do something drastic if I was left to my own devices. And honestly, I can't say that might not have happened on my lowest nights if she hadn't been there. But things were strained and it got tougher, especially for Trevor. I suppose he hadn't signed up for a moody adult son when he'd asked Mum to marry him. One day we were having this almighty row, and I'd said something about her backwards family and how she was just like them – I was being a twat, I already know this before you tell me so – and then it just came out. She told me she was adopted. She'd never said a word up until that day.'

'When I met your mum she told me she was sorry she hadn't been able to share the fact she was adopted with you. The truth was that she'd been rejected by Margaret, her birth mother – once when she was given away and then again when she tried to find her twenty years ago. She felt as if she'd be rejected by her real father too if she tried to find him. It hurt, and so I think she felt everyone she loved was better shielded from the thing that caused her so much pain, in case it caused them pain too. That's why she never told you.'

'You see, you already know more about it than I do. I suppose that's because people want to talk to you – they know you won't explode and behave like a complete dickhead when they do.'

'Hardly. So, when I came to your door that first time with George's letter, you knew?'

'Not exactly. I couldn't be sure. But I had an idea. I'd got some information from the adoption group Mum was a member of and I managed to track down Margaret to Wessex Road. Then I was online trying to find the house when I saw the flat at number eleven was up for rent. It seemed like too good an opportunity to miss and it felt like the right time to leave Blackpool. Mum and Trevor didn't want me around, and they didn't deserve such a drag in their lives. So I came to Bournemouth and I didn't tell them where I'd gone.'

'But your mum knew that Margaret had lived at Wessex Road? Might she have thought to look there for you?'

'She'd been there years before when she tracked down Margaret the first time. I didn't tell her I'd been doing some research of my own. I don't even know why I was doing it. Opening old wounds wasn't exactly what Mum needed but something in me just had to know. I needed to know about the people who'd made me, where I came from. Does that make sense?'

'It does,' Dodie replied, her thoughts going back to Isla, who had only just said a similar thing. She could understand very well. 'But what I don't understand is why you didn't tell me?'

'You're angry?'

'I'm hurt. Offended a little, but not angry. You could have helped me find my own answers a lot quicker and it would have helped you in the end. We could have worked it out together.'

'That's part of the problem,' he said quietly. But then he looked up and shook his head. 'I wasn't really much further on than you in my investigations. To tell you the truth, once I'd got here and moved into Margaret's house, I stopped searching. I wasn't sure if what I might find would make things better or worse. And I was settling here. I was alone, but that was OK because alone I couldn't screw anyone else up. Alone I wasn't a burden. But then you came and changed all that and made me feel like I didn't want to be alone any more. And then we started to make progress and the longer things went on, the less able I was to tell you because I thought you'd hate me for not telling you on the first night. I couldn't stand the thought of you hating me.'

'Ed,' Dodie said gently. 'I could never hate you.'

'I don't think you could hate anyone.'

'Especially not you.'

'I wish I could be like that. I've had so much hate…' He thumped his breast, and then his head. 'In here, and in here. So much anger and so much hopelessness. And I direct it all at the people who deserve it the least. Like my mum. I was so angry that she hadn't told me any of this before.'

'She did it to protect you. She thought it was the right thing to do. She said it and I believe her. You weren't there at the meeting – you didn't see her face when she read that letter; all the years of pain and rejection she'd had to bottle up was plain for anyone to see. She read George's words and it was like she'd had every answer she'd ever wanted. I wish you could have seen it.'

He looked up at her. 'If we'd been in contact I suppose I would have done,' he said, a note of bitterness creeping into his tone. 'I suppose I would have been there with her, supporting her, like a good son should. I bet Trevor was there, wasn't he?'

'Yes, but… what's the deal with you and Trevor? You don't like him?'

'He's OK. It's me who's the problem. Or so he says. But then I guess he's right.'

Dodie appraised Ed silently for a moment. 'He's the reason you took off. It's not just about the adoption and your row with Julia?'

'Not exactly. I suppose he just told me in no uncertain terms what a selfish pain in the arse I was and how much better off Mum would be without me in her life. She had enough to deal with as it was without me adding to that burden, or so he said. And he was right – she is better off without me.'

Part of Dodie had to agree with Trevor if what Ed thought was true. That particular comment made him sound like a maudlin pain in the arse right now, but she smiled patiently. She didn't know what he'd been through and perhaps he just needed time and understanding to work it out. There was no way of knowing whether he'd had that in the past, but Dodie was here now and more than willing to give all she had.

'One thing I'm confused about… your mum says she comes from a place called Cleveleys. But you're from Blackpool.'

'It's only up the road. She moved out where it was quieter when I joined the army but it's just easier for me to tell people Blackpool still; they usually have more of a clue where that is.'

'No wonder I didn't make the connection.'

'Even if you'd known that's an unlikely connection to make, if only because it's so weird and random.'

'It *is* weird,' Dodie acknowledged. 'Apart from the fact the flat came up for rent just when you wanted to get away, that the letter would end up in my possession at the same time is one hell of a coincidence. In fact, if coincidences were monkeys this one would be King Kong.'

He looked up at her. But then he broke into a bemused smile. 'I've just realised that it can get weirder. *If coincidences were monkeys this one would be King Kong*? What does that even mean?'

'I don't know,' Dodie said, breaking into a smile of her own. She joined him at the table, the kettle forgotten again. 'You need to go and see your mum. Talk to her. This is too big for you both to ignore and you should be working it out together. Your mum has already been rejected once by her birth mother, don't make it so she's rejected by her son as well.'

'She doesn't want me or need me in her life – I only complicate things.'

'Of course she does! She misses you like crazy and she needs you now more than ever. Even Trevor said so. Surely it can't be that hard to swallow your pride.' Dodie paused. 'What happened? What started it all off – your mental problems, I mean. Did you kill someone?' she asked quietly. 'In the army, I mean. Did you?'

'Not personally,' he said. 'I…'

'Yes? You can tell me; I won't judge, you know I won't.'

'I know. It's hard. I'm not proud of what I was like when I was discharged. I went home, then my girlfriend left me and I went off the rails. I moped, raged… some days I thought about ending it all. I had no idea Mum had all this pain of her own that she kept hidden every day. If I had…'

'Sometimes it's hard to be the person we want to be. You can talk to me. Why did you want to end it? Because of what you saw? Because of things you did? I can only imagine—'

'There was a landmine,' he cut in. 'I made a stupid mistake. It blew. My mate, Evan… he was closest. Gone. Me… I survived. But it was my fault. It should have been me, not Evan.'

'God…' Dodie grabbed his hand. And then she saw the scar, a deep curve from his thumb to his middle finger.

'It doesn't work that well any more,' he said, his gaze following hers. 'I find it hard to grip stuff. But that's the least of my worries.'

'Did it hurt?'

'It would have done if my leg hadn't been taking my mind off it,' he said with a hollow laugh.

'Your leg?' Dodie's gaze went to the table. His legs were tucked beneath it. 'Is it bad?'

'Bad?' he said, meeting her eyes as they travelled back to his face. 'Not now. It's a bit of a mess but the doctors managed to save it. More than I deserved really.'

'Can I see?' she asked, but instantly blushing. Another case of her mouth moving before her brain had engaged, but now the question was out and all she could do was wait to see how he reacted.

He simply frowned. 'You want to look?'

'It was that bad? I mean, you walk OK.'

'I manage fine; medics did an amazing job. I don't know that you'd want to see it, though.'

'Why not?'

'It freaks people out.'

'It wouldn't freak me out.'

'It freaked Sadie out.'

'Your girlfriend?'

He nodded.

'That's why you split up? Not because she was seeing your best friend behind your back?'

'Oh,' he gave a wry smile, 'she was doing that too.'

'It won't freak me out,' she insisted. 'Considering what you came here to tell me I doubt one more thing can shock me.'

He studied her for a moment. Then he pushed his chair away from the table and rolled up his trousers to expose the map of scars and burnt skin the length of his leg. He looked up at her.

'That's it. Lovely, isn't it?'

'I've seen worse.'

'Liar.'

'But it's not gross. It's part of you, the story of your past. You have to accept it.'

'I'm used to it, but I don't think I'll ever accept it.'

They lapsed into silence. Dodie looked up, into the depths of his eyes, and she saw his pain, how much he needed someone to heal him. She could be that person. But this wasn't the time to say so, and perhaps her need was greater than his, because right now she didn't give a damn about the leg or his family history, all she could think about was kissing him.

The spell was broken as he cleared his throat and rolled his trouser leg down again. 'I felt bloody sorry for myself,' he said. 'Mum did everything she could for me once I was home, but it was never enough. I'm not proud of this, by the way, and I know I was awful. One day Trevor told me they'd had enough and if I didn't buck my ideas up I'd be looking for a place of my own. I don't know how much of that had come from her and how much he'd taken upon himself to say without her knowing.'

'So there was no pin and no map?' Dodie said with a faint smile.

'No.' Ed cleared his throat. 'Sorry about that.'

'That one was a white lie – I suppose I can forgive you that one.'

'Either way, I didn't wait around to get my marching orders; I took off and Bournemouth looked as good a place as any.'

'And then I landed on your doorstep and shattered your peace.'

He gave a slight nod. 'But I'm glad you did. So, Miss Oracle, what should I do now?'

'Right now? Go and see your mum.'

'She might be on her way home.'

'Excuses, excuses. She might not be. And even if she was, what's to stop you going to Blackpool to see her? You still have her phone number?'

'Yes. Unless she's changed it.'

'Even if she has changed her number Sally Chandra will have the new one so we can always get it. Try the one you have first – call her.'

He blinked. 'Now?'

'Why not?'

He hesitated, looked set to argue, but Dodie cut him off.

'Remember all you've just said to me. She's having a tough time right now and hearing your voice will make it a lot easier to bear. She needs you, and this is your chance to make amends.'

He smiled, and this time it was something close to genuine. 'I can hardly argue with such a compelling case.' Pulling his mobile from his jacket pocket, he dialled the number.

Dodie waited, watching his expression waver between anxiety and outright fear. But then she heard a faint voice at the other end of the line.

'Mum,' he said. 'It's Ed. I just wanted to say… I just wanted to say, I'm sorry.'

Dodie hadn't heard most of the phone call; having decided that whatever Ed and Julia needed to talk about was private, she'd left him on the phone in the flat and taken herself down to the shop to open up again. Not that she could concentrate on what was going on in the shop, her head spinning with so many new revelations. In hindsight, the connection should have been obvious and Dodie had missed a huge trail of clues, but that was hardly the point. Ed had followed her down twenty minutes later and asked if she knew where the Sea Spray Hotel was.

'West Cliff, I think,' Dodie said. 'Is that where your mum's staying?'

'She's planning to travel home this evening,' he said. 'I need to go there now.'

Clapping her hands together, Dodie beamed at him. 'She wants to see you? That's brilliant!'

'Can you tell me how to get there?'

'Yes! If it's the one I think it is. Better still I'll drive you – the sat nav will take us.'

'But the shop…'

'Oh bugger the shop,' she said. 'This is far more important and I'm hardly likely to miss a stampede if I'm closed for an hour or two.'

It was a clear indication of his emotional state that he didn't argue. He stood silently as Dodie locked the till and switched off the shop lights before grabbing her coat and securing the front door.

'My car is parked a few streets away,' she said, nodding up the street. 'No spaces here. You're OK to walk to it?'

'You're not going to ask me that every time I need to walk a few yards, are you?' he asked. 'My leg is still there you know, even if it looks like shit.'

'Oh, no… I didn't even mean your leg…' She blushed. 'I'm so sorry, I—'

'No,' he cut in. 'No, please. *I'm* sorry. Of course you didn't mean my leg. I know I have to stop doing that.'

Dodie was about to reply when her foot connected with a box on the floor by the doorway, almost sending her flying across the pavement. She frowned, bending down to open the loosely fastened flaps. 'Oh.'

'What's that?' Ed peered over her shoulder. 'Has someone left it for the shop? I didn't think it worked like that.'

'My things,' Dodie said, a hard edge to her voice as she rifled through a jumble of hairbrushes, lipsticks, clothes, straightening irons and CDs. 'Ryan must have left them here while the shop was closed. Either that or he didn't want to come in and face me.'

'Ryan? Your boyfriend?'

'Ex,' Dodie said briskly. 'This is all the stuff I had at his house. I suppose I should be thankful he didn't just throw it in the bin.'

'You've split up?' Ed asked, following as Dodie started to walk. 'Where are you taking that?'

'I might as well put it in the car for now, save unlocking the shop again. Besides, we need to get you to your mum's hotel and this can wait.'

'Let me carry it,' he said, taking the box from her. Dodie didn't argue. 'Do you want to talk about it?' he added.

'There's honestly nothing to say,' Dodie replied, eyes fixed straight on the pavement ahead. It was easier than giving him any sort of clue of the tumult of her emotions right now. There were far more important things they needed to worry about than Ryan's actions; Dodie could mull those over later but now they needed to get Ed reunited with his mother. If only one good thing came out of this whole business, Dodie was determined that it should be this. She shook her head. 'We'd been on the way to this moment for a long time. If anything, it's a relief.'

There was a significant pause. Then: 'So you don't still have feelings for him…?'

Dodie turned to see that Ed was looking straight ahead too, her box hugged to his chest as he walked.

'I feel bad about the way it ended, and at first I thought I would miss him but… no, I don't have *that* sort of feeling for him any more. I'm not sure I ever really did. He's clearly OK with it too, as he's brought my stuff back.'

'He could have brought it back to make a point – not to signal that it was over but in the hope that seeing it will make you change your mind…'

'Undoubtedly, knowing Ryan.'

'Because he's hurting?'

'I don't doubt he thinks that too. But I know him – in a few weeks he'll see that this was never going to work and I think he'll realise it was a good thing after all.'

Ed offered no reply and Dodie quickened her steps to keep pace with his long strides. But then he spoke again. '*You* don't feel it was a mistake then?'

'No.'

Dodie waited for more to come, but would he ask it? There was unfinished business between them, and now they'd broached the subject of her split with Ryan she wondered if it was on Ed's mind, as it was on hers, that she was free, and that she knew he *had* been interested. Perhaps not now, however, and so she could have asked but it didn't seem like the right thing to do; it might create new awkwardness just when they'd finally managed to get over the old one. And perhaps not when she considered that he had far bigger thoughts to occupy him today, like having a whole new branch of his family to discover and that he was about to see his estranged mother for the first time in six months. Inwardly, Dodie chided herself. She needed to stay on point, at least for now, and she could mope and overanalyse later when all this was over.

'Here we are,' she said, pointing to a cherry-red car, tucked untidily in the corner of an alleyway.

'The 1975 Beetle?' he asked. And to her surprise, he broke into a chuckle. 'I might have known you'd have an old VW!'

'I don't need anything fancy,' she said, a defensive note creeping into her tone. 'And I happen to like it.'

'I'm not insulting it; I like it too,' he replied, smiling down at her. 'It's so very you. So absolutely, perfectly, wonderfully you.'

She threw him a sideways look as she dug in her handbag for her keys. 'What, small and scruffy?'

'Cute and feisty. With more power than would first appear. Strong and dependable. One of a kind. Want me to go on?'

She bit back a grin as she unlocked the car and opened the map function on her phone. 'Pop the box on the back seat for me, would you? Sea Spray Hotel you said?'

He nodded as he reached in and deposited her belongings.

'Got it,' she said, studying her phone. 'Just where I thought it was. Shouldn't take us longer than ten minutes to get there.'

She climbed in the driver's seat and started the engine as he got in the other side. It was hard not to laugh as she noted how close his head was to the ceiling.

'Sorry it's a bit cramped,' she said. 'Size was never an issue with Ryan.'

'Lucky Ryan,' he mumbled, folding his legs beneath the seat, and Dodie's smile burst free.

'You're OK?' she asked. 'I'm sorry but I think the seat might be as far back as it can go so we're all out of leg room.'

'Apart from feeling like a contortionist, yes I'm OK, thanks.'

Dodie pulled away from the kerb, emerging from the alleyway before swinging the car in the road to do a U-turn in the direction of the cliffs.

'Julia does know you're coming, doesn't she?'

'Yes,' he said, and she noted with a glance that any humour he'd just displayed had evaporated again. His anxious gaze was trained on the thin ribbon of grey sea on the horizon, hands restless in his lap.

'Good. I suppose you've got a lot to discuss. It's a shame she's got to go home tonight. It's Christmas Eve… maybe you'll go with her? Spend Christmas Day with her?'

'I don't know yet. She might not want that. And I said I'd feed Albert's cat for him while he went to visit family in Hong Kong.'

Dodie could tell an excuse when she heard one, but she let it slide. 'I could feed Albert's cat if you wanted to go,' she offered.

'I know you'd do it in a heartbeat – that's you all over – but I said I would. I can always go to see Mum over New Year and it might be better; give us both time to think about stuff before we spend any proper time together.'

'Is that how you feel about it? As if it might be awkward today, something you might need time away from? I don't think she's going to reject you if that's what's scaring you—'

'No,' he cut in quickly, 'I know she wouldn't do that. It's just… there's a lot to take in. A lot to discuss. I don't even know where to start. I imagine Mum will be feeling the same. And I didn't exactly behave like a good son before…'

'You'll be fine.' She reached out to give his arm a brief pat before returning her hand to the wheel and setting her gaze on the road again. 'From what I can tell, she'll be thrilled to see you again.'

They were silent for a moment as Dodie navigated some of the narrower side roads that wound down towards the coast. She could only imagine how he must be feeling right now, the uncertainty, the overwhelming guilt. What he'd been through over the past year or more was probably more than anyone should be expected to bear, and all she could offer were meaningless words of comfort to let him know that he had a friend. She wished she could do more.

'I would have walked you home that night,' he said suddenly.

Dodie frowned. 'What night?'

'The night we went for chips.'

She gave a slight smile. 'You mean the night *I* had chips. You bailed on me, remember?'

'Yeah. I'm sorry I didn't walk you home.'

'It doesn't matter; I didn't need walking home. I had my deadly hairspray to keep me safe from muggers.'

'But it does. It was just me being an arse. I've been an arse quite a lot lately. But that night it was just... well, I...'

Dodie could almost see the words hanging on the air, and she wanted to pluck them out and give them to him to speak. But he just exhaled in defeat.

'Never mind,' he said. 'Ignore anything I say today because I'll sound like an idiot.'

She didn't push him for an explanation because she'd guessed part of what had driven him away that night. Maybe she didn't need those words that had dissipated on his breath because the things he'd said to her on the beach a week later had told her what she needed to know. The bigger question for her was: did he still feel the same way or had she blown it? She'd behaved pretty idiotically herself, now that she thought about it and she'd certainly made a hash on the relationship front with him *and* Ryan.

'It's OK,' she said. 'I understand.'

He was silent again for a moment. But then lurched into a different subject. 'I was supposed to have counselling, you know.'

'You told me that once, I think. You still haven't sorted it?'

'Not since I came to Bournemouth. I kept thinking I should but I couldn't bring myself to admit I needed it; it felt like a weakness, you know? And then I met you and it made me think about it again.'

'I'm glad to hear I make people feel they need counselling,' she retorted.

'You don't,' he said, offering a weak smile. 'I just meant I felt it would make me a better person, more whole. More like you.'

'Being like me is easy – simply dye your hair red and divorce yourself from reality.'

'That's just it. You don't realise just how you embrace and deal with reality in a way that's far better and kinder than anyone else I know. You cling onto your values in the face of reality and that's rare.'

Dodie fought another blush. 'That's not how it is at all. Anyway, will you get your counselling now? It might help rebuild things with your mum.'

'I should, but it's weird; I don't feel like I need it now.'

She nodded. 'You *do* seem better to me, actually. Since I've known you I can see a change.'

He turned to her. 'Dodie… how do you be the way you are?'

'I have no idea!' she laughed. 'How does anyone be the way they are? They just are!'

'It amazes me,' he said. 'How you can see the good in everyone, and how you're always so optimistic and so kind, even to people who are arses with you. You always want to do the right thing even when it puts you out. Like now, helping me when you should have told me to go and die in a hole.'

'Why on earth would I do that? What's the point in treating people so horribly? Life is complicated and everyone has their reasons for the way they behave. Usually, if you give someone a chance, you'll see it for yourself and then you can understand it better. Obviously, there are people who are just horrible and they're beyond saving, but I find it's not as many as you might think.'

'I wish I could say that's been my experience, but it hasn't.'

Ahead a pristine white villa rose up, surrounded by verdant lawns and rows of winter-wrapped palm trees, the cliffs beyond dropping sheer to the beach below.

'I think this is it,' Dodie said, swinging into the car park. 'Your mum's hotel.'

'It's nice,' he said, gazing out of the window as Dodie pulled on the handbrake and killed the engine.

'I'll bet it's not cheap,' Dodie said, peering up through the windscreen. A row of flags fluttered on poles at the entrance, elaborate black ironwork on every balcony in stark and beautiful contrast to the gleaming white stone of the building. It looked impressive now, in the depths of winter, but in the summer you could be forgiven for thinking you were in a chic suburb of Southern France. 'Take me a month of Sundays and a lot of Crimplene dress sales to afford a week here.'

'She deserves a treat every now and again; I'm glad Trevor's putting his hand in his pocket for her. I know he's got a bit put aside but I never saw much evidence of them spending it.'

'Perhaps they couldn't think of a good enough reason until now.'

'Maybe.' His expectant gaze met hers and it seemed she was meant to say something else. But what?

'Good luck, then,' she offered, not knowing what else to give him. She forced a bright smile. What did she do now? Hug him? Shake hands? Their connection had deepened fundamentally during the last few hours, and yet she was more uncertain of him than ever.

His gaze went back to the hotel – thoughtful, introspective. Was he thinking of turning around and leaving again? Running away as he had done before? He turned back to face her, and she saw that same uncertainty in his eyes. 'I don't know what to say to her.'

'You've already spoken on the phone,' she said with an encouraging smile that had to look more certain than it felt. If she had been in his position now, she would have been running for the hills. But she couldn't let him know how she felt because this mattered more than anything that had gone before – more than George's letter or Margaret's actions, more than their confused friendship, more than the promise of his new family. Getting his mother back in his life was the first step to healing, Dodie was sure of that much, and she had to help him do that.

'I know,' he said, 'but that feels different. I can't explain it.' He let out a deep sigh. 'This is ridiculous – nervous about seeing my own mum.'

'A lot's happened. You'll be fine; I know it. Julia will be happy to see you.'

'You should come with me,' he said suddenly.

Dodie stared at him. 'Me?'

'You found the letter. If not for you we wouldn't be talking at all, let alone finding new family. You should come and see her with me.'

'Do they even know about me? I mean, do they even know that I know you?'

'Of course – I told her all about it on the phone. She'll want to see you because you were the one who made all this possible.'

'I hardly think that's true—'

'It is! Come up with me.'

'Ed…' she began slowly, 'this is about you and Julia. It's not a situation for strangers…'

'But you're not a stranger, you're…' He stopped, stared up at the gleaming façade of the hotel. 'You're my friend,' he said. 'At least I hope so.'

She smiled. 'I've always been that, even when you ditched me at the chip shop.'

'OK, don't make me feel any worse about that. But I could do with a friend right now… Please come up to the room with me. Just for a short while.'

She let out a breath and nodded. She was never going to say no anyway – how could she when he'd laid his soul bare, confided in her just how much he needed her support?

'I'll come up but only for ten minutes and then you need to talk things through properly, mother to son, and that means family only.'

'I know. But this is the hardest bit – just seeing her again for the first time. So thank you.'

As they walked across to the entrance, Dodie felt his hand brush against hers. She closed her eyes, his touch doing things to her she shouldn't be thinking of right now. At that moment, she realised they would never be friends, not for her, not in the way he'd talked about, because other feelings would get in the way. For now, she would do her best to be there for him, but afterwards there would need to be distance if there wasn't to be anything else. He was screwed up already, that much was certain, she'd only just split from Ryan, and a complicated relationship probably wasn't what either of them needed right now.

Julia had given Ed the room number and nobody at the hotel reception seemed concerned at the two people just walking through to the lifts. They travelled up to the third floor in silence, Dodie shooting an encouraging smile whenever he looked up from the plush red carpet of the lift interior. She could only imagine what it would be like to face this situation with her own parents but, with all that he'd been through before, she guessed he was finding it tough. Her biggest worry was only ever her gran's latest nutty scheme. For Ed and Julia there would be a lot of soul-searching, recriminations, guilt, apologies, recalibrating of their relationship, and that would take patience and time. But from what Dodie knew of both Julia and Ed now, she felt sure they would get there. The main thing was they both wanted to make things good between them again. That had to count for something.

Trevor answered Ed's knock on the door of their suite, momentarily thrown by the sight of Dodie standing alongside him, but then giving her a stiff smile before turning to Ed and offering his hand.

'Good to see you,' he said warmly. 'Your mum's so happy you've decided to come.'

Dodie hovered awkwardly at the doorway as Trevor beckoned Ed in.

'I should let you all get on,' she said, backing away into the corridor. 'I just came to give Ed a lift…'

Ed turned back. 'Just say hello to Mum. You promised me ten minutes.'

Before she could reply, Julia appeared from a side room. With an exclamation of joy she grabbed Ed and pulled him into a hug.

'My boy!' she cried. 'I've missed you so much!'

She began to weep, her head buried in his shoulder, and Dodie wiped away a sudden tear of her own as she saw Ed bow his head, arms wrapped around Julia's delicate frame, his own eyes misted.

'I'm sorry,' he said. 'I'm sorry for everything.'

Julia looked up at him. 'It doesn't matter. You're here now, that's all I want. You've no idea how much I've worried about you.'

'I didn't mean for that to happen,' he sniffed, dragging a thumb beneath his eyes. 'I thought you'd be better off without me. I know it was wrong and I'm sorry for all the pain I've caused you.'

Dodie glanced at Trevor as she fished in her handbag for a tissue, and even he seemed moved by the scene, staring very deliberately at the window as if trying to hold his own tears at bay. On the way up, Dodie had wondered whether she ought to be here to witness such an intense and private moment, but now she felt that it was just so beautiful, so life-affirming, that she would simply be grateful to carry the memory of it to her grave. They had a long way to go, but they had love, and there was no better starting point than that.

Ed turned, his arm around Julia's shoulder, and smiled at Dodie. 'Mum, Dodie… I think you two have already met.'

'Yes.' Julia laughed through her tears. 'Yes, we have met.'

'In the weirdest plot twist ever,' Dodie added.

'The more I think about it, the more amazing it is to me,' Julia agreed. 'Of all the places Ed could have wound up he's here, where the story began with my birth mother, living in the same street she lived in—'

'The same house,' Ed cut in.

'Yes,' Julia smiled. 'The same house. And then Dodie found the letter and met you. You found me again, without even meaning to. It makes me wonder… It's as if my mother's up there, finally reunited with my dad, and she looked down on the mess we were in and wanted to put everything right, to make up for the years she never knew us. And so she sent you to live in that street, and she made the letter end up in the hands of someone who would care about it, and she helped bring us all together.'

'But none of it would have been possible if not for Dodie,' Ed added. 'Most people would have thrown that letter away.'

Julia walked to Dodie, arms outstretched, and Dodie knew that her last bastion of control would disappear. In Julia's embrace, she began to cry, and Julia began to cry again too, and when she looked around Ed was wiping his eyes and Trevor was like a statue, staring at the window as if he was Superman trying to laser it.

'Thank you,' Julia said, kissing Dodie's cheek. 'Thank you so much for everything.'

'I didn't do anything apart from be curious,' Dodie excused. 'There's no need to thank me. I'm just glad to see you together again.' Wiping her eyes, she made a show of checking her watch. 'God, I really should go and get the shop open again,' she said. 'And I'm sure you have lots to discuss. You'll be OK to get back from here?' she asked, looking at Ed.

'We can run him wherever he needs to be,' Trevor said. 'Don't you worry about anything – you've done enough.'

'Right then.' Dodie turned to Julia. 'It was wonderful to meet you, and I hope you find your family. That is, if you want to.'

'Thank you,' Julia said.

Dodie looked uncertainly at Ed. 'I guess I'll see you around?'

'You can count on it,' he said. Dodie smiled stiffly, still not sure that was such a good idea. But dealing with it would wait.

Trevor followed her to the door. 'Thank you, lass,' he said in a low voice. 'You're an angel, one of a kind.'

With a short nod, Dodie hurried from the room before she started to cry again.

Seventeen

What looked like a mother and her teenage daughter were staring up at the closed sign as Dodie arrived back at Forget-Me-Not Vintage. As they turned to walk away, Dodie called them back.

'Sorry… Just about to open now if you wanted to come in!' she panted, racing over with her keys.

They retraced their steps as she opened the door with a tight smile, switching the sign to open before letting them in and flicking the lights on as the door closed with a clatter behind them. As the customers perused the rails, Dodie set about opening the till, switching on the radio and generally making the shop welcoming again. Puffy-eyed and red-nosed, standing behind the counter was the last thing she needed, but there was nobody else to do it and she'd lost enough business for one day. The only thing to do now was put the morning's events firmly out of her mind and get back to making a living.

'Can I try this on?' the girl asked, holding up a corduroy pinafore dress.

'Of course… changing room is just there behind that curtain. Shout if you need anything.'

The girl disappeared into the cubicle while her mother stood in front of the curtain like a sentry guarding a queen. Dodie turned her attention to wiping a duster over the counter and came across the copy of the *Echo* she'd stashed there that morning. Had it really only been that day she'd seen Sally's coverage of Julia's story for the first time? Was it really only that morning that Ed had raced in with his earth-shattering revelation? It felt like a lot longer, and even though it was only just lunchtime, Dodie was exhausted. She opened the pages and read the story again. They'd all been shocked by the coincidence, but the more she thought about it, the more she felt Julia might have been on to something when she'd said Margaret herself could have had a hand in it. Crazy, of course, to think that such a thing could have been influenced by a dead woman, but there was no denying that the likelihood of them all meeting in the way they had was infinitesimal in the scheme of things. Ed had got himself to Wessex Road in the first instance, of course, but the rest had all just fallen into place. It seemed fated, as if some higher power was at work. If so, the bigger question wasn't how, but why? Gran would have had an opinion on it, no doubt, and she'd be fascinated to hear the story. Dodie made a mental note to call her later, wish her a merry Christmas and tell her all about it. She also decided that perhaps she ought to come clean about Ryan. He wasn't coming back and there was no point in keeping it to herself any longer.

As she continued to read, and her gaze went to the photo of Julia, her thoughts wandered. What was happening at the hotel now? Were they still getting along? Were they coming to a new understanding about their relationship and how the world worked? Every question fired up a new one, like a chain of burning fuses. She wanted to phone Ed to find out but resisted the temptation. They were probably still deep in conversation and perhaps it was better to leave things alone for now. They'd tell her eventually – at least she hoped someone would.

There was a call from the changing cubicle.

'Mum… can you ask if she has this in a bigger size?'

Dodie tried to resist rolling her eyes. If she'd had a pound for every time she'd had to explain that a stock consisting entirely of vintage clothes meant that it was highly likely there would be just one of everything, and that it was kind of the point of shopping there, she could close the shop for a week and take off to Barbados. OK, maybe not Barbados, but possibly Weymouth.

'Sorry, there's just that one,' she replied, smiling at the girl's mother. 'But I think there's something quite similar in a slightly bigger size on the rail…' Wandering over, she pulled out another pinafore dress – this one in a heavy wool with a pinstripe design – and handed it to her. 'Not exactly the same but worth a try? It's a similar cut and it would look lovely with opaque tights.'

The woman nodded gratefully and passed it through a gap in the curtains to her daughter.

'I'll leave you to it,' Dodie said, going back to the counter to continue her dusting. It wasn't until the girl and her mother were standing before her holding the bigger dress that she realised she'd been staring out of the window for at least ten minutes.

'We'll take this one,' the mother said, laying it on the counter while she fished in her handbag for her purse.

'It's very cute, this one,' Dodie said, folding it into a carrier bag after making a note in her book of the item number. 'And you can always keep checking to see if something more like the first one arrives in – I get lots of stock all the time.'

'You have a cool shop,' the girl said. 'My friends would love it here.'

Dodie smiled. 'Please don't be shy about bringing them in. I'm always happy to let you mooch as often and as long as you want and I won't stand over you; I don't believe in the hard sell.'

'Oh, I hate that,' the mother agreed as she opened her purse. 'The first thing I do in a shop like that is walk right out again. We're perfectly capable of calling for your attention if we need it and hovering over us just makes us feel like shoplifters or something.'

'I don't like it either, which is why I don't do it,' Dodie said, handing the carrier bag to the girl.

'Thanks.'

'Thank *you*!' Dodie smiled. 'I hope to see you again.'

The girl's mother took her change. 'Merry Christmas!'

'And you too,' Dodie said, waving them from the store. Checking her watch, she noted that she'd completely missed lunch. Not that she was all that hungry.

Deciding it was a sensible idea to continue working through lunch because she'd been closed for a good part of that morning, Dodie made herself a quick cup of tea and pulled out her stock ledgers. But her thoughts kept returning to families and the strange events of the past few weeks, and then it suddenly struck her that today she ought to have been at a wedding. Gran's brief and doomed match to Bernard whatever-his-name-was should have seen them tying the knot today. If it had ever been a thing at all, and with Gran there was no way of knowing. In many ways her gran was a complete loon and she drove Dodie mad, but there was no doubting how her heart swelled with love for the family nutjob. A life without Gran in it, a childhood bereft of her eccentric, bohemian sense of fun, her warm laughter, her kind words and even kinder deeds… it was unimaginable. And yet, though Ed had his adopted grandmother, he'd missed out on what Dodie took for granted – knowing where he came from and loving the people who made him. She wondered whether it felt different for him, whether he saw his adopted family in the same way. Did it change you? Or did he cling onto the knowledge that the people who had really made him were the ones who'd brought him up, determined not to forget or forsake them?

She shook herself, endeavouring to concentrate on her books. Gran wasn't getting married today and at least that was one less thing to worry about.

The afternoon dragged. Dodie watched the street outside the window as people hurried to and fro with gift bags or arms full of food and drink. It was still trying and failing to snow and Dodie, ever a white Christmas enthusiast, hoped for just that tomorrow, despite the weather reports saying otherwise. Even a sprinkling would do, though if it could wait until she'd done her charity dip in the morning and was back in warm clothes that would be perfect. Part of her wished she could be out on the streets now, soaking up the atmosphere, maybe stopping for a mulled wine at the markets to take off the chill, bags of carefully chosen gifts hanging at her sides. Time for Christmas gift shopping had been a luxury. She'd managed it all at the last minute and not with the consideration she wished she could have given it. An amber-inlaid pendant for Isla that she now wouldn't be able to give her until she got home, a beautiful dress brooch shaped like a sunburst that had come into her shop for Gran, along with a hamper of tea, biscuits and preserves from Waitrose. For her mum, new driving gloves and some of her favourite perfume and various bits and pieces for other family members that represented more money than she could probably afford.

There had been a grand total of five customers that afternoon and only three had resulted in sales. Dodie was philosophical about it – she'd been ready for a quiet day in the knowledge that everyone would be getting ready for Christmas and vintage clothes shopping was really the sort of thing you did for yourself. She was looking forward to a quiet night on her own – Christmas carols on the radio, maybe a walk into town to see what was going on, tracking Nick down to wish him a happy Christmas… As the clock eventually crawled around to five, Dodie switched off the radio, ready to shut up shop. But then she spun around at the sound of the doorbell tinkling. She opened her mouth to tell them she was closing, but then stopped. From behind an enormous bouquet of red and gold seasonal flowers peeked Ed.

'Mum asked me to bring these,' he said. 'And of course, they're from me too,' he added quickly.

'That's so thoughtful!' Dodie hurried across to take them from him, burying her nose into their rich scent. 'They're gorgeous! I can't remember the last time I got a bunch of flowers this enormous and beautiful.'

Ed shrugged, almost apologetically. 'I'm glad you like them. It's not much but we wanted to say thank you… Properly, you know?'

'You've already thanked me a million times and I hardly did anything but be nosey,' she laughed. 'But I love them. I'll be locking up in a minute… Do you have time to stay for a while?'

'Why not? I've got nowhere else to be right now.'

Dodie walked back to the counter with the bouquet. 'You're not going back to the hotel to see your mum before she leaves for home?'

'She's tired and I think it will do her and Trevor good to talk about everything without me there. They've decided they're not travelling back now until after Christmas, and she wants me to go home to Blackpool with them when they do, but I can see on his face that he's not so keen and he's just trying to make her happy. We're seeing eye to eye at the moment, me and Trevor, but I don't think he trusts me not to hurt her again just yet. I sort of understand that and I'm glad he's looking out for her, although I suppose other people would see it as weird that I agree with him. I *was* a pain in the arse, though, and I'd probably have done the same if things had been the other way around. It's something they need to sort out and I should let them talk freely about it.'

'That's all very fine and noble but what do *you* want to do?' Dodie laid the flowers carefully down before she took her keys from a drawer under the counter and went to lock the shop door. 'You need to think about that too, or you run the risk of ruining what you've built again. There's nothing like a little resentment to kill a relationship, and if you go home just to please her and it's not what you really want that might happen.'

'Honestly?' Ed scratched his head. 'I don't know. It depends…'

Dodie turned to him. 'On what?'

He shrugged. 'I don't know about that yet either.'

'You're being very cryptic.'

'I know… sorry about that. It's just…' He took a deep breath, plunging his hands into his pockets. 'I should go, let you get on. I've taken up enough of your time today. In fact, I've taken up enough of your time full stop; you must be sick of the sight of me.'

'Of course not,' she said, and she wanted to ask him to stay, but she couldn't find the words. Perhaps their moment had been and gone and it was already too late. Perhaps she'd damaged his fragile heart beyond repair when she'd spurned him at the beach that time. Maybe second chances weren't a thing he gave readily. He'd called her his friend and perhaps that was all she was now. She forced a smile. 'You know you're welcome any time you want to talk. Don't think you have to endure everything alone.'

'Thank you.'

'So you'll be having dinner with your mum tomorrow?'

'It's Christmas Day and we've got a lot to celebrate, so I think so. Unless she changes her mind. I'm sure you'd be welcome to join us. But I suppose you've already got plans.'

'Sort of. I'll be with my parents and my gran.'

'Right.'

'And in the morning I have this daft charity sea-dip thing on the beach,' she added, not even sure why she was telling him this. She only knew there were gaps, huge gaping holes that were supposed to be full of the things they needed to say but weren't, and she had to fill them with something. It didn't seem to matter what any more. 'Gran says I'm mental but it's actually good fun.'

He'd just opened his mouth to answer when the shop phone rang.

'You want to get that?' he asked.

'We're supposed to be closed but—'

'It might be important… Don't ignore it on my account.'

Dodie nodded and went over to pick up the call.

'Gran? Why have you called me on this phone?'

'You weren't answering your other one,' Gran said. 'And you told me to phone if they wanted help at the homeless shelter.'

'Oh, so I did,' Dodie replied absently, her eyes following Ed as he went to the window and looked out at the street.

'They'd be thrilled to get more help tonight,' Gran continued. 'Can you get here for seven? And would you mind picking me up if you're coming this way anyway?'

She hesitated. Ed looked around and gave a brief smile before turning back to the window again. What was the point of sitting alone and dwelling on what could have been? The letter was back with its rightful owners and Julia had been reunited with her son. All in all it was a good result and to expect anything else was plain greedy. She'd got nothing else to do so why not make herself useful?

'Yes,' she said finally. 'I can help and I'll come and get you on the way through.'

Eighteen

Spirits were high at the shelter. Dodie had helped out a couple of times before but she'd never seen it this full or this rowdy. Groups were sitting around tables eating good, wholesome dinners, playing cards and drinking coffee, or deep in conversation with old friends. Christmas songs played on an old radio, a threadbare plastic tree was strewn with faded tinsel and paper chains stretched the lengths of the walls. No sign of Nick, though, and as Dodie stood behind the hot plate wearing a far-from-fetching apron and cap she wondered where he was. His usual excuses, she supposed, though even if he didn't spend the night she had wondered if he'd celebrate Christmas Eve by having a hot meal there. She glanced down at the hot plate and gave some of the sauces a stir to stop them congealing. There was a choice of peri-peri chicken, curry and rice, fish pie or an early Christmas lunch for those who wanted it, all cooked by volunteers with as much love and care as any top chef at any restaurant. At any other time the smells under her nose would have driven her mad considering the long and hectic day she'd had with little time to do more than snack. But though she tried to stay cheerful for the sake of everyone around her, her low appetite was the real giveaway of her actual mood.

'Francesco says you can help yourself if you're hungry,' Gran said, tottering past with an armful of dirty dishes.

'Maybe later,' Dodie said with a vacant smile. She shook herself. 'Hey, what are you doing with all that? Let me take some.' Without waiting for a reply she grabbed the top plates and followed her gran to the pot wash.

'Are you alright, love?' Gran said as they loaded the crockery into the washer.

'Of course.'

'Only you don't seem quite yourself. Fallen out with Brian?'

Dodie sighed. 'We've split up.'

'Well, I expect you can fix it again.'

'No we can't. It's not a spat. We've split up. For good. That's it, no more Ryan.'

'What happened?'

'I happened. I'm an idiot, Gran…' Tears squeezed her throat, unexpected and unwanted. Damn it, why did she have to react this way at the most inconvenient times? She swallowed them back. If her love life was a mess she had only herself to blame.

'I'm sorry,' Gran said. 'You must be so sad. And at Christmas too. You'll find yourself another nice man in no time.' She reached up and stroked Dodie's hair behind an ear with a fond smile. 'Sweet little thing like you won't be on your own for long so don't worry.'

How could Dodie tell her gran that it wasn't about being alone? How could she tell her she wasn't crying for Ryan because she knew now that they'd never really been in love? How could she tell her she was crying for what might have been because, no matter what everyone said about her supposed goodness and wisdom, she'd got it so woefully wrong with the man who might just have been the real thing – actual true love?

'I don't care about that,' Dodie said, forcing a bright smile. 'I don't need a bloke because I have enough to keep me busy as it is.'

'That's the spirit,' Gran said, patting her hand. 'Right, I'd better get the rest of those tables cleared or we'll be here until midnight.'

Dodie nodded and as Gran went back to the common room she pulled her mobile phone from her pocket. Not a single message from anyone. As she took her place behind the hot plate again, she looked up to see Nick coming in, greetings from all directions as he walked through the common room. As he set eyes on Dodie he broke into a broad grin.

'Merry Christmas to me! What are you doing here?'

Dodie shrugged. 'My gran was helping out so I thought I'd come along.'

'Well it's made my night.'

'I wondered if I'd see you here this evening. What are you having?'

He planted a hand to his chest. 'Please… it's got to be turkey, right? Today of all days it's got to be a lovely bit of turkey.'

Dodie smiled. 'I suppose it has.'

'So I saw your fella yesterday,' Nick said as Dodie scooped some mash onto his plate.

'Who?'

'Blimey, how many you got? That Ed fella.'

'Oh, he's not mine. We're just friends.'

'Sorry, I forgot. You've got that other one, haven't you? Sour-looking youth.'

'Ryan.' Despite the melancholy and the mention of a painful subject, she couldn't help but chuckle at Nick's description of her ex. 'I suppose he had his moments. We're not together any more either.'

'Footloose and fancy free, eh?' He tilted his head around to the dining room and called out, 'Form an orderly queue – she's available!'

Dodie turned puce as the room erupted into laughter. Gran smiled across from where she was stacking plates, though Dodie didn't think she'd quite caught the joke.

'Only joking, sweetheart,' he said. 'Any of these renegades try anything I'll knock them out.'

'Oh God, don't do that on my account!' Dodie squeaked. 'I'm sure it won't come to that!'

'Just saying,' Nick added, rolling his shoulders like an East End boxer. 'So you and Ed… you're an item now?'

'No. Why do you ask?'

'No reason. Just asking. Cos if you were it couldn't happen to two nicer people. You like him?'

'He's pretty busy at the moment so I doubt he's interested in romance. And like I said, we're just friends.'

'He can't be that busy; he was asking me about volunteering here. And I see him around town now almost as much as I see you. Always gives me a handful of change or gets me a cup of tea. Top bloke.'

'Ed?' Dodie blinked. The surprises just kept coming. She'd imagined him holed up in his flat feeling sorry for himself night after night, and that was how he made his life sound. But all the while he'd obviously been making an effort to reach out to Nick and help him. Had he been doing more than that, modesty dictating that he kept it to himself? Nick had already told her about one time Ed had given him money, but it sounded as though it was happening regularly. There had been many strange coincidences over the past few weeks but Ed running into Nick by accident so often definitely wasn't one of them. He had to be seeking him out with the intention of helping him, and the thought squeezed Dodie's heart just that little bit tighter. He'd made mistakes and he'd told some lies, but underneath it all he was a good man. The sort of man who could make Dodie very happy.

'He'd be good in here,' Nick said. 'Ex-army, he tells me. Straight down the line, no bullshit, capable of a bit of banter and looks like he can handle himself.'

'I suppose he would,' Dodie said. She handed Nick his dinner and he nodded his thanks.

'You're one of the good ones, you know that.'

'I don't know about that,' Dodie said with a small smile. 'We're all just getting by the best way we know how, aren't we? Sometimes we do the right thing, and sometimes we mess it up, but the important thing is we keep trying.'

On Christmas morning she'd woken at seven, though the alarm still had half an hour to go. Opening her curtains, she looked across the strangely silent street to see two magpies perched on the opposite roof engaged in a rowdy exchange. *Two for joy*, she mused, and with a shake of her head and a wry smile went through to put the kettle on.

After opening a box of special Christmas tea she'd treated herself to when she'd bought Gran's hamper, Dodie sat at the table with her mug, fragrant with the warm scents of cinnamon and star anise, and stared, yawning, at the kitchen wall. It didn't feel like Christmas, but perhaps that was because she was tired. Her thoughts kept going back to the previous day. It was no wonder she was tired when she considered just how much had happened, and that was without her evening shift at the shelter. She wondered what Ed was doing now. She hoped he was getting ready for a day with his mum – they had a lot of ground to cover to fix their relationship but she was certain that they'd be OK.

Breakfast was her usual of toast and jam – she didn't see the point in overdoing it when she was going to be throwing herself into the sea in a couple of hours and later on she'd be eating enough for three people anyway. She savoured the peace and quiet for a while – the time to collect her thoughts. There would be enough excitement and noise later too.

As she washed up the breakfast dishes, the radio on the kitchen shelf played the early morning Christmas church service, the pure voices of the choristers singing carols giving her a contented smile as she worked.

Despite the fact she'd only be ruining it all in a matter of hours as she splashed around with hundreds of other mad people on the beach, she took half an hour to fix her make-up and hair. Her outfit was a strange, stiff felt Christmas tree dress that did nothing for her figure, but then, what did it matter?

By 8.30 a.m. she was dressed and ready, drumming on the kitchen table as the local radio began its broadcast of more contemporary music and Wizzard expressed their earnest desire that it should be Christmas every day. A silly notion by anyone's standards, but something felt different about this Christmas already. Maybe she'd have a different opinion on the matter by the end of it.

While she waited she wished that she'd been able to sleep in a little later but her racing brain had seen to that. But now she had time to kill and it was driving her mad waiting to go out. There was no point in starting any little jobs and no point in waiting around at the beach unless she wanted to stand around in sub-zero temperatures dressed in a felt Christmas tree. Probably not her best idea. But the longer she sat around in her flat with time to think, the more she decided it wasn't a good thing. More times than she could count she'd been so tempted to phone Ed. To say what? *Merry Christmas, how's it going with your mum? By the way I think I love you and I wondered if we might rerun that scene on the beach where you ask if you can kiss me, only this time I'll say yes and I'll snog your face right off.* Would he thank her for dropping such a bombshell? Didn't he have enough to deal with already without her complicating things? Maybe she would make that call one day, but today wasn't it, no matter how much she wanted to.

With a sigh, she looked up at the clock. It would be freezing down on the beach but at least there'd be plenty of people around to take her mind off silly notions. Grabbing her keys and her kitbag, she headed for the door.

The skies were a thick, heavy blanket of white cloud that stretched out to sea. On the horizon it was hard to see where the ocean ended and the sky began. But the waves were tame, gentle white-topped rollers ambling in and out, which had to be better than the churning conditions Dodie had endured the year before when she'd done the Christmas Dip with Isla.

She pulled into a parking space overlooking the sands. The beach along here was quieter than the main Bournemouth beach and it was easier to park close, particularly today and particularly as the event organisers seemed to have made provisions for it. It would save Dodie walking through the town looking like a mad Christmas junkie. There might not have been many people wandering the streets at this time on a Christmas morning, but even one person seeing this was one too many.

The weather app on her phone had predicted snow, and while Dodie was the biggest white Christmas fan this side of Dorset, even she was hoping it would hold off for a little while. The sea would be cold enough without snow as well.

She'd barely walked twenty yards from the car but already she was feeling the chill beneath her flimsy costume. There hadn't been much point in wearing lots of layers to get wet and heavy, though, so she'd stashed her bag containing a woolly jumper, fluffy socks and leggings in the boot for when the dip had finished so she could drive home warm and dry.

Dodie turned her attention to the crowds on the beach as she reached the railings that separated the sand from the pavement that ran along its length. It was flanked by pastel beach huts and seaside shops, people with pushchairs, prams, wheelchairs and bikes standing aside to watch the action on the beach.

It looked like a good turnout already; there must have been 700, maybe 800 people waiting at the seashore itself, all dressed as Santas, reindeer, snowmen, pirates, elves, hula girls, aliens and some things that weren't even vaguely recognisable. One or two very sensible people had turned up in scuba gear, while others had gone for the simple Speedo look. Another sprinkling of spectators stood further up the beach, dressed more appropriately in heavy coats, scarves and hats, pointing and waving at people. It had to be the coldest day they'd had so far since winter had arrived, and Dodie clung to her own coat, determined to leave it on until the very last minute. As she smiled vaguely at fellow bathers, the sense of being alone struck her more keenly than ever before. Doing things on her own had never really bothered her but today, as everyone waited to begin the event with their families and friends in tow to support them, she realised how much she missed that. Isla should have been there, of course, and that had always been enough. She'd phoned her parents and told them not to worry about travelling over from Dorchester as she'd be going back that way to meet them for dinner anyway. And she'd told Gran to stay home where it was warm and dry, knowing she would have been tired out from her evening helping at the homeless shelter and needed the rest. Other friends had partners and children and had moved on. On good terms with Dodie still, but not close enough to expect them to give up their Christmas morning for an event like this. She half wondered if she'd see Nick, but this was too far down the seafront from his usual haunts.

'Finally! I've been calling and calling you! Where's your phone?'

Dodie whipped round and found herself face to face with Ed.

'What are you doing here?'

'I've been looking all over for you.'

'Looking for me?' Dodie blinked. 'Is something wrong?'

'No… God, no. In fact everything's amazing. I remembered you'd said you were doing this today and I thought I'd come down – offer a bit of support. And then I thought, what the hell, I can do more than offer support. So I've signed up.'

'To this?' she asked, angling her head at the sea.

'Yeah. I've not got much in the way of sponsorship but I suppose I can collect after I've done it. Mum and Trevor have sponsored me, of course.'

'That's amazing!' Dodie said, breaking into a bemused smile.

'It's only a little bit of money.'

'I mean it's brilliant that you've come. Really brilliant.'

'I wouldn't have missed it for the world,' he said.

Dodie's heart leapt. Did he mean that? And was he speaking as a friend, from gratitude for all she'd done to help get his life back on track, or did he have another reason for wanting to be there today?

'You must be the best-looking Christmas tree I've ever seen,' he said, breaking into her thoughts.

'I'm sure you say that to all the Christmas trees,' Dodie laughed, feeling weirdly giddy at the sight of him looking rested and handsome, even if he was in his scruffy old sports clothes, his smile for her warm and his eyes making her feel like nobody had ever done before. He looked better today than she'd ever seen him look, but she couldn't decide whether that was down to the new inner peace he seemed to have found or whether she was just seeing that as a consequence of the decision she'd made to bare her soul and the anticipation of what that might mean for them. Because as he stood there, she knew she would have to tell him how she felt. She had no choice but to risk it, to go all or nothing because the alternative – a half measure where she got to see him but didn't get to touch or kiss him, where she didn't get to lie in those arms and feel those lips upon her – was unthinkable. Denial was no longer an option, and pretence even less so. And if she didn't say something today, then he might go back to Blackpool with Julia and never come back.

'What time do they start this madness?' Ed asked, pulling her back to reality.

'Soon, I think,' Dodie said. 'They're never strict on times; I think when they feel everyone who's registered has pretty much arrived they go for it. It looks like a good turnout,' she added, eyeing the colourful crowd gathered at the shore. 'Better than last year I think.'

Ed stamped his feet and blew into his hands. 'I can't believe you've done one of these already and knowing how cold it was agreed to do it again.'

She shrugged. 'It's weirdly fun. There's a great sense of camaraderie and, in the end, what's a few minutes of discomfort in your life compared to the world of good the money it raises does?'

'I couldn't have put it better myself,' he said. 'I didn't say I didn't like that you decided to do it again, just that I was surprised. A lot of people wouldn't. Then again, a lot wouldn't do it in the first place.'

'The way I see it, none of us knows what's in our future and one day we might need the help of charity ourselves. I mean, look at Nick. I'm sure when he was living in his nice house with his wife and kids he didn't imagine a few years later he'd be on the streets. But it happened.'

'Nick has a wife? And kids?'

Dodie nodded.

'Where are they now? How did he end up on the streets?'

'He never says, but I know he's more choked about it than he lets on. He likes you, though,' Dodie added. 'Maybe when you start your homeless work he'll open up to you, and you might even be able to help him connect with them again. After all, you went through something similar with your mum.'

'Maybe,' Ed replied, deep in thought. 'Hang on a minute… how did you know about the homeless work?'

'I saw Nick last night when I worked at the shelter with Gran,' she replied with a small smile. 'He told me all about it. He tells me you've become quite pally of late…'

'Like you said, he's an interesting bloke once you get talking to him. Victim of circumstances – it can happen to the best of us. We've got a lot in common really.'

Dodie smiled vaguely as those eyes assaulted her senses again. She wasn't thinking about Nick now. She wasn't thinking about Ed's past or his future. She wasn't thinking about the hardships he'd suffered and the pain he'd both endured and caused. She wasn't even thinking about George and Margaret. She was thinking only of how much she wanted to lay her hands on his chest, how she wanted to run her fingers down his torso and feel the heat of his skin beneath them, how she wanted to explore every inch of him with every inch of her.

She'd never wanted a man the way she wanted him right now, and it terrified and excited her in equal measure. She wanted to shout it to the crowds on the beach, but she wanted to run and hide and give herself time to cool down too. She barely knew what to do with herself. *Hurry up and start the dip*, she thought. At least the cold water might do something to douse the fire stoking inside her.

'Mum wanted to come too,' he said. 'She's here with Trevor… Somewhere, at least. Want to say hello?'

Dodie nodded and gave silent thanks that mind-reading was not an actual thing because she was pretty sure Julia didn't need to see the thoughts she was having about her son right now. Ed began to walk and she fell in step alongside.

'I told them to wait by the parking spaces,' he said, frowning as they reached the tarmac and saw no sign of Julia and Trevor. 'Typical.' Turning to scan the beach, he was silent for a moment. 'Bloody hell, can't see them anywhere. Come on, we'll have to walk around a bit until we find them.'

It took ten minutes to finally locate Julia and Trevor, who greeted Dodie warmly while she thanked them for the flowers Ed had brought to the shop the night before. Julia was brighter than Dodie had ever seen her. She was happy to see that relations seemed a lot more relaxed between them both and Ed too, and they even shared gentle banter as they waited.

'I'm almost tempted to join you,' Trevor said, angling his head at the crowds waiting to take the plunge. 'Spirits are certainly high.'

'That's probably what they've been necking to keep warm,' Ed replied with a wry smile. 'Now that I think of it, a skinful of whisky would probably have kept the chill at bay.'

'Or you'd have been too drunk to care,' Trevor said.

'You'll be alright?' Julia asked, her gaze switching from Ed to Dodie and then back again. 'You'll be careful not to stay in too long, won't you?'

'There's not much danger of that.' Ed glanced at Dodie. 'A quick in and out is the strategy I'm going for.'

'We have to make it count, though,' Dodie said. 'If it's not a hardship then you haven't earned the sponsor money.'

'As long as it has the same end result I'm with Ed,' Trevor said cheerfully. 'No point in killing yourself over it.'

'What are you up to for the rest of the day?' Julia asked Dodie.

'Nothing much after this apart from the usual. I'll pick up Gran and head to my parents' house for dinner and then we'll watch an old film before we all fall asleep.'

'Oh, that sounds nice. We'd do that ordinarily, but of course we're not home today so it will be a bit different this year.' She offered Ed a fond smile. 'Not that I mind, of course. I always watch *It's a Wonderful Life* on Christmas Day. Sort of a tradition.'

'Oh, I love that film so much!' Dodie cooed. 'One of my all-time favourites!'

'Absolutely. Such a beautiful story,' Julia agreed. 'Eddie loves it too, don't you?'

Ed turned to her, a slight flush on his cheeks. 'Eddie? Since when did you call me Eddie?'

'Since always,' Julia said, that peculiar maternal indignation in her voice that all mothers have when they don't see why childhood indulgences have to change.

'It's been Ed for years,' he sniffed.

'I think it suits you,' Dodie said, biting back a grin. 'It's cute. So, how about it, *Eddie*? Ready for our dip?'

'If you call me Eddie once more I'll be throwing you in,' he said, now holding off a grin of his own.

Dodie stripped her coat off and Trevor took it for her. She turned to Ed, who took off his trainers and then hesitated, glancing around at the crowds.

'Nobody is going to care,' Dodie said in a low voice. She reached to give his hand a quick squeeze. 'If anything they'll be in awe of your strength and bravery.'

He looked up at Julia and Trevor, who were smiling with encouragement too.

'I'm so proud of you,' Julia said, tears misting her eyes. 'I don't tell you that often enough, but I'm incredibly proud of the man you've become. And this, today, makes me prouder than ever.'

With a deep breath, he pulled off his tracksuit trousers to reveal his swimming shorts and his scarred leg beneath. And then he stood up straight, scanning the crowds again. Barely anyone noticed, and those who did gave a silent nod of encouragement or a smile of goodwill.

'In the end,' Dodie said, 'all that matters is that we're here for the same reasons today, and nobody thinks you're any less of a man because of your leg.' She blushed. 'If you see what I mean.'

'Thanks,' he said. 'It means a lot to hear you say it.'

The PA system crackled into life to announce the imminent start of the event.

'We'd better get down to the shore,' Dodie said. 'Ready?'

'I was born ready!' He grinned, and he reached for her hand.

She was shivering as they walked across the sand, clammy and wet beneath her feet, but the cold wasn't the only reason. She could pretend it was because she was falling for Ed, but the truth was she'd already fallen. His hand was warm and solid around hers as they fell into step, the pace of her heart just that little bit faster at the feel of his skin on hers. This was driving her crazy, the not knowing, it was like torture. *Today*, she thought, *when this is done, come what may, I have to tell him*. If it ended badly, if he walked away, if he'd decided to go back to Blackpool never to return, if she'd hurt him so deeply the last time they'd shared their feelings that he couldn't forgive her then so be it, but at least she'd have tried, at least she'd have told him, because to carry on pretending was driving her mad.

They lined up at the shoreline, watching the white-crested waves darken the sand where they touched. He squeezed her hand, gave her a manic grin, and her heartbeat picked up speed. And then someone fired a starting pistol and he began to run with everyone else, pulling Dodie behind him. The sea came to meet them, sharp as an icy slap around her legs.

'*Oh my God!*' she squealed, alternately laughing and trying to catch the breath that the cold had stolen from her lungs. 'IT'S BLOODY FREEZING!'

'I don't know what you expected,' Ed shouted, laughing too. He must have been as cold as she was, but she didn't think he'd ever looked happier. Even the awkwardness he'd first shown revealing his scars amongst the crowd of bathers had gone. All she saw now was a beautiful man, a friend, someone she desperately wanted in her life. She wanted to fling her arms around him, to whisper in his ear how she felt, for time to stop while they kissed. She shook the thought away. Later, when she could explain properly how she felt, when they were both sober-minded enough to talk it through.

'I expected it to be cold!' she cried, grinning even though her legs were quickly becoming numb. 'Just not this cold!'

'Wishing you hadn't come? I did try to warn you.'

'Never!' she said, stamping up and down to keep warm, though it succeeded only in splashing the seawater further up her body and making her colder. She glanced around at the other bathers, shrieks of delight and horror in equal measure coming from the crowd, but sheer joy on every face. To be alive, on this day in this place, felt like a wonderful thing, the reasons they were here even more so. Nothing made Dodie feel more complete than the thought of the good she was doing.

But when she looked back, Ed seemed to have forgotten the cold and he was standing stock still, his smile faded, watching her intently.

'What?' she asked, her own smile faltering.

He shook his head slowly, a bemused expression. 'You.'

'Have I done something wrong?'

'I don't think you could ever do anything wrong. You're just… you. That's what you've done. You're… I've never met anyone like you.'

'I'll take that as a compliment.' She gave an uncertain laugh, arms folded tight around her body to keep out the cold.

'You should,' he said. 'Dodie…' He paused, and the world around them suddenly seemed to pause too. 'You're amazing. That's all. Just amazing. And I wondered…'

'Yes?'

'Could I get that kiss now?'

The widest of smiles stretched her face, her stomach flipping and her body shivering from more than the cold. She nodded and he stepped forward, pulling her close and placing his lips over hers. They were salty, chilled, but they warmed as they kissed, and she liked the taste of the sea on them. Everything she had ever wanted was in that kiss.

Pulling away, he leaned his forehead against hers and looked into her eyes. 'I'm sorry,' he murmured.

'What for?'

'Because I'm going to tell you something you might not want to hear.'

'What?' she whispered, aching to have his lips over hers again, almost wishing he'd stop talking.

'I love you,' he said. But then he frowned. 'Is that OK? I mean, is that too soon?'

She smiled slowly. 'More than OK. Because I'm pretty sure I love you too.'

The anxiety drained from his face and he grinned. 'Now isn't that a coincidence?'

'It wouldn't be the first one.'

'Oh, God,' he said. 'You have no idea how much I've wanted to say it to you. I've been scared in my life but the thought of saying that to you… it was worse than anything I've ever faced.'

Dodie's mind went back to the thoughts she'd had that very morning, how desperately she'd tried to figure out what to do, how to tell him. And he'd been feeling it all along. They both needed to open up if they were going to avoid this every time something needed saying.

'It's OK,' she said. 'I have to tell you that I've felt the same. I've wanted to say something for ages; I didn't know how you'd react but… I guess it doesn't matter now.'

'Well,' he said, 'that makes us a pair of idiots, doesn't it?'

'I suppose it does. As long as we can be idiots together I don't care.'

'Me neither…' He pulled her into another kiss, long and hot enough to turn the freezing water around them into steam 'There's one more thing,' he whispered as their lips parted.

'What's that?'

'I think we might get hypothermia if we stay in here any longer.'

Dodie giggled, and she leaned back to see that people were now making their way to the beach. Some watched her and Ed with raised eyebrows and smiles but most were just desperate to get into their warm, dry clothes. Somewhere up on the sands Julia and Trevor were probably watching, but she didn't care.

'It's funny, but I don't feel so cold any more,' she said, reaching to kiss him again.

He grinned down at her. 'There's something else.'

'What now?' she replied, pretending to be annoyed.

'It's snowing.'

She looked up. The first flakes drifted from a white sky. 'That's OK, I love snow.'

'Of course you do; why doesn't that surprise me? But I suspect the sea is about to get a whole lot colder.'

'Let it,' she said, but then squealed as she was suddenly swept off her feet, into Ed's arms. He began to stride towards the beach, not hampered in the slightest by her weight.

'Put me down!' she giggled, but he carried on walking.

'I'm not letting you get pneumonia,' he said. 'There's a severe shortage of girls willing to stand in a freezing cold sea while a man tells her they love her so now I've found one I'm keeping her.'

'What if I don't want to be kept?'

'Well then, I'm afraid that's too bad.'

Ed dropped her gently onto the sand. One of the organisers rushed over to hand him a towel and he wrapped it around her, drawing her into his arms again.

'Now I'm lovely and warm but you're still cold,' she said, her eyes locked onto his. 'What if you get pneumonia? There's a severe shortage of men willing to run into a freezing cold sea for me and then tell me they love me. Now I've found one I'm keeping him.'

'What if I don't want to be kept?' he asked, dipping his head to kiss her.

'Well then,' she whispered, smiling as he broke away, 'I'm afraid that's just too bad.'

A Letter From Tilly

I really hope you've enjoyed reading *A Very Vintage Christmas* as much as I enjoyed writing it. You can sign up to my mailing list and will get all the latest news this way. The link is here: www.bookouture.com/tilly-tennant

A Very Vintage Christmas is one of those rare things – a book that the author herself is in love with. Often I'm self-critical and sometimes the process of writing a novel is, while enjoyable, fraught with difficulties and frustrations. But writing this was different because Bournemouth is the place where I was born, a place where I've spent many happy hours, and I was very proud and excited to share this wonderful, vibrant town with my readers. I hope you've fallen for its charms and love it as I do.

If you liked *A Very Vintage Christmas*, the best and most amazing thing you can do to show your appreciation is to tell your friends, or tell the world with a few words in a review. It can be as short and sweet as you like but it would make me so happy. In fact, hearing that someone loved my story is the main reason I write at all.

If you ever want to catch up with me on social media, you can find me on Twitter @TillyTenWriter or Facebook.

So, thank you for reading my little book, and I hope to see you again soon!

Love Tilly x

Acknowledgements

The list of people who have offered help and encouragement on my writing journey so far must be truly endless, and it would take a novel in itself to mention them all. However, my thanks goes out to each and every one of you, whose involvement, whether small or large, has been invaluable and appreciated more than I can say.

There are a few people that I must mention. Obviously, my family, the people who put up with my whining and self-doubt on a daily basis. My colleagues at the Royal Stoke University Hospital, who have let me lead a double life for far longer than is acceptable and have given me so many ideas for future books! The lecturers at Staffordshire University English and Creative Writing Department, who saw a talent worth nurturing in me and continue to support me still, long after they finished getting paid for it. They are not only tutors but friends as well. I have to thank the team at Bookouture for their continued support, patience, and amazing publishing flair, particularly Kim Nash, Peta Nightingale, Jessie Botterill and Lydia Vassar-Smith. Their belief and encouragement means the world to me.

My friend, Kath Hickton, always gets a mention, and rightly so for putting up with me since primary school. Louise Coquio also gets an honourable mention for getting me through university and suffering me ever since, likewise her lovely family. And thanks go to Storm

Constantine for giving me my first break in publishing. I also have to thank Mel Sherratt and Holly Martin, fellow writers and amazing friends who have both been incredibly supportive over the years and have been my shoulders to cry on in the darker moments. Thanks to Tracy Bloom, Emma Davies, Jack Croxall, Dan Thompson, Renita D'Silva, Christie Barlow and Jaimie Admans: not only brilliant authors in their own right, but hugely supportive of others. My Bookouture colleagues are also incredible, of course, unfailing and generous in their support of fellow authors – life would be a lot duller without you all. I have to thank all the brilliant and dedicated book bloggers (there are so many of you but you know who you are!) and readers, and anyone else who has championed my work, reviewed it, shared it or simply told me that they liked it. Every one of those actions is priceless and you are all very special people. Some of you I am even proud to call friends now.

Last but never least I have to thank my agent at LAW, Philippa Milnes-Smith, for her counsel and support.

Made in the USA
Lexington, KY
16 November 2017